Alice-Miranda
in China

Books by Jacqueline Harvey

Alice-Miranda at School
Alice-Miranda on Holiday
Alice-Miranda Takes the Lead
Alice-Miranda at Sea
Alice-Miranda in New York
Alice-Miranda Shows the Way
Alice-Miranda in Paris
Alice-Miranda Shines Bright
Alice-Miranda in Japan
Alice-Miranda at Camp
Alice-Miranda at the Palace
Alice-Miranda in the Alps
Alice-Miranda to the Rescue
Alice-Miranda in China

Clementine Rose and the Surprise Visitor
Clementine Rose and the Pet Day Disaster
Clementine Rose and the Perfect Present
Clementine Rose and the Farm Fiasco
Clementine Rose and the Seaside Escape
Clementine Rose and the Treasure Box
Clementine Rose and the Famous Friend
Clementine Rose and the Ballet Break-In
Clementine Rose and the Movie Magic
Clementine Rose and the Birthday Emergency
Clementine Rose and the Special Promise
Clementine Rose and the Paris Puzzle

Alice-Miranda in China

Jacqueline Harvey

RANDOM HOUSE AUSTRALIA

A Random House book
Published by Penguin Random House Australia Pty Ltd
Level 3, 100 Pacific Highway, North Sydney NSW 2060
www.penguin.com.au

Penguin
Random House
Australia

First published by Random House Australia in 2016

Addresses for the Penguin Random House group of companies can be found at
global.penguinrandomhouse.com/offices.

National Library of Australia
Cataloguing-in-Publication entry

Creator: Harvey, Jacqueline, author
Title: Alice-Miranda in China/Jacqueline Harvey
ISBN: 978 0 85798 520 0 (pbk)
Series: Harvey, Jacqueline. Alice-Miranda; 14
Target Audience: For primary school age.
Subjects: Student exchange programs – China – Juvenile fiction
          Sabotage – Juvenile fiction
          China – Social life and customs – Juvenile fiction
Dewey Number: A823.4

Cover and internal illustrations by J.Yi
Cover design by Mathematics www.xy-1.com
Internal design by Midland Typesetters, Australia
Typeset in 13/18 pt Adobe Garamond by Midland Typesetters, Australia
Printed in Australia by Griffin Press, an accredited ISO AS/NZS 14001:2004
Environmental Management System printer

Penguin Random House Australia uses papers that are natural, renewable
and recyclable products and made from wood grown in sustainable forests.
The logging and manufacturing processes are expected to conform to the
environmental regulations of the country of origin.

For Ian and Sandy, as always.
For Shannon and her students —
thank you for your inspiration!

Prologue

Lionel Wong leaned forward on his elbows and clasped his hands together. On the other side of the desk his two sons, Bernard and Charles, remained silent. 'Well, what do you think?' he asked.

Bernard ran his palm over the top of his cleanly shaven head. 'Are you certain this is what you want, Baba?'

The older man stroked his long grey beard. 'The ancestors have blessed us with rare talents. It is time to share our good fortune.' He turned to his younger son, Charles. 'And you?'

There was a distant clashing of cymbals and the rumbling of a timpani drum, followed by shouts and a series of thuds.

Bernard grimaced. 'I've told the troupe not to practise their tumbling in the hall. One day they will find themselves face to face with Mama, and I wouldn't want to be in their shoes when that happens.'

'It is fortunate, then, that they are not wearing any,' Lionel quipped, a wry smile playing on his lips. He looked at his younger son, whose face was always impossible to read.

Finally, Charles spoke. 'If this is your wish then it is my wish too.'

It was just as well because there was no turning back. Lionel had already made a verbal agreement, which, if all went to plan, would be formalised soon. 'Then it is settled,' he said.

'Would you like us to help you with the negotiations?' Bernard asked.

'No,' Lionel replied sharply. 'And you will not speak of this to *anyone*.'

The brothers exchanged a look. There was an edge to their father's voice they had rarely heard.

'What about Mama?' Charles asked.

Lionel's face crumpled into a smile. 'Whose idea do you think it was in the first place? When we received the letter of interest, it was your mother who pointed out that this may be the most fortunate opportunity that has ever presented itself.'

'But why do they want us?' Charles asked.

Lionel scoffed. 'Because we are the best acrobatic troupe in all of China, of course.'

In the distance the music was building, but before it reached its climax, there was a loud crash and the sound of smashing crockery.

Bernard grinned. 'What was that you were saying about us being the best, Baba?'

Lionel shook his head. 'I should have bought shares in a plate factory. Ah well,' he sighed, 'you cannot expect perfection without a few hiccups along the way. Come, it is time to rehearse.' He walked out from behind the enormous teak desk and patted Charles on the shoulder. 'This will bring great honour to our family.'

'Yes, Baba,' Charles replied.

As Bernard reached for the doorhandle, a figure receded into the shadows of the hallway and disappeared around the corner.

Little did they know that the walls had ears.

Chapter 1

Alice-Miranda Highton-Smith-Kennington-Jones was already dressed and on her way to see Mrs Howard. She'd offered to help with the school pennant the woman had been busily sewing for their upcoming trip and had a little window of time before breakfast to work on it. Alice-Miranda's tummy fluttered – she couldn't believe that she and her friends would be in Hong Kong by Thursday night.

'I'll see you at the back door,' Alice-Miranda said, and gave Millie a wave.

The girl was frantically finishing the Maths homework she'd forgotten to do the night before. 'Okay, I won't be long,' Millie said. She looked at the multiplication sum in front of her and bit her lip.

As Alice-Miranda stepped into the hallway, she was met by Fudge, the school's newest recruit. The cavoodle pup trotted out of Sloane and Caprice's room with a sandal wedged in his mouth.

'What are you doing with that, you naughty boy?' She scooped him into her arms, trying to dislodge the shoe, but Fudge growled and bit down harder. He never gave up his treasures without a fight.

Alice-Miranda chuckled and went to close the girls' bedroom door when she noticed Caprice was still in bed. 'Caprice? Are you feeling unwell?' she whispered, tiptoeing into the room.

There was a rustle as the covers were pulled higher.

Sloane arrived back from the bathroom and the two friends smiled at one another. 'Good morning,' Alice-Miranda said quietly.

'Not so good for some,' Sloane replied, lowering her voice and gesturing to Caprice.

Fudge dropped the sandal and wriggled out of Alice-Miranda's arms to jump onto Caprice's bed.

The pup had developed a curious attachment to the challenging young girl and promptly made himself at home on her feet.

'Are you getting up?' Sloane asked. 'Howie will be back any minute and she's not going to be happy.'

'I don't care,' Caprice grumbled from beneath her duvet.

Sloane rolled her eyes and began lacing her shoes. 'Are you still grouchy because you're not coming on the trip?'

'No,' Caprice snapped. 'Why would anyone want to go to China, anyway? It's overcrowded, polluted and, worst of all, they eat dogs.'

Fudge raised his head and whimpered.

'That's not true,' Sloane bit back.

Caprice threw off the covers and propped herself on one elbow. 'Uh, yes it is, and that's not the only disgusting thing on the menu. You can ask my mother – even though I'm not speaking to her ever again. Fancy some fricasseed chicken's feet or shredded snake? How about steamed fish eyes? Or, my personal favourite, sautéed pigs' livers in seaweed sauce?'

'I'm sure we're not going to have any of that,' Alice-Miranda said. 'Think of all the delicious dumplings, steamed buns and roast pork we'll get to eat.'

Sloane hoped Alice-Miranda was right. She turned around and hung her towel on the back of the door.

Alice-Miranda thought for a moment. She wondered what Caprice's mother had done to upset her this time. 'Why aren't you speaking to your mother?' she asked the girl.

'Because it's her fault that I have to spend the holidays at home,' Caprice fumed. 'She was too busy with her stupid show and forgot to send the forms in time.'

'So you *are* still cross about not coming,' Sloane said.

Caprice threw herself back on the bed. 'No, I just hate my mother, and now I have to spend two whole weeks with her.'

'There will be other trips,' Alice-Miranda said gently. 'I know Miss Grimm intends to establish a biennial excursion. The Bright Star students will visit us next year and then you'll have your chance the year after that. The time will come before you know it.'

'But it won't be the same because you'll all have been together and you'll just leave me out of everything, like you always do.' Caprice leaned forward and picked up Fudge, hugging him to her chest.

Sloane actually felt sorry for the girl. After the fire earlier in the term, Caprice seemed to have turned a corner. Even when she only came runner-up in the National Eisteddfod, she'd taken it surprisingly well. But when Caprice had learned that her mother had missed the deadline for the trip, after having spent a week bragging about her knowledge of Chinese cuisine and Mandarin, there had been an explosion to rival Plumpy's worst experimental disasters. Although, she'd been smart enough to avoid doing it in front of the teachers this time.

Mrs Howard's voice floated down the corridor. 'Girls, hurry along. We'll be leaving for breakfast in ten minutes.'

Caprice quickly scrunched up some tissues and scattered them around her. She pinched her cheeks and mussed her hair, then dropped back onto the bed, with Fudge nestling in beside her.

When the woman reached their room, she was shocked to see the girl under the covers. 'Good morning,' she said, smiling at Alice-Miranda and Sloane, then looked over at Caprice. 'Are you ill?'

'I've got a cold,' Caprice moaned, putting on her best nasal voice. She rolled away and covered her head.

Howie raised her eyebrows at Sloane, and the girl shook her head in reply. The elderly woman winked conspiratorially. 'Well then, it sounds like you should spend the whole day right there. No television for you and I'll keep Fudge out of the way too – you won't get any rest if he's in here.'

Caprice huffed loudly.

'What was that? You're feeling better, are you? Yes, I thought you might.' Mrs Howard consulted her wristwatch. 'If you want to have a shower, you've got three minutes starting from now.'

The girl leapt out of bed, gathered her things and stormed down the hall. Fudge jumped out of the way, running to the corner of the room, where he plonked himself on top of one of Caprice's trainers and began to chew the laces.

'Goodness me, I don't envy Mrs Clarkson getting that one next year,' Howie said, referring to the housemistress who was in charge of the older girls at Caledonia Manor. 'I hear she takes no prisoners. Perhaps that's just what Caprice needs.'

Sloane grimaced. She'd heard the same thing.

'Are you doing anything special in the holidays, Mrs Howard?' Alice-Miranda asked. 'Will you be spending time with your daughter and her family?'

'Actually, they're off on a camping holiday. They asked me to join them, but the thought of navigating muddy camping grounds and sleeping on an air mattress doesn't really appeal to these creaky old bones of mine. For the first time in a long while, I have no plans and I have to say that I'm looking forward to it immensely,' the woman said cheerfully. 'Although, I will be busy looking after that little mite.' She reached down and picked up the pup, who nipped her finger. 'I think I might take him to some extra puppy-training classes. He's getting a bit too cheeky for my liking and his shoe fetish has got to stop.' She looked down at Caprice's trainer, which was now covered in drool.

The thudding of wet feet sounded in the hall. Caprice reappeared with a towel wrapped around her and a shower cap on her head. 'Can't a girl get any privacy in her own bedroom?' she grouched, pushing past the group.

Mrs Howard exhaled loudly. 'Did you lose something on your way from the bathroom?'

Caprice threw her toiletries bag onto her bed, where it fell among the tangle of duvet and sheets. She rummaged about to see what was missing. 'No, everything's here.'

'I meant your manners, young lady,' the old woman said.

Caprice scrunched her nose.

'Come along, girls. Caprice, I will see you at the back door in five minutes, along with those missing manners.' Mrs Howard arched her eyebrow and pulled the door shut.

Aldous Grump turned the page and glanced across at his wife, who was buttering a piece of toast. Rather, she had been buttering it but now seemed to be frozen in time. He cleared his throat and set aside the newspaper.

Ophelia startled, then resumed her task.

'How are the last-minute arrangements coming along?' he asked. 'Are you looking forward to the trip?'

'Ridiculously so,' she said, flashing him a tight smile. It lingered for a moment before a frown creased her brow. She set down her knife and looked at her husband worriedly. 'Do you think I'm mad to undertake all this at such short notice?'

'Darling, it will be wonderful,' he assured her. 'In fact, I saw Sep Sykes in the village yesterday afternoon and he told me Thursday couldn't come soon enough.' Aldous raised his teacup to his lips.

'That's only because I've wangled them two days off school.' Ophelia smiled to herself. She thought back to the day, two months ago, when a letter postmarked from China had arrived on her desk. Much to her surprise, it was an invitation. A dear friend from her university days was now head of the Bright Star Academy in Beijing, a prestigious bilingual school, and had asked Ophelia if she would like to bring a group of students to stay for a week – and in return they might visit Winchesterfield-Downsfordvale the following year. Given that she'd recently introduced Mandarin to the curriculum, it was an incredibly serendipitous venture.

Ophelia had swiftly taken it up and extended the invitation to the neighbouring Fayle School for Boys on the other side of the village. While Professor Winterbottom wholeheartedly supported the idea, he expressed his deep regret that he and his wife, Deidre, would be unable to join them as they were booked on a long-planned cruise to the Mediterranean. Ophelia wasn't overly concerned as the Fayle boys had proven themselves most reliable on their choir trip to Paris – well, apart from Figgy and Rufus and that candle incident at Sacré Cœur, but she was certain they had learned their lesson. Anyway, they were apparently terrified of her and she was confident that a withering look would be all that was needed to bring them back into line.

Many hours of planning later, Ophelia and her husband, along with the newly wedded Livinia Reedy and Josiah Plumpton, were about to set off with ten students and a small group of parents on a ten-day cultural exchange. They would have a couple of days in Hong Kong, three days in Shanghai and the remainder of the time in Beijing, where the children would attend school and stay with host families.

'I'd better hurry up and get dressed,' Ophelia said, finishing the last bite of her breakfast. 'I need to finalise the billeting list with Livinia before assembly.' The woman stood up and deposited her cup and plate in the sink, then kissed her husband on the top of his head. 'I'll see you later, darling.'

'Have a good day.' Aldous waved and went back to his paper.

Chapter 2

Just as the alarm began its slow morning beep, a hand reached out to shut it off. Coco smiled, clinging to the remnants of her delicious dream.

'Time to get up, little one,' Wai Po whispered. She pulled a plain black leotard from the top drawer of the chest and laid it on the end of the bed.

Coco rolled onto her back and stretched like a cat. Within seconds, she had changed into her morning uniform consisting of the leotard, tights and a tracksuit over the top.

The old woman picked up a hairbrush from the bedside table. Despite her crooked fingers, tormented by arthritis, she tamed the child's locks into a perfect bun. 'There is congee for breakfast.'

Coco pulled a face. She wasn't a fan of the thick rice porridge. 'Could I have cereal instead?' she asked.

'Since when do good Chinese girls eat that American birdseed?' Wai Po squinted at Coco over the top of her narrow glasses.

'It's yummy and it doesn't sit in my stomach like a rock,' Coco replied. She picked up her bag, which Wai Po had already packed with her school uniform and textbooks.

'I will see what I can find,' the woman said, shuffling from the room in her brocade slippers.

The little girl cartwheeled out of her bedroom and along the open veranda of the family compound. She hurled her bag into the air, watching it spin over and over, then caught it with her right foot and flicked it onto a hook on the wall. Coco scampered out the front door and onto the top of the wall, where she tumbled and flipped all the way down the alley to the communal bathroom at the end of the narrow lane. Her double somersault dismount was magnificent and she landed with feline grace on the ground below.

Their neighbour Au Shen, who was on his way to work, paused to clap. 'That was very good!' he said. 'You become more impressive with each day, Coco. I think you will soon be the best acrobat in all of China.'

Coco grinned and bowed. 'Thank you, Au Shen. Enjoy your day!' she replied, before charging into the white building.

A petite woman emerged from a toilet stall just as Coco rushed into the one beside it, struggling out of her leotard. The tiny acrobat wished she didn't have to get dressed before her morning ablutions, but her mother insisted that no daughter of hers would ever walk the *hutongs* in her pyjamas.

'Good morning, Mama,' she sang out.

'Good morning, Coco,' the woman said with a yawn. 'One of these days we won't have to share a bathroom and it will be even better.' She turned to find their ancient neighbour Sun Ming, whose face was scrunched up like a dried prune, picking at a boil on her chin. Lucille shuddered. Sun Ming offered a toothless smile before shuffling outside.

Coco flushed the toilet and bounded out of the stall. 'Wai Po says that our bathroom is a luxury compared to what she grew up with in the provinces,' she said, pushing up the sleeves of her tracksuit top to wash her hands.

'You shouldn't call her Wai Po – she isn't your grandmother,' Lucille reprimanded. 'And of course this is luxury. She was a peasant from the fields.'

Coco soaped her hands, then held them out for her mother to pour water over them from a bucket. 'But, Mama, she says that I am just the same to her as Sunny.'

'I would prefer it if you didn't. You know that it upsets my mother – your *real* grandmother.' Lucille tightened Coco's bun, causing the girl to wince.

Mother and daughter walked out into the alley. Coco rose onto the tips of her toes and was about to launch into a series of cartwheels when Lucille gripped her arm.

'Don't you even think about it,' she warned. 'The ground is filthy. How many times do I have to tell you not to tumble out here?'

Coco frowned and walked beside her mother, although it was more of a frustrated skip.

The girl opened a door into a large courtyard. An ancient pomegranate tree sat in the centre of the complex, skirted by a veranda lined with doors that shot off into various living areas and bedrooms. Each room also had a window overlooking the courtyard. While running water had been installed some time ago, the Wongs had not yet added any internal bathrooms, much to the displeasure of their elder daughter-in-law, Lucille. Altogether, there were nine residents: Coco's paternal grandparents, Lionel and Winnie Wong, who she called Ye Ye and Nai Nai; her mother and father, Lucille and Bernard; her Uncle Charles and Aunty Cherry and their boy, Sunny. Last of all there was Cherry's mother, who Coco called Wai Po.

Coco's maternal grandparents lived in Beijing too. Her grandfather was an important official in the government, and he and his wife lived in a modern high-rise apartment. Coco rarely saw them, and when she did, her grandmother was always complaining about some irritation or another. Coco would never have told her mother this, but she often wished Wai Po was her real grandmother.

Coco raced into the dining room and sat opposite her cousin, Sunny. Nai Nai and Wai Po were there too, as well as her Aunty Cherry.

Winnie looked up from her bowl of congee, her eyes sparkling. She was dressed in her trademark red, her silken hair pulled back into an immovable French roll. 'Good morning, Coco.'

Without warning, she flicked an empty bowl towards the young girl. Coco effortlessly caught it with one hand, but just as she was about to set it down, Winnie threw another along with a pair of chopsticks.

'Good morning, Nai Nai,' the child replied, as she spun the two bowls above her head. They twirled in perfect unison, each balanced on the end of a chopstick.

The old woman nodded approvingly and slurped her breakfast. 'Now one hand.'

Coco did so without missing a beat. She looked over at her cousin, who was reading a comic book at the table, and seized her chance to catch him out. She flicked the bowls towards him, but he caught them with two hands and began to juggle. Coco pouted, her ruse foiled.

Winnie winked at her granddaughter and spun a third towards him, followed soon after by another. Nonplussed, the boy juggled the four bowls in the air until he was given permission to stop.

The cousins grinned at one another. Coco glanced at the calendar on the wall and shivered with excitement. 'Our visitors will be arriving soon,' she announced happily.

'Do you think they speak Mandarin?' Sunny asked.

Coco shook her head. 'Miss O'Reilly says they've only just begun learning. I'm looking forward to practising my English with them.'

'I wonder what they're like,' Sunny said, pouring himself a bowl of cereal.

'They will be the same as you but with different experiences of life,' Winnie said. 'You can show them what it is like to grow up in the most famous acrobatic troupe in all of China.'

'I imagine they live in houses with inside plumbing,' Lucille said bitterly. She stole a look at her mother-in-law. 'This will be a big shock to them. What if they are unhappy and cry the whole time?'

'Children can handle almost anything. It is only if they grow up spoilt that they can't,' Winnie replied pointedly. 'You could always buy your own house and live somewhere else if it is so terrible here.'

Coco sank into her chair. Her mother and grandmother often clashed and it usually ended with her mother storming off. She wished her mother would learn to keep quiet like her Aunty Cherry, but the two women couldn't have been more different.

Lucille pinched her lips together. She would have left years ago but her husband was so devoted to his parents that he couldn't bear the thought of the family being apart. Lucille contented herself with the fact that Lionel and Winnie wouldn't be around forever. There would be big changes when she took over, that was for sure.

'We're going to find out about our billets at school today,' Coco said, trying to lighten the mood. 'Miss O'Reilly said we'll be matched with someone who shares similar interests and skills. Do you think our guests will be gymnasts?'

'Bah!' Winnie scoffed. 'It would only be a hobby to them, if that were the case.'

'Yes, I can't imagine the children would have any proper skills,' Lucille said.

At least her mother and grandmother were in agreement about something, Coco thought to herself. She hadn't imagined her father would agree to host the foreign students when she'd initially raised the idea. Her mother had been horrified by the proposal, but the rest of the family decided that it would be a wonderful learning experience for them all, even if Nai Nai complained about having extra mouths to feed. Coco knew she didn't mean it. They often took in young acrobats when they first arrived in the city. And she and Sunny both had large bedrooms of their own with plenty of extra space.

'That reminds me, I must get the beds sorted,' Wai Po said, gingerly rising to her feet.

'Lucille will help you with that,' Winnie offered, and took pleasure at the sight of the woman's face twisting. 'What's the matter, daughter? You look as though you've bitten into a durian.'

Coco wrinkled her nose at the mention of the smelly fruit.

Sunny shuddered. 'Remember when Ye Ye made us try it? The house stank like a toilet for a whole week.'

Lucille held her tongue and smiled at her mother-in-law. 'Of course I will help. It will be my pleasure.'

Chapter 3

Jacinta Headlington-Bear closed her diary and yawned. She secured the lock, then popped the key inside the trinket box on her bedside table. Instead of dreaming about the upcoming trip, she'd spent the past few nights lying awake and worrying about Lucas. It was stupid, of course, but she couldn't seem to shake the niggling feeling in the pit of her stomach or the fact that her legs went to jelly every time she saw him. Surely that wasn't normal?

She desperately needed to talk to someone, but none of the girls in her own year were remotely interested in boys and Millie and Sloane would just make a joke of it. There was only one person she could rely on to listen and give proper advice, and although Alice-Miranda was so much younger than herself, she seemed to know about most things in life. It also helped that Lucas was her cousin.

Jacinta slipped her diary under her pillow and hurried out of the room, narrowly avoiding a collision with the new housemistress.

'Oh my, someone's in a hurry.' Petunia Clarkson straightened the tower of towels in her arms and tucked a stray strand of hair back into her otherwise perfect brown bob.

'Sorry, Mrs Clarkson,' Jacinta said, with flushed cheeks. 'May I use the telephone, please?'

'Yes, of course, but you have to be up to lessons in fifteen minutes,' Mrs Clarkson replied. She looked more closely at Jacinta. 'Is everything all right? That's a very serious face, my dear.'

'I'm fine,' Jacinta answered, forcing a grin. 'Thank you for asking.'

Petunia Clarkson smiled back and, suddenly, the hallway felt a whole lot brighter. Although the girls were still getting to know her, and Mrs Clarkson had proven stern on a couple of occasions, Jacinta had warmed to the woman immediately. She had one of those faces that seemed to radiate sunshine.

'Have a good day, my love,' Petunia trilled, then continued on her way.

Jacinta rushed off to the sitting room. She dialled the number for Grimthorpe House, hoping that Alice-Miranda was still there.

Coco raised her left leg against Sunny's shoulder and leaned into a standing split. She arched her back and flipped herself over with the elasticity of a rubber band.

'Have you finished your warm-ups?' their grandfather called from the centre of the stage.

'Coming, Ye Ye,' the pair echoed, and jogged over to join him.

The old man smiled at his grandchildren while absently stroking his long beard. 'Do you realise that once we have perfected this routine we will be the only acrobats in the world to have three generations of the same family undertake such a breathtaking feat?'

Sunny's mouth formed a perfect 'O'. 'Wow! Is that true, Ye Ye?'

'Have you seen any other grandmothers out there riding bicycles and spinning plates?' Lionel asked.

The lad grinned. 'I don't think so.'

A loud squeal cut through the air. A red bicycle shot out of the wings and began circling the group.

'Nai Nai!' Coco shouted. 'You are going too fast!'

The old woman's feet rested on the handlebars while she lay back with her head dangling above the rear wheel. Then, in one swift movement, she leapt to a standing position on the seat and gracefully swept out her arms. 'Ta-da!'

The children giggled.

'Will you be part of the act too, Ye Ye?' Sunny asked his grandfather.

Lionel's eyebrows formed two happy half-moons. 'Of course, my boy. I may be old but I am still strong, and your father and uncle can tumble with the best of them. You will all be doing flips while the ladies circle us on bicycles. However, it is our last trick that will be our most mind-boggling feat ever,' the man replied.

Sunny's father, Charles, ran into the ring and stood beside the old man. 'Baba, I want to speak with you about that. I think it's too risky.'

'Rubbish,' Lionel scoffed. 'When we started the motorcycle cage with three riders you said it was too dangerous, but how many are there inside the cage now?'

Charles gulped. 'Nine.'

'When we started the Wheel of Death you said that someone would be killed. Has that happened?'

'No,' Charles conceded.

'You worry too much, my son. I am not going to allow anything to happen to a member of this troupe. They are all my family – blood relative or not. Surely you know that?'

Charles sighed, defeated. 'Then we must begin rehearsals at once.'

'Yes!' The old man clapped his hands. 'We will debut our performance next week.'

'Impossible!' Charles spat.

Coco felt a twinge in her stomach. She had never seen her uncle so distressed. 'What's the final trick?' she asked.

'Your father will somersault onto my shoulders, your uncle will be atop his shoulders, then Sunny will catapult to the top. We will be a giant tower! Hopefully more like the Pearl Tower than the Leaning Tower,' Lionel said, snickering at his own joke.

'Sunny will then tumble off Charles and onto the handlebars of the bicycle that your grandmother will be riding. Your mother and aunty will be hanging from either side spinning plates, and you will be doing the same while straddling their shoulders.'

'How am I to land?' Sunny asked uneasily. It was a long drop to the bicycle below.

'In a handstand,' Lionel replied.

The boy was aghast. 'But I will break my arms!'

'I am just kidding, Sunny. Even I wouldn't have attempted that at your age. You will be on your feet, of course.'

Sunny swallowed hard and looked at his cousin.

'You can do it,' Coco said. Truthfully, she was worried about her own trick. It was going to be a challenge standing on the shoulders of her mother and aunty while spinning plates and hoping that her grandmother didn't fall and get them all killed.

'Why do we need a new act?' Sunny asked.

Charles was about to say something when the old man's eyes warned him not to.

'We are performing for an important guest,' Lionel said. 'We must bring honour to our family and to all of China, and no one has attempted anything like this before.'

Coco wondered who it could be.

Sunny's eyes widened. 'Is it a film star?'

He had recently hit on the idea that one day he would give up acrobatics and go into the movie business instead, putting his skills to good use as a stuntman.

'It is not for you to know just yet,' Lionel replied with a wink. 'Rou,' he called out to the woman lurking in the doorway. 'Gather the rest of the family. We need to get started.'

Chapter 4

As soon as their lessons were over, Alice-Miranda and Millie quickly changed into their riding gear and headed to the stables via the dining room, where they picked up a couple of Mrs Smith's cheese toasties for afternoon tea. In no time flat, the pair had their ponies tacked up and ready to ride. The weather was warm and the girls trotted along, enjoying the breeze on their faces.

'Do you think Jacinta's going to quit gymnastics?' Millie asked.

'I'm not sure. She was being rather mysterious on the telephone,' Alice-Miranda replied. 'I don't really know why she needs to see me so urgently.'

'Because you're good with advice,' Millie said, 'and I'm excellent at eating cake, which is exactly what I'm going to do at Caledonia Manor while you're dealing with Jacinta and her dilemmas.' Millie smacked her lips at the thought of Miss Hephzibah's chocolate cake.

Alice-Miranda sighed happily and looked across at her friend. 'Do you wish we could stay here forever?'

'What? Here at school?' Millie wrinkled her nose. 'No way! We're going to Hong Kong on Thursday, and I'll have two glorious weeks without Caprice.'

Alice-Miranda, trying to look reproachful, giggled. 'I didn't quite mean it like that. I just think it would be lovely if we could be children forever. It seems such a shame to have to grow up,' she mused.

'I can't wait until I'm old enough to drive and I don't have to do homework and I can make all my own decisions,' Millie said. 'Imagine eating chocolate for breakfast and cake for lunch and no one banging on about rotten teeth.'

'That does sound like fun,' Alice-Miranda agreed. 'But Mummy says that we should make the most of every minute of our childhoods because one day we'll wake up and wonder where the past thirty or forty years have gone.'

Millie looked at her friend with a knowing smile. 'Have you been reading those weird philosophy books again?'

Alice-Miranda shook her head. 'Just thinking, I suppose. Can you imagine us all grown up? What will we be doing in ten or fifteen years from now?'

'Well, that's easy,' Millie said. 'I'll be training for my second Olympics, where I will add to my medal collection, having won gold in the eventing and showjumping four years earlier. Jacinta will have already won an Olympic medal in gymnastics – it'll probably be a silver medal because, let's face it, she'll be up against the Russians and Chinese, so silver would be incredibly respectable. She'll marry Lucas, who'll be a famous movie star, just like his father. Sloane will be an international model travelling the world, or perhaps she'll shock us and become a teacher. No! Better still, she'll be the headmistress, here, at Winchesterfield-Downsfordvale. That would be hilarious! And Sep will be a human-rights lawyer or a doctor working in some dreadful part of the world where they still don't have running water. Sadly, Caprice will be in jail because, by then, someone will have realised that mean girls should be separated from the general population . . .'

'Millie,' Alice-Miranda chided, laughing.

'Okay, she won't be in jail,' Millie relented. 'She'll be in some manufactured pop group because she is a very good singer. I'll give her that.'

Alice-Miranda nodded. 'Better. What about me?'

'You'll be running the Highton's empire, of course,' Millie said, as if it were the most obvious thing in the world.

Alice-Miranda frowned. 'That's a lot more than ten or fifteen years away. I'm only eight!'

Millie shook her head. 'You turned nine a while ago, remember?'

'Oops, I keep forgetting. It's a bit tragic to be in age denial at nine,' Alice-Miranda said with a grin. 'That all sounds like fun, but wouldn't you rather us ride our ponies and dream about the future? It seems far too complicated to be in it.'

'Well, if you'd rather stay in the moment, I'll race you to the gate,' Millie said. She clicked her tongue and dug her heels into Chops's flanks.

'Come on, Bony!' Alice-Miranda called, and for once her little black brute did exactly what he was told.

⭐

Alice-Miranda and Millie tied up the ponies outside the boarding house.

'Bony must be getting faster in his old age,' Millie said, giving the beast a pat on the neck.

'Or Mr Charles has been feeding him too much oats,' Alice-Miranda said. Bony plunged his head into the water trough and then proceeded to spray slobber all over her. 'Did you really have to do that?' she said, wiping the slime from her chin.

Millie looked at her watch. 'What about I meet you back here in forty-five minutes?'

Alice-Miranda nodded. 'Say hello to Miss Hephzibah and Miss Henrietta for me and tell them I'll try to visit before we leave for China.'

Millie secured the lock on the yard and skipped off up the gravel driveway towards the main house.

Alice-Miranda hurried across the cobblestoned courtyard and through the large glass doors that had replaced the dilapidated stable entrance. She paused for a second and thought about the first time she'd been there – when Bonaparte had bolted on their way back from a picnic and sniffed out the abandoned vegetable patch. That was when she had first discovered Miss Hephzibah and Caledonia Manor. It was one of the best days of her young life;

finding a friend like her had been wonderful. She could hardly believe everything that had happened since.

Alice-Miranda walked down the wide hallway towards Jacinta's bedroom just as the housemistress emerged from her office at the end of the passage. Alice-Miranda smiled. 'Good afternoon, Mrs Clarkson. I was just looking for Jacinta.'

'Hello, my dear. She's in her room,' the woman replied. 'Are you excited for your holiday?'

Alice-Miranda's brown eyes sparkled. 'Yes, very. I can't believe we're going to China. It's going to be fantastic, although I wish I could speak a bit more Mandarin. I suspect it's going to be a little hard to communicate with everyone.'

'I'm sure you'll have a marvellous adventure no matter what.' Petunia gave a wave and headed off upstairs.

Having heard Alice-Miranda's voice in the corridor, Jacinta poked her head out of her room and waved her in. She quickly closed the door and the two girls hugged, Jacinta more fiercely than usual.

'It feels like I haven't seen you in ages,' Jacinta said.

'I know, we're all so busy. Have you been training a lot?' Alice-Miranda asked.

Jacinta nodded. 'I thought I'd stick with it until the next round of competitions and then I'll make a decision.'

Alice-Miranda noticed that Jacinta seemed agitated, fiddling with her hair and biting her nails.

'Are you all right?' Alice-Miranda asked. It wasn't like the girl to be so vague and anxious. 'What did you want to talk about?'

'It's going to sound stupid,' Jacinta replied, looking at the floor.

'You know you can tell me anything,' Alice-Miranda said, shooting her an encouraging smile.

'I know and that's why I only wanted to talk to you.' Jacinta cast a wary glance around the room and lowered her voice. 'Promise you won't breathe a word to anyone else?'

'Of course,' Alice-Miranda replied, crossing her heart.

Jacinta took a deep breath and sat down. For the first time, she spoke aloud the worries and fears that had been crowding her head for the past few weeks. Alice-Miranda took her hand and, together, they talked it all through. Jacinta was surprised to find that she didn't feel stupid at all. On the contrary, it was as if a weight had been lifted off her shoulders.

Chapter 5

Ophelia Grimm ran her finger down the list of names. She and Livinia had spent an hour before lessons confirming the children's host families, going over the information the Bright Star Academy had supplied and ensuring that the students' interests and talents matched as best they could.

There was a meeting with the young travellers after dinner – Charlie was taking the school minibus to collect the Fayle boys who were going on the trip, so Ophelia could go through the final plans with everyone. She was armed and ready to answer the inevitable barrage of last-minute questions and concerns.

There was a knock on the door and Louella Derby poked her head inside. 'May I have a word?' she asked. There was a nervous inflection in her voice that Ophelia didn't miss.

'Yes, of course.' The headmistress pointed to the chair on the other side of her gigantic desk. 'Have a seat.'

Louella Derby scampered in and perched on the edge of the seat. 'I've just received a call from Mrs Ridout –'

'Oh, yes. Sofia's due back tomorrow, isn't she? It's probably a good thing to have a couple of days at school with her friends before the trip. Losing a grandparent is never easy,' Ophelia said. 'But having her mother along as one of our parent helpers should be a welcome boost to both their spirits.'

Louella ran her hand across her sweep of brown fringe, pushing the hair from her eyes. 'That's just it,' she said. 'They won't be going. Sofia's been rushed into surgery for an emergency appendectomy.'

'Oh, heavens! Poor girl. We must organise flowers and a card from all the girls and I'll telephone tonight.' Ophelia sighed. 'What a dreadful turn of events. We'll have to cancel their tickets immediately and reorganise the groups now that we'll be one parent down.'

Louella gulped. 'I'm afraid that's not all.'

'Surely there isn't any other bad news? That's more than enough already.' Ophelia picked up a pen and hovered it above her writing pad.

'Well, it might not be bad news, per se,' Louella said slowly. 'It seems that Mrs Ridout ran into Venetia Baldini a few days ago and apparently Ms Baldini was terribly upset that she had missed the deadline for the trip.'

Ophelia had a sneaking suspicion she wasn't going to like where this was heading.

'So when Sofia took ill this afternoon, her mother telephoned Venetia. Now Ms Baldini and Caprice are going in their place. They've already had the tickets reissued from the travel agent this afternoon,' Louella blurted.

'What?' the headmistress exclaimed. 'So much for me being in charge around here. Perhaps I'll go on a long holiday and leave Mrs Ridout and Ms Baldini to run the school.'

Louella bit her lip. 'I'm sure Mrs Ridout was only trying to be helpful, and it does solve the problem of the extra supervision.'

Ophelia Grimm sighed loudly. 'Well, I can't say I'm thrilled with the idea. Granted, Caprice has been better behaved this term. I do hope she can keep it up, especially during the homestay. We certainly don't need any international incidents.'

'Mrs Ridout said that Venetia would be thrilled to help with anything you need – particularly the food – and she's going to organise a couple of special activities for the parents while the children are at school in Beijing. She's very well connected,' Louella said with a tentative smile.

'You'd better get Ms Baldini on the telephone, then,' Ophelia said. 'We may as well make the most of her contacts, but I will be having a quiet word with Mrs Ridout, once Sofia has recovered, about the importance of school protocols.'

'Would you like a cup of tea?' Louella offered, already heading for the door.

'Strong and black, please. And after you've called Ms Baldini, can you find Livinia and tell her I need to see her before dinner?' the headmistress said, sinking back into her chair.

★

'So is Jacinta giving up gymnastics?' Millie asked. On the way back from their visit to Caledonia Manor, she'd been so busy babbling excitedly about the upcoming trip she'd forgotten to ask Alice-Miranda. Miss Hephzibah and Miss Henrietta had wanted to know every last detail and had got the girl thinking about nothing else.

'She's just a bit unsure about a few things,' Alice-Miranda said, hoping to steer the conversation in a different direction.

From behind the servery, Doreen Smith wiped her hands on her apron and watched the enthusiastic faces of the girls and staff with great satisfaction. The usual chinking of cutlery had all but disappeared as most diners endeavoured to master the wooden chopsticks she'd ordered some weeks ago, although the noise level was certainly no less than usual. This evening she'd produced her most ambitious buffet yet, even attempting steamed pork buns, which had taken up far more

41

of the afternoon than she'd intended. Fortunately, they were a triumph.

'I tell you what, Mrs Smith's really outdone herself with this chicken. I've loved all the Chinese dishes she's been whipping up lately,' Sloane said.

Caprice smirked. 'Puh-lease, this isn't *real* Chinese food. But I'm sure you'll all enjoy your canine casseroles next week.'

Alice-Miranda was about to say something when the headmistress appeared.

'Hello, girls,' Ophelia said, looking rather flustered. 'Gosh, it's very noisy in here, isn't it?' She looked around for Miss Reedy, who was supposed to be in charge of the evening's supervision. The woman was usually a stickler for a quiet dining room. 'Good grief,' Ophelia muttered, when she spotted Miss Reedy and Mr Plumpton staring into each other's eyes at the head table. The headmistress added another mental note to the long list of tasks she had to complete before the trip, then returned her attention to the table. 'Caprice, may I have a word?'

The girl, who until now had been focused on her plate, turned around. She wondered if Mrs Howard had dobbed her in for being rude this morning. 'Am I in trouble?' she asked.

Ophelia Grimm shook her head. 'No, not this time.'

Caprice stood up and walked with the headmistress to the corner of the dining room, where they spoke for a minute or so.

Millie looked at them warily. 'What do you think that's about?' she asked.

Before anyone had time to answer, Caprice yelled out and started leaping about. 'Yes! Yes, yes, yes, yes!' she bellowed.

'Sounds as though Caprice has received some very good news,' Alice-Miranda said, dipping her dumpling into a saucer of vinegar.

Sloane and Millie looked at one another.

Caprice sped back to the table, clenching her fists and grinning like a Cheshire cat. 'I'm coming to China!' the girl cried.

Millie's jaw dropped. 'What? That's stupid! How come everything always works out for you at the last minute?'

'I thought the trip was full,' said Sloane.

'Sofia's appendix burst, so she can't go,' the girl said happily.

Alice-Miranda gasped. 'That's terrible!'

'Not for me.' Caprice shrugged. 'Besides, it's just an appendix. People get them taken out all the time.'

'Caprice, appendicitis can be very dangerous, especially if you get septicaemia,' Alice-Miranda said.

'What's that?' Sloane asked.

'Blood poisoning,' Alice-Miranda replied.

'Well, Miss Grimm said she's fine but she has to take it easy over the holidays,' Caprice gloated.

'We should send her a card and some flowers right away,' Alice-Miranda said, and Millie and Sloane nodded.

'Whatever,' Caprice said, rolling her eyes.

Sloane gulped. 'Aren't we going to be billeted in pairs for the trip?'

Millie looked at her in horror.

'There's no need to worry about it now. We'll find out at the meeting straight after dinner,' Alice-Miranda said.

But Millie's mind was racing. Surely Miss Grimm was far too sensible to have her and Caprice together. That just wouldn't be fair at all.

Chapter 6

Fuchsia Lee sat opposite her boss, her pen poised to take dictation. She looked around the office, noting the man's love of monochrome with the stark white walls and black bookcase laden with black leather-bound notebooks. She was by far the brightest thing in the room with her patent hot-pink heels and matching lipstick, which contrasted beautifully with her emerald-green suit. She glanced at her watch and wondered if he'd forgotten she was there.

Benny rubbed his temples and cradled his head in his hands. He stared at the spreadsheet, then leaned back and stretched his arms above his head. Fuchsia flinched at the sight of the two enormous damp patches under his arms. 'I'm thinking of putting Beluga on the market,' he said, finally.

Fuchsia's eyes widened in surprise.

'Don't look so nervous. I'm not letting you go. In fact, if I sell the studio, it will free up capital for more investment. I'm keen to diversify my interests,' Benny said as a bead of sweat formed on his forehead.

Fuchsia exhaled, relieved to hear that she wouldn't be forced to search for another job, especially because this one was a cinch. She was pretty much left to her own devices for the majority of the year as Benny Choo divided his time between Los Angeles, where his family was based, and Hong Kong. Some days she left the office early to run errands, and it didn't hurt anyone if she also squeezed in a manicure or lunch with her fiancé. It suddenly occurred to Fuchsia that if Benny sold Beluga Studios he might intend to spend a lot more time in Hong Kong.

Benny fingered the page in front of him, glancing momentarily at the bottom line. His eyes swirled and he felt his heart thumping vigorously inside his chest.

'Are you all right, Mr Choo?' Fuchsia enquired. 'You look a little off-colour.'

The woman jumped up and disappeared, returning a minute later with a tall glass of iced water.

Benny took it from her and gulped it down. 'Thank you,' he said, taking a few minutes to recover. 'So,' he resumed, 'do you agree that it would be best to put Beluga Studios on the market?'

Fuchsia had no professional training beyond a short secretarial course, so the fact that he was consulting her about such a huge decision was confusing to say the least. She hesitated before answering. 'Why do you want to sell?' she asked. 'I thought you loved making movies.'

'The movie business has been good to me and I've made a lot of money. So much money. More money than you can imagine a man could make.' Benny seemed to be working himself into a frenzy. 'I just think it might be time to move on,' he said.

Fuchsia clicked her pen twice as she processed this. 'It sounds as though you've made up your mind. How do you sell a movie studio?'

'I'll have to play my cards right to make sure there's a line of bidders begging to take it off my hands. We are one of the biggest and the best, so I will quietly spread the news.' Benny smiled to himself, already feeling better. 'And don't worry, I'll still be in Hong Kong. The Circus of Golden Destiny is based here, after all.'

The phone rang, and Fuchsia instinctively stood up to answer it but he batted her hand away. 'Good afternoon, this is Benny Choo speaking,' he said cheerily. His large face grew pale and he laughed nervously. 'O-of course it is good to hear from you, my friend.'

He shot a dark look at Fuchsia and wildly gestured for her to leave. She promptly scurried from the room and pulled the door closed behind her.

Chapter 7

It seemed that every last student and staff member had turned out on the driveway to farewell the Chinese tour delegation, despite their dawn departure. Once bags had been loaded and daypacks stowed, it was time for the giddy travellers to say their final goodbyes.

Doreen Smith smiled as Alice-Miranda hugged her tightly around the middle. 'Have a lovely time, dear.'

'I'm sure we will.' Alice-Miranda nodded, then gave Charlie Weatherly and Mrs Howard hugs too.

'Come along, everyone,' the headmistress ordered. She looked up at Benitha Wall, the PE teacher to whom she had, with some trepidation, handed over the reins. 'I trust there won't be any disasters in the next two days. Just get the rest of the girls off home for term break and I'll see you when we're back. Mrs Derby will know what to do if there are any problems – heaven knows the woman could run this school with or without me.'

Benitha suppressed the grin that was tickling her lips. There was no doubt about that, but it was still funny hearing it from Miss Grimm herself.

The children and accompanying adults piled on board the coach. Venetia Baldini insisted on sitting beside her daughter, while Ambrosia Headlington-Bear sat with September Sykes. Lawrence Ridley was also set to join the group, but he was meeting them in Hong Kong later that evening, flying directly from Los Angeles.

'Has anyone seen Fudge?' Mrs Howard asked the girls and staff standing beside the bus. She was sure she'd seen one of the children carrying him earlier. The little mite had probably taken himself off to the staff-room door, where he'd recently learned that, if he whined long enough, someone would give him a tidbit.

Inside the coach, the girls pressed their faces against the windows, waving furiously to their friends left behind. 'Goodbye!' they squealed as the vehicle rumbled down the driveway and into the village.

Alice-Miranda looked across at Jacinta, who was spread out in the seat opposite. 'Are you okay?' she whispered, wondering how the girl was feeling about seeing Lucas again. Jacinta shrugged, and Alice-Miranda patted her arm. 'Just be yourself.'

Jacinta swallowed hard and mustered a brave smile. The trouble was, she hadn't been feeling much like herself at all lately.

'You know we're going to have the best time,' Alice-Miranda said, her eyes twinkling.

Millie was staring out the window and thinking about all the famous landmarks she was keen to see, like the Great Wall of China and the Summer Palace. Her father had sent her a guidebook, but she'd resolved to keep a lid on her obsession for trivial facts on this trip as this seemed to drive some of her fellow travellers mad.

The coach pulled into the driveway at Fayle, where Figgy and Rufus could be seen throwing a rugby ball on the lawn while Professor Winterbottom's West Highland terrier, Parsley, ran after them.

Ophelia Grimm peered out the window. There was no sign of a staff member anywhere. She tore off after the coach like a thoroughbred from the starting gate. 'Good morning,' she called loudly, trying to get their attention.

Sep Sykes and Lucas Ridley appeared from the side of the building, trundling their suitcases. 'Hello Miss Grimm,' the boys chorused. 'Would you like us to load the bags?'

'Thank you,' the woman said gratefully, casting a look in Figgy and Rufus's direction. The unruly lads were still charging around with Parsley, apparently oblivious to everything. 'I'm glad two of you are organised.'

The coach driver opened the door to the luggage compartment and was shocked when a bundle of caramel curls leapt out at him.

'Fudge!' Ophelia exclaimed. 'What are you doing in there?'

The pup took off at pace, rushing at Parsley and nipping at his heels.

'I'll get him,' Sep called, and raced away.

Jacinta sat up in her seat. 'Is that Fudge?' she said, watching Sep sprint after the pup.

Venetia Baldini arched an eyebrow at her daughter.

'Hey, don't look at me,' Caprice protested.

Harold Lipp walked onto the front porch with a steaming mug of tea in his hand. Ophelia Grimm blanched at the sight of him. He was still wearing his pyjamas, with a garish yellow-and-pink plaid dressing-gown over the top and cobalt-blue slippers on his feet. The girls had also spotted him and were in fits of laughter.

'Mr Lipp's got the same pyjamas as your father, Sloane,' September Sykes remarked, to even greater guffaws.

'Right, boys,' Ophelia barked. 'It's time to go!'

Professor Winterbottom hurried out of the main foyer, apologising profusely for not being on hand to meet her. He'd had to take an early call from a parent who was overseas and had left the organisation of the boys to Mr Lipp – regrettably, as he now realised.

'Good heavens, Lipp, couldn't you at least have put some clothes on?' the professor tutted under his breath.

The Drama teacher quietly slipped away before he could get into any more trouble.

The headmaster quickly had the boys in order, checking they had their passports and belongings. To the man's surprise, Sep Sykes was also in possession of a canine.

'Oh, hello Fudge, what are you doing here?' The man stroked the pup's head.

Ophelia sighed. 'He was a stowaway. We'll have to go back.'

The headmaster squinted at his watch. 'Oh no, dear, leave him with me. I'll take him over to Mrs Howard now. You don't want to be late.'

Mr Plumpton ticked off the boys' names as they hopped onto the coach. Although there were only four of them, he was a stickler for protocol.

Lucas walked along the aisle and spied the empty seat beside Jacinta. 'Is this seat taken?' he asked.

Jacinta dragged her eyes to meet his and felt a strange churning in her stomach. 'Sloane's sitting here,' she said, the words flying out of her mouth before she had time to think.

Lucas looked a few rows up the aisle, where Sloane was sitting beside Susannah. He wondered if he'd done something to upset Jacinta, but decided to find out later. 'Okay, I'll sit with Sep,' he said with a smile.

Alice-Miranda, having witnessed the exchange, frowned. She wasn't sure what else she could say or do to convince the girl to just be herself. Over by the opposite window, and seemingly a world away, Jacinta was kicking herself for being so stupid.

Chapter 8

Millie spotted the island first as the plane descended out of the clouds. 'Look, that must be Hong Kong!' she declared, pressing her nose against the window.

Alice-Miranda leaned over to see. 'There are so many high-rise buildings,' she marvelled. 'And what about all those ships.'

Alice-Miranda began to count but stopped once she reached one hundred. The plane continued its descent into Hong Kong International Airport, which was located on its own small reclaimed island outside the city.

'Daddy said that they used to have to land among the apartment towers and offices before the new airport was built,' Alice-Miranda said.

Ambrosia Headlington-Bear shuddered. 'I hated coming into Kai Tak because you could actually see people in their living rooms watching television. I remember one chap waving to me, and I felt as if I could have reached out and touched him.'

'That's ridiculous,' Millie gasped.

'Terrifying, more like it,' the woman said, shaking her head.

The school group was seated together in the economy cabin of the Boeing 777. All up, their party of seventeen, including four accompanying staff members and three parents, plus the ten children, occupied almost two full rows.

'What are we doing when we get there?' Jacinta asked. She glanced across the aisle at Lucas, but quickly averted her gaze when she realised he was looking right back at her.

Sloane pulled some stapled sheets of paper from her daypack, which was tucked under the seat in front of her. 'Going to the hotel and having dinner,' she said.

'Oh, yum,' Caprice said sarcastically. 'I wonder if we'll be having pickled pigs' trotters tonight or jellyfish salad.'

'Stop it, Caprice,' Sloane ordered. She'd been worrying for days about whether she might be tricked into eating something disgusting.

Venetia Baldini looked up from the magazine she was reading. 'Is something the matter, girls?'

Caprice smiled. 'Of course not, Mummy. We were just talking about what we might have for dinner tonight.'

'Oh, there are so many fabulous restaurants in Hong Kong,' Venetia gushed. 'I do hope we go somewhere that serves pickled sea cucumber. Do you know they're nigh on impossible to find at home?'

Sloane's face turned a peaky shade of green.

'Are you all right, sweetheart?' Venetia asked. She hoped the girl knew where the sick bag was.

'Fine,' she replied weakly.

Venetia noticed her daughter's wicked smile and cottoned on. 'Sloane, it's true that the Chinese enjoy quite a lot of foods we would consider exotic, but I can assure you there will be plenty of things you'll be happy to eat and you won't be made to sample any of the things I imagine Caprice has been threatening you with. Although, *she* might enjoy them. I think a mother-daughter evening at Wangfujing Snack Street might be just the ticket – the tarantulas and millipedes on sticks are a marvellous delicacy.'

Caprice's face suddenly took on the same shade as Sloane's, and Venetia returned to her magazine with a feeling reserved only for a job well done.

'Isn't Venetia fabulous?' Jacinta whispered to Sloane.

Sloane nodded and couldn't resist poking her tongue out at Caprice, who immediately poked hers out too.

Alice-Miranda was thumbing through her copy of the itinerary. 'It says that we have a surprise after dinner. What do you think it could be?' she said.

'I bet it's a cruise on the harbour,' Millie said.

'Or a really long walk,' Jacinta groaned. 'Remember when we went to Paris and Miss Grimm made us walk everywhere?' She stole another look across the aisle at Lucas, but dropped her gaze to the floor when their eyes met.

The in-flight PA system crackled to life and the purser directed all passengers to return to their seats along with the usual information about tray tables, seatbacks and seatbelts. Ophelia took the opportunity to stand up and count the heads of her charges. She stopped at the empty seat beside Rufus in the row ahead of her.

'Where's George?' she asked the boy.

Rufus turned around. 'He went to the toilet an hour ago.'

'An *hour*! Why didn't you tell me he'd been gone that long?' Ophelia blustered.

Rufus shrugged. 'Sometimes I go to the toilet for that long.'

'And you don't want to go in after him, that's for sure,' Lucas quipped.

Swallowing her horror, Ophelia turned to Miss Reedy, who had her headphones on and was glued to the screen in front of her. Mr Plumpton was snoring gently beside her, with his monitor tuned to the flight path.

'Livinia,' the headmistress said loudly, but the English teacher remained firmly fixated on the romance unfolding in front of her. She sniffed and dabbed at her eyes with a tissue.

'I'll have a look, darling,' Aldous offered. He stood up and wobbled down the aisle towards the toilets at the rear of the plane before a terse young flight attendant blocked his path.

'I'm sorry, sir. You need to take a seat,' she said in a tone that suggested she wasn't sorry at all.

'Yes, but one of the children is missing,' the man said. 'I think he may be attending to . . . matters.'

The flight attendant shook her head. 'I've just checked the toilets. He's most certainly not in any of them.'

Aldous sighed and turned back.

'Have you found him?' Miss Grimm asked, peering past her husband and scanning the seats.

'Not yet, but he can't have gone too far,' the man said.

'I'll have a look up front – perhaps he used the toilet there,' Ophelia muttered, ignoring the seatbelt sign that was flashing an angry red. 'George Figworth, where on earth are you?' she called, leaving her seat to march down the deserted aisle. She shrieked as the plane passed through a vicious patch of turbulence and grabbed a sleeping passenger's arm to steady herself. The elderly lady awoke with a jolt and, realising someone had hold of her, shrieked back. Ophelia apologised, quickly let go and clung to the back of the seat instead.

Millie was enjoying the show from the safety of row thirty-eight. 'Where do you suppose he is?' she said.

Rufus snorted. 'He's probably parachuted out of here because he did such a stinker he couldn't face anyone.'

'Or he's in the cargo hold looking for snakes,' Sep said.

'Wrong!' Sloane grinned and wiggled her eyebrows. 'He's flying the plane.'

After regaining her balance, Miss Grimm continued to stalk down the aisle, examining each row of faces. She grimaced at a middle-aged businessman who was very busy with his finger up his nose until he caught sight of Ophelia's death stare and pretended he had an itch.

The feisty flight attendant was in the middle of returning a woman's hefty handbag into an overhead locker when she spotted the errant passenger. 'What do you think you're doing?' she called out. 'Madam! *Madam!* Sit down!'

'Not while one of my students is missing,' Ophelia yelled back. The plane dropped suddenly and she toppled into a spare seat.

Within seconds, the flight attendant had pounced on the woman and strapped her down with a seatbelt, pulling it tightly to ensure that she wasn't about to get away. 'Stay there until we land,' the woman ordered before hurrying to her own seat.

Ophelia fiddled with the buckle and was about to stand up when a voice spoke.

'Hello Miss Grimm.'

She turned and found herself looking at George Figworth, who was sitting across the partition beside her. 'What in heaven's name are you doing there?' she demanded. Her face was red and she was still furious at having been manhandled and yelled at.

'I had to go to the toilet and, while I was on my way back, the seatbelt sign came on. One of those nice flight attendants told me I had to sit down immediately, so I did. When the bumps stopped, she asked if I wanted something to drink. I felt like a chocolate milkshake, so she brought me one as well as a really nice cake.' Figgy wriggled around and rearrange his two pillows. 'The seats up here are very fancy. I even managed a proper nap because I could lie all the way down.'

Ophelia glanced back at her husband, who was leaning out of his seat at a ninety-degree angle. 'He's here,' she mouthed.

Aldous smiled with relief.

'What did Miss Grimm say?' Millie asked, craning her neck to see.

'Figgy's living it up in business class,' Rufus shouted. 'Wish I'd thought of that.'

'I'm sure he only ended up there by accident,' Alice-Miranda said, 'and you can't blame him for wanting to stay.'

Mr Plumpton roused from his slumber. 'Wh-what's going on?'

Miss Reedy removed her headphones and sighed as the movie she'd been watching came to a most satisfying conclusion. She turned to the seat beside her and was surprised to find it empty. A look of concern flashed across her face. 'Oh, where's Ophelia?' she said.

'It's all right,' Aldous said as the plane touched down on the runway. 'She's up front with Figgy.'

Livinia and Josiah frowned at one another, wondering what excitement they'd missed.

Chapter 9

In no time flat the group was on their way to the city, passing over bridges and through tunnels to Hong Kong Island. Mr Grump took it upon himself to provide a commentary, as he had travelled to the city many times over the years. 'If you look to your left, everyone,' he said, sweeping an arm in that direction, 'you'll see the Kwai Tsing container terminal. Hong Kong has one of the busiest ports in the world, with around half a million ships arriving and leaving each year.'

'Where's Disneyland?' Rufus Pemberley called out.

'It's back towards the airport,' the man replied.

'Can we go?' the boy asked. There was a chorus of support from the other children.

'I'm afraid we don't have time,' Miss Grimm interjected. 'We're only here until tomorrow evening and we've got a full day planned, but we do have a surprise for tonight that I'm sure you're going to love.'

There were a few groans of disappointment before the children began to speculate about the mystery treat. As the bus crossed over onto Hong Kong Island, the children gawped at the city with its contrast of gleaming skyscrapers and much older apartment blocks.

'Look at those washing lines,' Millie said, pointing at rows of bamboo poles that stuck out horizontally from the windows and balconies of the flats. Many were laden with clothes, and she watched, mesmerised, as an old lady used a long stick to retrieve her underwear.

The bus wound its way through the bustling streets before pulling up in the driveway of a hotel. The children hopped off and waited for their bags to be unpacked before wheeling them inside the enormous marble foyer.

'Well, this looks lovely,' September Sykes said, and promptly began to reapply her lipstick and powder.

'Mummy, do you have to do that right here?' Sloane asked through gritted teeth. She'd noticed a few of the hotel guests eyeing the woman.

'I haven't had a second to freshen up since we landed.' September pouted and smacked her lips together. 'I must look dreadful.'

'No, you're gorgeous, Mrs Sykes,' Figgy blurted, wanting to swallow his words as soon as he opened his mouth.

Sloane pulled a face. 'Gross, Figgy. That's my mother you're talking about.'

'Thank you, George,' September said, ignoring her daughter. 'That's very sweet of you to say.'

'When's your dad arriving?' Alice-Miranda asked Lucas, who was standing with Sep.

'He's due in tonight,' the boy said. 'I can't believe he agreed to come along. I thought there was no way he'd have the time, but he was really keen. I don't think he's done much travelling in China before.'

'I hope he has lots of photographs of the twins,' Alice-Miranda said. 'I'm so pleased Mummy's getting to spend some time with Aunt Charlotte and the babies.' When Lawrence had volunteered to act as a chaperone on the trip, Cecelia thought she'd take the opportunity to visit her sister for a week.

'Can I talk to you in private?' Lucas said quietly.

'Of course,' Alice-Miranda replied, and the two of them moved away from the others. 'What's the matter?'

'I was going to ask you the same thing,' he said. 'Have I done something to upset Jacinta? She's hardly spoken to me since we left school, and looked away every time I was trying to catch her attention on the plane.'

Alice-Miranda gave him a sympathetic smile. 'I think you should speak to her.'

'I tried,' Lucas said miserably. 'She acted all weird and made up something about having to talk to her mother. I thought we were friends – good friends.'

'Of course you are,' Alice-Miranda said.

Lucas shrugged. 'I'm worried that she's changed her mind about me. We used to talk – a lot – but now it's as if I've done something to offend her and she doesn't like me anymore.'

'I think you'll find that's not true at all,' Alice-Miranda said, 'but you two do need to chat. I think she's just scared.'

'Of me?' Lucas looked shocked.

'No, silly.' The girl grinned. 'Of growing up and having lots of different feelings that she doesn't know how to handle.'

Lucas let out a deep breath. 'Well, that's a relief. I think I know what you mean about getting older. It's way more complicated than I ever thought it would be.'

Chapter 10

Lucille Wong flinched as Deng Rou set to work. 'Ow,' she moaned.

'I have to release the tension or you won't be able to perform tonight,' the woman said. Her child-like hands massaged the knotted muscles of Lucille's right shoulder.

'I'd do anything not to perform tonight,' Lucille grouched. 'I don't understand why my father-in-law insists that we go on with it, and now this ridiculous new act – three generations of the one family performing a stunt that will likely kill us all.'

'You grumble about performing all the time. What I wouldn't give to have your agility.' Rou paused to rub some more oil on her hands. 'You could always leave the troupe,' she said, a devilish smile upon her lips. 'Except I would miss you and you would miss me more.'

Lucille rolled over to face her. Sadly, Rou's words were true. Over the years, despite the woman's meddlesome ways, and probably because of them, they had become allies of a sort. 'You know what you speak of is impossible. I will live and die in this troupe, but maybe, if we keep doing such stupid tricks, death will come sooner.'

Rou flipped Lucille back over and resumed her work.

'Must you use such force?' Lucille complained. 'You should be weakening with age, not growing stronger.'

'You will not be right if I don't get this knot undone,' Rou said. 'I never understood why you became an acrobat if you hate it so much. You are not like your sister-in-law, a peasant from the provinces. She married up with Charles. You,' the old woman scoffed, 'you married down. You could have been the wife of an important official, like your mother, but instead you ended up with Bernard. Don't get me wrong, he is very handsome and strong, but you confuse me.'

'I confuse me,' Lucille huffed.

She lay on the table, her mind wandering. Ever since she could remember, her mother had made it abundantly clear that she would have much preferred a son. With all the travelling her parents did, Lucille had been packed off to boarding school at age four. But it was no ordinary school. From the very beginning, Lucille had shown great potential as a gymnast, so she decided to work hard and prove that she could make something of herself. Her mother had been embarrassed at first, but when Lucille had met and married Bernard, the mere fact that she was no longer her concern had seemed to improve their relationship, for a short while at least. But Lucille had always felt like an outsider with the Wongs. Her sister-in-law, Cherry, was far more talented than she and it hadn't seemed to matter how hard she tried or what she did, it was nigh on impossible to impress her mother-in-law, Winnie. Over the years, Lucille had grown bitter. She would love to have lived her mother's life these days, instead of having to train and perform endlessly. And what she wouldn't give to have an inside bathroom.

'At least *you* can still perform,' Rou said, jolting Lucille back to reality. 'You are not a cripple like me.' A shiver of pain ran the length of the older woman's spine.

'Why do you always do that? I was almost asleep,' Lucille barked. 'I am just so bored, and look at my feet. Have you ever seen anything –'

Rou screwed up her face. 'So ugly.'

'I was going to say "tortured",' Lucille said tartly. 'Anyway, you know my problems. You have been in this troupe longer than anyone, apart from Lionel and Winnie.'

'I have been here longer than Winnie,' Rou snapped. She eased up on Lucille's right shoulder and began on the left.

'Hmph. I'm just waiting for the day when my father-in-law kicks the bucket and we can move out of that hideous *siheyuan* and buy a real house with indoor plumbing. Or better still, we could move to Hong Kong.'

'Maybe you will not have to wait that long,' Rou said.

Lucille tensed. 'What are you talking about now? Is my father-in-law unwell?'

'No, but perhaps you should ask your husband,' Rou said, and slapped her on the back. 'There, you are done. How does it feel?'

Lucille slid off the massage table and stood up. She arched her neck and rolled her shoulders.

'You couldn't do that before, could you?' The old woman chuckled and flexed her wrists. 'That is because I have the hands of a magician.'

Lucille arched an eyebrow. 'And the tongue of a troublemaker.'

'How can you say that?' Rou pouted, feigning offence. 'You hurt my feelings.'

'Because it is the truth,' Lucille said. 'Now, tell me what you know.'

Rou grinned slyly. 'What is it worth?'

'You tell me, old friend,' Lucille said, her eyes narrowing.

Chapter 11

Millie stared out of the hotel window at the city skyline. 'This place is amazing. It sort of reminds me of Tokyo but with a harbour and mountains,' she said. 'Actually, it's totally different. Tokyo was super flat and way bigger.'

'It's pretty, though, isn't it?' Alice-Miranda said. 'And I love how it feels. There's so much energy.'

Millie grinned at her friend. 'I'm glad we got to be together for Hong Kong and Shanghai.'

'Me too,' Alice-Miranda said with a smile. 'I suppose in Beijing they matched us with the host student according to our interests. I can't imagine there are too many horseriders in the city, so I wonder why I ended up with Jacinta. I mean, I'm not a gymnast or anything.'

Just before they left on the trip, Miss Grimm had told the children the names of their host families and who they would be paired up with from school. Alice-Miranda, along with Jacinta, was spending her time in Beijing with the Wong family. Millie and Sloane were with the Chans, and Caprice and Susannah had ended up with a family called the Fangs.

Millie shrugged. 'Maybe it was choir. What else did you write on your form?'

'I said that I liked travelling and trying new things.'

'Perhaps my billet plays tennis,' Millie said. 'Or Miss Grimm might have decided to mix it up a bit. We're together for most things, after all. Anyway, at least I'm not with Caprice. That would have been the worst!'

Caprice and Millie had both breathed a sigh of relief knowing they weren't spending the week together.

Alice-Miranda looked at her watch. They were waiting for one of the adults to collect them for dinner.

'We should be going soon,' the child said, just as there was a loud tap on the door.

'Don't forget your keys, girls,' Miss Reedy trilled from outside.

Millie stowed her camera into her daypack and Alice-Miranda picked hers up from the bed. With a grin and an air of curiosity, the two friends set off on their first adventure in Hong Kong.

The children followed the headmistress and her husband along the main road and down an alleyway. Each parent was stationed intermittently along the line of pairs, which left Mr Plumpton and Miss Reedy to bring up the rear.

The city was a heady cocktail of smells and sounds. Pedestrians powered towards them unperturbed and several times the children had to leap out of the way to avoid being clobbered by a wayward briefcase or market vendor's cart. Pretty lanterns and restaurant shopfronts lined the alley. On the sidewalk, touts competed for business, shouting their specials to entice the punters inside.

Caprice gagged. 'Sheesh. Does it smell this bad everywhere in Hong Kong?'

'I think you'll find that's a special scent.' Millie pointed at the overflowing industrial waste bins at the end of the laneway. She sniffed the air dramatically. 'Ah, yes, I think that's called *eau de garbage*.'

Alice-Miranda giggled.

Caprice pinched her nose. 'It's rank!'

Miss Grimm made a hard right into one of the restaurants and left the rest of the group to wait outside while she checked that all was in order. The headmistress reappeared with a slim woman dressed in a traditional cheongsam and clutching a clipboard. She smiled and indicated for the group to follow her inside.

'That smells better,' Millie said, breathing in the food aromas. On top of the curved reception desk, a gold ceramic cat waved its paw at the patrons, and behind it an intricate screen of red and gold partially hid a large fish tank teeming with sea creatures.

The restaurant was jam-packed. The hostess spoke quickly into a small microphone headset before ushering the group up a wide flight of stairs. To the left, customers were enjoying their meals, while on the right a series of doors led to private dining rooms.

'The food here must be really good,' Millie whispered. 'There's not a tourist in sight.'

Alice-Miranda nodded. 'It smells delicious.'

Venetia Baldini leaned in. 'It's one of my rules of thumb when I'm away overseas to eat where the locals do.'

'Everyone looks so happy,' Alice-Miranda said. She couldn't resist waving at an elderly lady who smiled at her. '*Ni hao*,' the girl chimed.

Ophelia Grimm noticed that lots of the patrons were now waving at the children, and quickly herded everyone into the room their hostess had entered and closed the door. She wondered how they were going to cope when Lawrence Ridley eventually joined them, which reminded her that he should have arrived by now. She looked around for Lucas and realised the boy was standing right next to her.

'Have you heard from your father?' Ophelia asked. Her brow furrowed when the boy shook his head. 'I hope he's not going to stand us up,' she said, wishing immediately that she hadn't when she saw the glum look on the boy's face. 'It's all right. I'm sure he'll be here soon. Probably just a delayed flight.' Miss Grimm hurried away to get everyone seated, leaving Lucas on his own.

Jacinta watched the exchange from the other side of the room. She wanted to go and talk to him but her legs felt as if they were set in concrete.

Alice-Miranda appeared beside her. 'Go on,' she whispered. 'He looks like he could use a friend.'

But Miss Grimm began ordering the children to be seated and the moment passed. Jacinta and Alice-Miranda sat down at the closest of the three round tables and were quickly joined by their friends. Alice-Miranda had tried to orchestrate for Jacinta to sit beside Lucas, but Sloane had rushed in.

'Do we get to see a menu?' Sloane asked tentatively.

Venetia shook her head. 'Miss Grimm and I pre-ordered a range of dishes for everyone to share. Don't worry, Sloane. There's nothing unusual. They didn't even have pickled sea cucumbers on the menu.'

'That's a pity,' Sep said. 'I'd have tried them.'

'As if,' Sloane quipped, hoping Venetia wasn't just telling her what she wanted to hear.

Minutes later, several waitstaff descended upon the room, setting down plates of fried rice, steamed fish, Chinese broccoli, braised tofu and sweet-and-sour pork on the lazy Susans in the centre of each table. Sloane started off rather slowly, but it wasn't long before she was tucking in with as much enthusiasm as the rest of the party.

'I hope the food's as delicious as this on the whole trip,' Sep said. He was wrestling some tofu onto his chopsticks and having a far greater degree of success than his mother, who had just managed to flick a piece of pork over her shoulder and onto Miss Grimm's plate.

'Good heavens!' Ophelia exclaimed as she was showered in soy sauce. 'Where did that come from?' She stood up and looked around. 'If anyone here thinks it's funny to throw food, you'll be on the first plane home.'

Miss Reedy and Mr Plumpton were both trying to suppress giggles, having seen exactly who had launched the offending missile.

'Mummy, I saw that,' Sloane muttered.

September looked at her sheepishly. 'I didn't mean it.'

'Would you like Mr Plumpton to assemble you a pair of training chopsticks?' Miss Reedy offered from the next table. The man had brought a container of elastic bands and tiny sheets of paper so he could modify the chopsticks for children who wanted a little more practise before going it alone.

Josiah Plumpton handed the woman a pair. 'Here you are, Mrs Sykes. They can be tricky little utensils to master.'

'Thank you.' September forced a smile, although her cheeks were a deep shade of red.

'Don't worry,' Ambrosia Headlington-Bear said quietly. 'It took me years to get the hang of chopsticks.'

'I just slipped, that's all,' September sniffed.

Sloane rolled her eyes. 'You're hopeless, Mummy.'

'Ease up on Mum, will you?' Sep mouthed across the table at his sister.

Sloane wrinkled her lip. 'I didn't say anything that wasn't true.'

Sep slid out of his seat and walked around to speak with his sister. He didn't want to have a slanging match with her across the table. 'Mum's really trying to fit in,' the boy whispered. 'You know this is her chance to show everyone how much she's changed. You were given a second chance – why can't you do the same for her?'

While September pretended that she hadn't, she'd heard every word of her son's speech. Sep was such a good boy – even if she didn't understand him at all. And she *was* trying. She'd recently begun a whole raft of activities for personal improvement in addition to her weekly grooming rituals. Her favourite was ballroom dancing. She had tried to talk Smedley into going along with her but, as always, he was too busy. So she'd gone on her own and found the most divine partner. Six foot two inches tall with a muscular physique, Carlos flung her around that dance floor like a puppet on a string. In the past few months she'd learned to tango and rhumba, and apparently she was quite good at it. Carlos had even entered them in a couple of amateur competitions, which, naturally, they'd won.

She'd been surprised when Smedley suggested that she accompany the children on their trip to China. It wasn't somewhere she especially wanted to go, but he'd thought it might be a way for her to bridge the ever-increasing chasm between her and the children – which was glaringly evident each time they came home from school. September decided that if Smedley was paying, it wouldn't do her any harm, and anyway, Carlos was off on his annual engagement on a cruise ship, teaching senior citizens how to dance.

Carlos had mentioned that the shopping in Hong Kong was outstanding and she could probably buy lots of great fabrics for all the dance outfits she'd be needing over the coming months. The problem was, there didn't seem to be any shopping time allocated. Surely the adults didn't have to babysit the children the whole time, September thought to herself. What sort of holiday would that be? She was planning to sneak off for a few hours in the morning.

'What's that awful noise?' Ophelia Grimm put her chopsticks on their rest and looked around the room. To her absolute horror, on the next table over, Rufus Pemberley was slurping short soup through his front teeth with great gusto. 'Pemberley, stop that at once,' the woman demanded.

'But it's a compliment, Miss Grimm.' The boy grinned, glancing at his dining companions, some of whom had begun to do the same thing.

'Not where I come from,' the woman fumed.

'It's true,' Mr Plumpton weighed in. 'Slurping isn't considered rude at all in China. It's actually good manners.'

The headmistress glared at the Science teacher. 'Thank you, Mr Plumpton. Next time you might like to keep your learned opinions to yourself.'

Rufus belched loudly, drawing howls of laughter from the other children and spontaneous applause from the waitstaff, who had come to clear the empty dishes.

'Mr Plumpton,' Miss Grimm said, lowering her voice. 'I really don't think that's appropriate, do you?'

The man shrugged. 'When in Rome . . . or Hong Kong, as it happens to be,' he said as he felt a firm jab in the ribs from his wife. 'Ah, no, I'll have a quiet word with the children later.'

At the end of the main course, Miss Grimm stood up to address the group. Figgy clattered his chopsticks against the side of his teacup to get everyone's attention.

'Good evening, children, parents and staff. I hope you'll agree that the meal this evening has been delicious, although perhaps we might like to consider that adopting every local custom might not be necessary.' She paused to look meaningfully at Rufus and Mr Plumpton. 'We've had a wonderful start to the trip – a smooth flight, with no luggage lost, and the hotel is lovely. I'd like to compliment the children on their behaviour, for the most part, and my heartiest appreciation to the parents and staff for volunteering to come along and help make these ten days a time that the students will never forget.'

Ophelia stopped as she caught sight of a man with a long bushy beard hovering around the door to the room. He seemed to be looking for someone.

Lucas spotted him too. 'Dad!' he yelled.

The man pushed open the door and hurried inside, embracing the lad in a bear hug. Alice-Miranda looked twice before realising who it was. She shot out of her seat and ran to greet him as well.

'That can't possibly be Lawrence Ridley,' September blurted. 'That fellow is a fat middle-aged man who looks like he's just climbed out of a bin – well, apart from that divine linen jacket he's wearing.'

Lawrence laughed. 'Fantastic! It seems I'm ready to start shooting my next movie as I *am* playing an overweight middle-aged man who's been in hiding in the woods for three months.'

September's jaw dropped. 'Good heavens, it *is* you!'

'Sorry I'm late, everyone. The flight out of Los Angeles was delayed,' Lawrence said. 'I'm just glad that I finally found the right restaurant. I walked into the place next door and was quickly shown the exit – I think they mistook me for a hobo.'

He grinned and there it was. Even with the bushy beard and chubbier features, that smile which could light up any room appeared and rendered every woman and girl in the place speechless.

Ophelia Grimm sighed. 'It's lovely to have you with us, Mr Ridley.' She stood up and shook hands with the man, as did the other staff, before introducing him to the parents.

Of course, he already knew Ambrosia and greeted her warmly. Lawrence then thanked Venetia for his new figure, explaining that his wife was completely devoted to her show, *Sweet Things*, and was whipping up all manner of sugary treats for him. Venetia smiled sheepishly and said she was glad to help. September was almost completely overcome and looked as though she might faint, but fortunately Miss Grimm stepped in.

'Would you like something to eat?' Ophelia asked. 'They've just cleared away the last of the main courses, but here comes dessert.'

Lawrence chuckled and rubbed his belly. 'I can't very well say no, can I? I've worked hard for this body.'

Aldous Grump quickly found a spare chair and squeezed it in between Sep and Lucas.

'Thanks,' said Lawrence. 'So what's happening after dinner?'

'I was just about to get to that,' Miss Grimm said, trying to remember where she'd been up to before the man had arrived. 'We're off to see a show called the Circus of Golden Destiny, which happens to be playing quite close by to our hotel.'

The children looked at each other and grinned. 'Cool!' they chorused.

'I hope they don't have any elephants or tigers or performing bears,' Jacinta said. Ever since the discovery of the puppy farm in the woods near their school, some of the girls had been very active in campaigning against cruelty to animals.

Miss Grimm shook her head. 'There are no animals in the performance,' she assured the girl.

'But how can it be a circus without animals?' Figgy said.

Lawrence Ridley picked up a second cup of mango pudding from the lazy Susan and chimed in. 'It's fabulous. I've seen them a couple of times in different countries and you won't be able to take your eyes off the acrobats.'

'Really?' Jacinta gasped. 'There are acrobats?'

'Oh, Jacinta, you'll love it,' Lawrence said with his mouth full. 'These guys are the best in the world.'

'I saw the advertising signs on one of the buildings on the way into the city,' Millie said.

Livinia Reedy looked at her watch. 'We'd better not dally. The show starts at eight and it's just on seven now.'

Ophelia Grimm turned to her colleague, impressed that the woman was finally paying more attention to their schedule.

'This is going to be amazing,' Jacinta fizzed.

'I quite agree, Jacinta,' Miss Grimm said with a nod. 'Eat up, everyone!'

Chapter 12

Millie walked ahead of Alice-Miranda as the young usher guided them to their seats just a few rows from the stage.

In the middle of the square platform was a solitary oversized bed, which looked as if it were made of glass. Jacinta nudged Alice-Miranda and pointed towards the ceiling, where a giant rig contained an overhead pulley system with ropes and harnesses. In the shadows of the shimmering gold backdrop, the children watched in wonder as figures, dressed head to toe in black, scampered up rope ladders and positioned themselves on the various spotlights that were dotted around another square metal frame. A few minutes later, in the darkened auditorium, several more silhouettes could be seen ascending the precarious scaffolding.

'I think they must be some of the performers,' Alice-Miranda said, unable to take her eyes off them.

'This is really different to any circus I've ever been to before,' Sloane commented loudly. 'I thought there'd be a big top and a ringmaster.'

'At least there are no revolting animal smells,' Caprice said. 'When Mummy and Daddy took me to the circus, an elephant did a wee the size of a lake right in front of us. It was disgusting.'

'Stop exaggerating, Caprice,' Venetia tutted. 'I'd have said it only qualified as a paddling pool.'

Jacinta felt a tap on her shoulder and turned around to find Lucas offering her a program. 'I bought this for you,' he said quietly. 'I thought you might like to know about the performers – especially the gymnasts.'

'Thanks,' Jacinta squeaked. Flushing bright red, she took it and turned back around. She'd wanted to tell him that she couldn't wait to read about the circus and the profiles of each of the acrobats, but nothing came out. Jacinta cringed in her seat, hoping the ground would open up and swallow her right there and then. Lucas had just done something really kind, but from her reaction anyone would have thought he'd handed her a rattlesnake.

Alice-Miranda smiled at her friend. 'That was very thoughtful of him.'

Jacinta glanced down, dumbly, at the program in her hands. It had been the perfect opportunity to talk to him, she berated herself, and now the moment was lost, again.

'Is everything all right with you two?' Lawrence whispered to his son.

Lucas shrugged and shook his head. 'I don't know. I'm so confused.'

The houselights dimmed and a drum rolled. Lucas looked at Jacinta in front of him and recalled how he'd hated her the first few times they'd met, ages ago at Alice-Miranda's house. But it hadn't taken long for them to realise they had a lot more in common than he could ever have imagined. She'd been so fragile and angry at the time and so had he. They'd bonded over absent parents and feelings of abandonment and in the past couple of years they'd become good friends. She was the girl who made his heart race and his palms sweat, but best of all she made him laugh – she was his closest friend apart from Sep.

A bright light shone on the bed, where a girl dressed in long pyjamas lay curled into a tight ball. She didn't move for quite some time. Then, all of a sudden, she began to toss and turn as if in the throes of a fever. She sat up just as three enormous dragons burst onto the stage, dipping and dancing around her. She clutched at her hair and face and stood up, gazing to the heavens.

'What do you think that's about?' Millie whispered.

'Maybe she's having a dream,' Alice-Miranda said.

The dragons disappeared and were replaced by silver angels overhead, suspended from gigantic lengths of sheer ribbon. Their gossamer wings glistened as they twirled and spun in the air.

One of them swooped down low and plucked the little girl from the bed, carrying her high above the audience, where they put her onto a trapeze swing.

Jacinta's heart was in her mouth. 'Oh my goodness, she's hanging from her toes!'

The swing began to move, arcing higher and higher. The child spun upwards and flipped to grab the rail with one hand, then just by a pinky finger.

'I can't look!' Millie said, covering her eyes.

The child mesmerised the crowd with her incredible strength and agility. At one point the swing she was perched on rose so high it disappeared into the rafters of the building, the girl along with it. She reappeared wrapped in a length of red satin. Without warning, she plunged to the floor, the satin ribbon rapidly unfurling from around her. The audience gasped and a few women screamed in horror. The girl pulled up mere centimetres from the deck and couldn't resist looking into the audience with a mischievous grin.

The show continued with clowns on unicycles, followed by acrobats dressed as strong men, hurling barbells and medicine balls as they sprang from high towers and catapulted from trampolines. There were death-defying trapeze artists, tightrope walkers and even a group of skipping chickens. The children had never seen anything like it before and spent almost the entire show with their mouths agape.

Jacinta's eyes were everywhere as she tried to take it all in. She watched yet another group of tumblers flip across the stage and marvelled at the way they made tricks that had taken her years to learn seem effortless. In that moment, Jacinta knew exactly what she wanted to do. She wasn't going to give up all those years of gymnastics at all. She was going to become an acrobat! Having finally made a decision about something that had been bothering her for months, an overwhelming sense of calm settled upon the girl despite the fervent activity around her.

Her eyes turned upwards as an eagle soared overhead. The girl fell from its back, tumbling and spinning, before landing onto the bed. She curled into a ball as the haunting strains of a lone flautist beckoned her to sleep. The lights went out and a final drumbeat echoed through the stadium.

Figgy was on his feet cheering before anyone else. 'Woohoo!' he crowed.

Soon the entire audience was up, clapping and cheering as the cast made their way onto the stage. The loudest applause was reserved for the tiny girl who had played the lead role. She looked up into the audience and waved. Jacinta waved back, in awe of the child's extraordinary athleticism and courage. Her heart felt as if it were about to burst through her chest. 'She was astonishing!' Jacinta gushed, and turned to Lucas. 'I wish I could meet her.'

Lucas grinned and leaned in to speak to his father. 'Dad, did you hear that?' he yelled over the noise. 'Jacinta said she'd love to meet the lead acrobat. Do you think you could pull a few strings?'

'*You* barely recognised me,' Lawrence said, laughing. 'How am I supposed to get anyone else to realise it's me? Besides, I think Miss Grimm might go into meltdown if I put the word out that I'm here.'

'You don't have to tell everyone – just the stage manager – and see if they can arrange for Jacinta to speak with the girl, that's all,' the boy said.

'What I do for you.' Lawrence winked and stood up. 'I'd better take Alice-Miranda too.'

He couldn't believe he was about to do this. A few weeks ago he'd mocked his friend George mercilessly when the man had used his star power to get them a table at an exclusive restaurant. It wasn't Lawrence's style at all and his wife, Charlotte, would have been mortified – she hated all that Hollywood 'who's who' nonsense.

Lawrence tapped Jacinta on the shoulder and the girl sprang into the air. 'Sorry,' he said as she spun around. 'Can you and Alice-Miranda come with me?'

'Okay, but where are we going?' Jacinta asked warily.

'Maybe nowhere, but I'd like to give it a go,' he said with a cheeky grin. He turned to Lucas. 'Tell Miss Grimm we won't be long.'

Chapter 13

Alice-Miranda and Jacinta followed Lawrence Ridley as they dashed through the building and down a long flight of steps. He had an overwhelming urge to stop at the ice-cream cart up ahead of them but decided they didn't have time.

'I can't believe you're doing this,' Jacinta said as they neared the stage door.

'Well, you can thank Lucas if it works out,' the man said.

Jacinta bit her lip and shot Alice-Miranda a guilty look. She felt so silly for avoiding Lucas, even sillier after he'd bought her the program, but it was as if every time he came near her, her tongue got tied in knots and she didn't know what to say.

'Excuse me,' Lawrence said to a stocky security guard dressed in a black suit. 'Would I be able to have a word with the stage manager?'

The man frowned and shrugged his shoulders.

Lawrence looked at the girls apologetically. 'This might be a bit trickier than I thought. I don't think this fellow speaks English.' Lawrence had another idea. 'Do you have the program with you?' he asked Jacinta.

Jacinta nodded and pulled it from her daypack.

Lawrence quickly flicked through the pages and found one of the child star sitting in the middle of the giant bed. He walked back to the security guard and showed him the photograph. 'We'd like to meet this girl.'

The burly fellow shook his head.

'Look, I'm not sure if you know me but –' Lawrence grimaced – 'I'm an actor. You might have heard of me? Lawrence Ridley?' He looked at the guard hopefully.

At the mention of the name, the man tilted his head and considered Lawrence. He squinted, then took a step back and laughed.

Lawrence sighed, his shoulders slumping. At least Miss Grimm would be pleased to know that no one recognised him. He turned away and walked back to the girls. 'Sorry, Jacinta. I'm embarrassed to say I even pulled the celebrity card and it didn't cut any sway with that guy.'

Jacinta smiled and took back her program. 'That's okay, Lawrence. Thank you for trying.'

The trio was about to leave when the stage door opened and a short, rotund man in a pinstriped suit walked out, flanked by two tall chaps dressed identically in black.

'He must be important,' Alice-Miranda said. 'They look like bodyguards.'

Lawrence glanced over and his face lit up. 'Benny!' he exclaimed, rushing towards the man.

The beefy guards set upon Lawrence in a split second, kicking his legs from beneath him, spinning him like a top before pinning him to the ground.

'Ow!' Lawrence groaned as one of the men kneed him in the back.

'Stop that!' Alice-Miranda yelled, and rushed over with Jacinta right behind her. 'Let go of him!'

'Benny, it's me – Lawrence Ridley,' the man said into the cement.

The rotund chap squinted over the top of his stylish red glasses. 'Ridley? What are you doing here? And why do you look like a fat hobo in a rich man's clothes?' The man tutted, then gestured for his bodyguards to help the fallen star. 'Get him up! Up! Don't you realise who this is?'

'It's okay, Benny. I'd rather not make a fuss,' Lawrence said sheepishly, as people around them began to stare.

'My gosh, Lawrence,' Benny said, then turned to his guards. 'You are sacked and you are sacked,' he said, pointing at them one by one. He shook his head. 'Idiots.'

'But, boss . . .' one of the men protested.

'Just get out of my sight,' Benny said, shooing them away with a wave of his large paw. He turned back to Lawrence. 'Why are you in Hong Kong? Are you shooting a movie? What movie? Why don't you make movies with my studio anymore?'

Lawrence was beginning to regret calling out to the man. 'No, I'm not working,' he assured him. 'It's a long story. Anyway, let me introduce you to my niece, Alice-Miranda, and her very good friend Jacinta.'

'It's lovely to meet you, Mr Choo.' Alice-Miranda held out her hand, which the man shook gently. She couldn't help noticing the trickles of sweat tracking down his temples and the dark patches under his arms. Alice-Miranda discreetly pulled a tissue from her pocket to wipe the moisture from her palm.

Jacinta simply nodded at the man and said hello.

'We were hoping to meet that phenomenal little gymnast who played the lead role. I think I saw her name is Summer,' Lawrence explained. 'You see, Jacinta's a gymnast herself and would love to chat with her. You don't happen to know someone who can get us in, do you?'

'Of course I do,' Benny said, puffing out his chest. 'That would be me, the owner of the circus.'

'How exciting!' Alice-Miranda exclaimed. 'I've never met anyone who owns a circus before.'

'Wow,' Lawrence said. He had only known Benny Choo as the owner of Beluga Studios, a big Hollywood production company. Lawrence had worked for him quite a few years back on a hugely successful franchise called The Lobster movies. The blockbuster films followed a group of down-and-out cat burglars who pull off the biggest heists in history. Since then, though, Benny had invested in a bunch of massive flops and word on the street was that the studio was struggling. 'So you're diversifying your interests then,' Lawrence said. 'This is quite some operation, the Circus of Golden Destiny.'

'Something like that,' Benny said. 'Right then. Shall I take you to meet the star of the show?'

Alice-Miranda and Jacinta nodded eagerly. 'Yes, please,' they said in unison.

'Come.' Benny turned around and walked back up the stairs to the stage door. This time the guard stepped aside immediately and Benny led the group into a long corridor, where they had to dodge jugglers and tumblers, spinning plates and batons.

'I thought the show was over,' Lawrence said as he spun around, narrowly avoiding a collision with a unicyclist.

Jacinta's eyes were on stalks as she took it all in. Her head was instantly filled with images of herself performing in the Circus of Golden Destiny. Alice-Miranda ducked to avoid being hit in the head by a plate hurtling through the air.

'Oh, it is never over.' Benny chortled knowingly. 'The only way to be the best in the world is to practise and practise and then, when you're fed up, you must practise some more.'

'That reminds me of how we had to rehearse for months on end for The Lobster movies. Benny actually set up some robberies we thought were real,' Lawrence said. 'Do you remember that time we were in Denmark and you had to come and bail us out after the Danish police thought we were trying to rob the Amalienborg Palace?'

'But why would you do that?' Alice-Miranda was shocked to hear it; Uncle Lawrence was one of the most honourable people she knew. Although, Jacinta had been recalling the time at Alice-Miranda's house when Lawrence had snuck about in the garden and she thought he was up to no good. He had proven her wrong in the end, but there was no doubting the man's abilities as an actor.

'It's called method acting, my dear,' Benny said, 'and your uncle is one of the best at it.'

'Why are they called The Lobster movies, anyway?' Jacinta asked.

'You can ask Lawrence to explain them to you later. They sound ridiculous but, trust me, it all makes sense in the end,' Benny said with a wriggle of his eyebrows. 'Here we are.'

He stopped at one of the many doors that lined the hallway and rapped on it sharply. A small voice answered and Benny pushed the door open. He then spoke quickly in a language Alice-Miranda assumed was Cantonese as it definitely wasn't Mandarin.

Benny turned to them and smiled. 'Miss Tan is happy to receive guests, but I'm afraid she speaks very little English, so you will just have to be patient,' he warned them.

Jacinta grinned upon hearing Summer's surname. She hadn't noticed it before when she skimmed the program.

Benny raised his eyebrows. 'I know – Summer Tan – funny name, hey?'

'I think it's sweet,' Alice-Miranda said, and Jacinta nodded. 'Are you coming in with us?'

The man shook his head. 'No, I want to speak with your uncle for a minute.'

'Of course,' Alice-Miranda replied.

'We can't be long or Miss Grimm will be wondering where we are,' Lawrence said.

Alice-Miranda thought Jacinta was looking a little pale. 'Are you all right?'

The girl nodded. 'I can't believe we're going to meet her. She's the most astonishing gymnast I've ever seen.'

Alice-Miranda took Jacinta's hand and the girls walked into the room.

Typical of dressing rooms the world over, there was a small vanity table and a mirror surrounded by naked light globes. But unlike most other dressing rooms, there was a balance beam on the opposite wall and a long satin ribbon hanging from the middle of the ceiling.

'*Ni hao*.' Alice-Miranda gave a wave and hoped that the Cantonese greeting for 'hello' was similar to that in Mandarin. 'I'm Alice-Miranda Highton-Smith-Kennington-Jones, it's a pleasure to meet you.' She turned to her starstruck friend. 'And this is Jacinta Headlington-Bear.'

Jacinta rushed forward. 'You're amazing,' she gushed, clenching the girl's hand in a vice-like grip. 'I've never seen anyone do the things you do. I can't believe it.'

'Thank you,' Summer said softly, attempting to manoeuvre her hand back, and bowed.

'Sorry! I'm crushing you, aren't I?' Jacinta relinquished her hold on the girl. 'How embarrassing.'

Summer was even more petite up close. It was hard to tell her age, but Alice-Miranda thought she was probably around twelve or thirteen at a pinch.

'We loved your show,' Alice-Miranda said, with some accompanying hand gestures.

Summer smiled again and nodded.

'Do you like being in a circus?' Jacinta asked. She thought about how she could do some actions that might help the girl understand, but came up empty.

'How have you been getting along?' Benny asked, walking into the room with Lawrence.

'Not too badly,' Alice-Miranda replied, 'but perhaps you could help interpret for us. Jacinta asked Summer if she liked working in the circus.'

Benny posed the question in Cantonese. Summer gulped and stared for a moment before Benny said something else. Then she nodded fiercely, a thin smile on her lips.

'It must be incredible,' Jacinta said. 'I do gymnastics too. I was actually thinking of giving it up altogether, but now Summer has inspired me to become an acrobat.'

'Perhaps you will come and work for me,' Benny said, chuckling.

'That would be a dream come true,' Jacinta sighed.

Alice-Miranda studied Summer's face. The girl was so expressive on stage, but in real life she almost seemed sad. For a few seconds, Alice-Miranda held her gaze and something passed between them, although she had no idea what it meant.

'How long in Hong Kong?' Summer asked, her words stilted as she worked hard to remember the right ones.

'We're leaving tomorrow night for Shanghai and then after that we're going to school in Beijing for a few days,' Alice-Miranda explained slowly, and waited for Benny to translate.

'Sorry, girls, but we'd better get moving, otherwise Miss Grimm will have my head,' Lawrence said. 'It's been a pleasure to meet you Summer.'

Jacinta couldn't help herself and, as they were about to leave, she rushed forward and hugged the girl.

Summer gasped, and Jacinta released her just as quickly. 'I'm so sorry. I don't know what came over me.' The words tumbled out faster than the gymnasts in the hallway as she turned bright red and scampered from the room.

'It was lovely to meet you,' Alice-Miranda said, giving Summer an affectionate squeeze.

The group filed out of the room and closed the door. Summer collapsed in her chair and looked at herself in the mirror. Finally, she allowed the tears to slide down her face.

Chapter 14

Alice-Miranda was awake long before it was time to get up. As Millie snored gently from the next bed, Alice-Miranda pushed back the covers and walked to the window, where the first rays of sunshine sparkled on the water below. She sat down on the ledge that doubled as a seat and watched the city wake up. A ferry made its way across the harbour while smaller fishing boats chugged along the coastline. There were yachts bobbing about in the marina and she spotted a couple of junks too. Huge ships steamed in and out of view. Others were moored, waiting to load or unload their cargoes. From eighteen storeys high, she could see shopkeepers thrusting up shutters and street vendors pushing carts.

Millie's eyes fluttered open and she squinted into the light. 'Oh, did I sleep in?' she yawned.

Alice-Miranda shook her head. 'No, I just woke up a while ago,' she said, and hugged her knees. 'The view from here is gorgeous.'

'What are we doing today?' Millie asked, propping herself up on one elbow. Miss Grimm had made some announcements the night before but she couldn't remember much of what was said. After the flight and their evening activities, Millie had felt like a zombie on the way back to the hotel. She couldn't wait to fall into bed and she must have been asleep before her head hit the pillow.

Alice-Miranda slid off the ledge and pulled the itinerary from her daypack. 'We're taking the tram to the top of Victoria Peak first of all. I hope the weather stays like this because the views will be stunning. Then we're going to some markets and having lunch, and after that it says we're off to the botanic gardens and the zoo and then we're flying to Shanghai.'

'That sounds exhausting,' Millie mumbled. She fell back on the bed and snuggled under the duvet.

'You can't sleep now,' Alice-Miranda said. 'I need an update on some of the sights we should be looking out for from your guidebook, and breakfast is in half an hour. We have to pack our bags too and take them with us. I'll have first shower, if you like.'

There was a knock on the door. Alice-Miranda walked over and stood on the tips of her toes to look through the peephole. It was Lawrence. She undid the latch and opened the door with a smile. 'Good morning, Uncle Lawrence, you're up early. Is everything all right?' She wondered why he was looking so serious.

'May I come in for a tick?' he asked, wiping some crumbs from the side of his mouth.

'Of course. Is there something the matter?' Alice-Miranda asked.

Lawrence walked into the room and waved to Millie. 'To be honest, I'm not sure. I've just had a call from Benny Choo. He wanted to know what you and Summer talked about.'

'Why would he want to know that?' Millie said.

Alice-Miranda thought for a moment. 'Well, let's see. We told her how clever she was and how much we admired her bravery and Jacinta hugged the poor girl like there was no tomorrow. Why? What's happened?'

'He didn't say exactly,' Lawrence said, scratching his head. 'In fact, he was being quite mysterious. Why would he call me at this hour to ask what you talked about?'

Alice-Miranda frowned, recalling the strange look that had passed between her and Summer after the girl was asked whether she liked being in the circus. 'There was one thing,' Alice-Miranda said, 'but I may have just imagined it.'

'What was it?' Millie asked, sitting up with interest.

'It was a feeling more than anything,' Alice-Miranda said. 'It was probably nothing.'

Millie's mind raced with possibilities. 'Maybe Summer hates being in the circus,' she said excitedly. 'Can you imagine how hard they must train to be as good as they are? Perhaps she's run away.'

'Golly, I hope not,' Lawrence said. 'Anyway, I told Benny I'd call him back once I spoke to you, so I'll see if I can get anything more out of him.'

'How well do you know Mr Choo?' Alice-Miranda asked.

'About as well as you really know anyone in Hollywood. In some ways I owe him my career. He took a big risk when he cast me in The Lobster trilogy – nobody had any idea who I was back then – and I don't know if I'd be anywhere these days without having had that opportunity,' Lawrence said. 'But to be fair, he made an absolute killing on those movies, which is just as well because I'm sure he hasn't had any good earners since then. I'm relieved I passed on a role he offered me in order to play Vector instead. His movie tanked while *Vector* turned out brilliantly for me.'

'Have you worked with him again?' Millie asked.

'Sadly not. He keeps sending me scripts, but they've all been pretty terrible. Anyway, I should let you get ready, or Miss Grimm will be more cross with me than she was last night. I'd better not wander off anywhere without telling her in future. I'll see you at breakfast,' Lawrence said, and walked out the door.

Millie looked at her friend. 'So what was this feeling you mentioned?'

'I don't know,' Alice-Miranda said, 'but there's something bothering me. I just wish I could work out what it is.'

'You know, you're usually right when it comes to your strange feelings,' Millie said as she hopped out of bed.

Alice-Miranda grabbed some clean clothes from her suitcase. 'Well, I hope I'm wrong this time. Summer is so talented and quite the sweetest girl. I'd hate to think she was in any trouble.'

Chapter 15

Caprice yawned and rubbed her sleepy eyes. Whoever was in the room next door to her and her mother had snored like a jet engine all night. She'd vowed to find out who it was and make sure that they were nowhere near them in the next hotel.

'You look tired,' Sloane commented as the group stood on the platform waiting for the tram.

'Yeah, you've got bags under your eyes,' Figgy chimed in.

'As big as my suitcase,' Rufus added.

Caprice shot them a fierce glare. 'You would too if someone had kept you awake all night with their snoring.'

'It was probably us,' Rufus said, grinning. 'We were in room three-oh-one.'

'We were miles away,' Caprice said, 'in three-six-nine at the end of the corridor – so there was only one room next to us.'

Figgy and Rufus had already lost interest in the conversation and skived off to see whether they could coax a free drink from a vending machine they'd spotted.

'Oh, we were in three-six . . .' Sloane stopped suddenly, realising that she and her mother had been in the room beside Caprice and Venetia. 'Six,' she fibbed. 'Three-six-six, down the hall.'

Sloane hadn't heard a thing last night. It must have been her mother, she thought, because if it wasn't, that could only mean one thing and that was too awful to contemplate.

Further along the platform, Jacinta had just finished telling her mother that acrobatics was the future direction she wanted to take. Ambrosia wasn't sure if she liked the idea – it seemed even more dangerous than gymnastics – but there was no point getting into an argument about it now. Jacinta had been on edge for weeks, something Ambrosia had put down to the moodiness of growing up. The woman was relieved when Alice-Miranda interrupted their discussion and even more pleased to see Venetia and Mr Grump arrive on the platform with two trays of takeaway coffees for the adults. She promptly excused herself from the girls and went to get one.

'Is everything all right with you and your mother?' Alice-Miranda asked, having noticed the serious expression on Ambrosia's face before she'd walked away.

Jacinta nodded. 'I just told her I'm going to be an acrobat. I don't think she's that keen on the idea, but that's her problem. She can't stop me.'

Alice-Miranda relayed her early-morning visit from Lawrence and the odd conversation he'd had with Mr Choo about Summer.

'I can't stop thinking about her,' Jacinta sighed dreamily. 'She's my idol.'

'Did you talk to Lucas this morning?' Alice-Miranda asked.

Jacinta shook her head. The boy was standing with Lawrence, who was eating a very large custard bun. 'I will, though,' she promised.

'Hey,' Millie called, and aimed her camera at the girls. 'Smile!'

The tram pulled up and the children and adults piled into the carriage. When everyone was safely on board, the tram lurched forward and soon began its ascent. Victoria Peak loomed large in the distance.

'Whoa, this thing's cool,' Figgy declared as he tried to force open the window.

'Sit down, George!' Miss Grimm barked. 'You need to keep your body inside the carriage at all times. You can take photographs through the glass.'

Alice-Miranda nabbed a seat beside her uncle. She was eager to find out if he knew anything more about Summer. Millie squeezed in beside her.

'Did you speak with Mr Choo?' Alice-Miranda asked.

'No, I've left a message for him,' Lawrence said. 'Did she tell you how old she was?'

Alice-Miranda shook her head. 'No, but I wouldn't have thought she was more than thirteen. It must be quite a burden to work so hard and carry a sold-out show at such a young age.'

'The poor girl's probably exhausted,' Millie said. 'Maybe they make her do loads of jobs on top of being the star of the show. What if she has to cook and clean and sew costumes and stuff, like a slave? She's probably run off so she can have a rest.'

Alice-Miranda frowned. 'I think your imagination might be getting the better of you, Millie. Mr Choo seems like a very nice man and lots of fun too.'

'Yes, Benny's a good fellow,' Lawrence said.

'I hope Mr Choo calls back soon, though,' Alice-Miranda said. Despite not wanting to give any credence to Millie's fanciful notions, Alice-Miranda knew she'd feel much better once she was sure the girl was safe and sound. She looked at her uncle. 'Have you talked to Aunt Charlotte?'

Lawrence nodded, and pulled a chocolate bar from his pocket. 'She and your mother are run off their feet. The twins are keeping them very busy.'

Alice-Miranda grinned. 'I bet. I can't wait to see them again. We'll have to make sure that we spend all of the long holidays together, or the next thing you know they'll be at school. I don't want to miss them in that cute toddler stage.'

'Cute toddler stage?' Lawrence tilted his head. 'That's one way to put it. I'm surprised you didn't hear Imogen's tantrum the other night – I know half of Beverly Hills did. I think she's destined to be a singer because she's already a diva, that's for sure.

The funny thing is, Marcus is the opposite. He is the calmest child you'll ever meet. He just stared at her and, at one point, I could have sworn he shook his head.'

'I bet you've never had a tantrum,' Millie said, looking at Alice-Miranda.

'Of course I did,' the girl replied.

'When?' Millie challenged. 'Can you remember one?'

The girl thought for a moment. 'Um . . . Oh, I know. When I was four, Mrs Oliver and I made a cake for Mummy's birthday and I insisted on carrying it to the table outside, where we were going to have a picnic. At the time we had a horrible goose called Gertrude, who lived on the lake beyond the garden wall. She spotted me and gave chase, nipping at my bottom. I tripped and sent the cake flying and it splattered all over the grass. She ate it up too, the naughty thing. You should have seen my meltdown.'

Millie rolled her eyes. 'That's not a tantrum. That's doing something nice and a stupid goose attacking you. Anyone would have been upset. Seriously, it's like you were born a grown-up. I've had so many tantrums I couldn't even pick the best one, although I grew out of them before I started at boarding school, unlike *some* of our friends,' she said, grinning at Jacinta, who was in the seat ahead of them.

Jacinta turned around. 'What? I don't have them anymore,' she said. 'And at least I was only ever known as the school's *second* best tantrum thrower, which is an honour I'm happy to hold on to. I mean, there aren't many girls who can lay claim to that.'

Alice-Miranda giggled as she recalled her first meeting with Jacinta, when the girl was sitting on the floor of the gymnasium and squealing with the might of ten elephants.

'I know,' Jacinta said, reading Alice-Miranda's mind. 'Who'd have thought we'd ever end up being such good friends?'

Alice-Miranda leaned forward and squeezed the girl's shoulder. 'I'm glad we are.'

The tram continued along, climbing higher and higher. The terrain alternated between being steep and flat, and the views were stunning.

'What are we doing when we get to the top?' Sloane asked no one in particular.

'We'll have a quick look around and then we have to go back again,' Miss Reedy said.

'Why did we bother coming all the way up here, then?' Rufus Pemberley complained from the other side of the carriage.

September Sykes couldn't have agreed more. She'd tried to sneak off and get in some shopping that morning, but when she'd asked the hotel concierge the best places to go, she'd been told that the stores didn't open until ten o'clock. What was the point of being in Hong Kong if she couldn't at least max out each and every one of Smedley's credit cards? Not that he seemed to care about her spending these days, ever since he and Leonard Nordstrom's property development business had begun to go gangbusters.

September had always been disappointed that her husband had missed out on the compere's role on her favourite game show, *Winners Are Grinners*. It had been a huge let-down when he'd had to make a career flogging vacuum cleaners on the home shopping channel, but all that had changed when they moved to Spain and money was no longer such a source of conflict for the pair of them. Her husband was a lot happier these days and she was too – especially now she could shop without getting told off all the time.

'What are we doing after that?' Rufus called out.

Miss Reedy exhaled loudly. 'If you'd been listening this morning, you'd already know,' she bit. Her husband reached over and patted her hand.

'Don't let the boy get to you, darling,' he soothed. 'Let's just enjoy the day.'

'We're going to the Ladies Market in Kowloon,' Sloane said.

September tingled with excitement. 'Finally, some good news.'

'What about the men's market?' Figgy griped. 'I don't want to look at handbags all afternoon.'

'There will be a range of goods, George – it's not strictly for women. Perhaps you could buy a gift for your mother,' Miss Reedy suggested. 'It's also an opportunity to learn the fine art of haggling. Anyway, we won't have a lot of time for shopping as we'll take a tour of the botanic gardens and zoo at lunchtime. Now –' she looked around the carriage at the students – 'it's very important that you stick with your groups in the markets as I'm sure it will be busy and we don't want anyone getting lost. We're flying out at half past five to Shanghai and I don't plan on missing that plane.'

September rolled her eyes. 'Great.'

The views from Victoria Peak were every bit as good as the group had hoped, with vistas extending back across the city and to the islands. Millie took masses of photographs, although she was just as interested in the people as the scenery and found herself snapping sneaky shots of the adventurous fashion statements.

Ambrosia Headlington-Bear caught her spying on a couple of very stylish young women. 'I love that look too,' she whispered to the girl. 'Maybe I could use some of your pictures for an article I'm writing about upcoming fashion trends in China.'

'Sure thing.' Millie snapped away with renewed vigour. 'But I have to warn you: my rates are pretty high these days.'

Ambrosia grinned. 'It looks like Miss Reedy wants a group shot,' she said, pointing at the woman, who was gesturing at the children to come together.

'Goodness me,' Livinia remarked. 'Hurry up, everyone.' She felt like she was herding cats. She'd just about have them all in place when someone would wander off. Finally, the teacher passed her camera to a tiny woman wearing a large electric-blue sun visor, a shimmery gold top dotted with diamantes and the skinniest of skinny jeans. She had on the most outrageous platform wedges made of denim and lace. Gold bracelets and crystals dripped from the woman's slender arms, and her bleached hair was pulled back into a high ponytail.

'I wonder which runway she got that look from?' Millie whispered to Ambrosia.

The woman raised her eyebrows. 'She certainly doesn't subscribe to the theory that less is more.'

Despite her diminutive size, their photographer began barking orders at the group, determined to get the perfect shot. She demonstrated each pose and then encouraged the children and adults to mimic her. First, she had them all standing to attention with sombre faces, which was tricky because everyone's natural inclination was to giggle. She then had them with their hands in the air, making peace signs, followed by hands on hips and then arms folded. A small group of tourists gathered and started taking photographs of their own too. When the woman pouted and made kissing noises, Miss Grimm stormed forward, snatched the camera and thanked her for her trouble.

'Perhaps next time you should avoid the fashionista photographers,' Ophelia said, passing the camera to Miss Reedy.

The English teacher bit back a smile and nodded. She quickly reviewed the pictures and stifled a snort as she came upon one of her husband making bunny ears above the headmistress's head. It was promptly deleted.

Chapter 16

An hour later, having caught the tram back down the mountain, the group was loaded onto the tour bus along with their luggage. They made the short journey through one of the tunnels to Kowloon, the mainland part of Hong Kong, where most of the population lived. The bus pulled up on a busy street perpendicular to a string of market stalls, and Miss Grimm spent the next five minutes on the microphone going over buddy groups and instructions on what the children should do if they got lost.

'Now, each of the adults is going to show you how to haggle with the shopkeepers,' she continued. 'It's an interesting art and I don't want to hear of anyone paying full price for anything out there. And please be sensible. Remember, you have to be able to fit whatever you buy into your bag and we still have a lot of the trip left.'

For this activity, Miss Grimm had decided that each parent would be paired with their own child. She put Venetia and September together with Caprice, Sep and Sloane, and Figgy and Rufus joined them. In hindsight, it did seem to be a somewhat diabolical grouping, but Sep was immensely sensible and Sloane was much better these days too. Besides, Venetia seemed to be a woman with her wits about her. Ophelia and her husband, along with Miss Reedy and Mr Plumpton, would bring up the rear, keeping an eye on everyone, from a distance.

Alice-Miranda was grouped with Millie, Jacinta, Lucas and Susannah, under the supervision of Lawrence Ridley and Ambrosia Headlington-Bear. Jacinta made eye contact with Alice-Miranda, who raised her brows, hoping to convey to her friend that now would be as good a time as any for her to snatch a few minutes with Lucas, but the boy seemed glued to his father's side.

The group walked into the market and was immediately set upon by vendors eager to sell their wares. First up was an endless display of handbags and wallets.

Ambrosia shook her head. 'I suspect they're of dubious origin,' she said, looking at the designer labels with prices a fraction of what one would pay in a boutique.

'Are they fakes?' Jacinta asked.

'Sometimes it's hard to tell, but sadly there are lots of factories which produce knock-offs. It's highly illegal but difficult to police, so as long as there are people who buy them, supply will always equal demand,' Ambrosia explained.

Alice-Miranda walked further along and found a shop that sold traditional Chinese merchandise. There were little porcelain figures hanging from red string – dogs, roosters, monkeys – in fact, every animal of the Chinese zodiac. 'These are sweet,' she admired.

'Five for twenty dollars,' barked the old lady manning the stand.

Alice-Miranda went to pull out her wallet.

'Not yet, you don't,' Millie whispered, stopping her. She shook her head, then eyeballed the woman. 'Five for ten dollars.'

The woman's jaw dropped. 'You rob me,' she cried. 'My family will starve.'

'Oh no, it's all right,' Alice-Miranda said quietly. 'I can pay what she asked.'

Lawrence, Ambrosia and the other children watched with wonder as Millie took over. 'Sorry, I think we'll leave it for now,' she said, grabbing her friend's hand and walking away.

Alice-Miranda frowned. 'But they were lovely.'

'Just follow my lead,' Millie said under her breath. 'It's not over, trust me.'

The girls moved on to the stall opposite when the old lady rushed across. 'You drive a hard bargain, little girl,' she said with a wry smile. 'Five for sixteen dollars, okay?'

Millie looked at her evenly. 'Fifteen, and you have a deal.'

Alice-Miranda grinned at Millie and then at the old woman. 'Thank you,' she said, retrieving the right change and handing it over.

The old woman plonked the trinkets into a plastic bag with a swirly gold print and gave them to Alice-Miranda. 'Your friend is a good haggler. You can learn a lot from her. She will never pay too much.' She winked at Millie, whose smile couldn't have been any bigger.

As the group continued on its way, Lucas spotted a man selling kites in all shapes and sizes. He raced over to have a look with his father. After some furious negotiating, the boy was soon the happy owner of a colourful dragon, which folded up neatly into a small bag. He wished there was time to fly it, but the humid air was so still and thick they'd never have got a kite off the ground, even if there was an opportunity.

Ambrosia found some beautiful silk cushions, which she decided would be perfect for Jacinta's bedroom, so mother and daughter spent a few minutes haggling to get the price down. Jacinta eventually sealed the deal and was very pleased with herself. Meanwhile, Susannah purchased a lovely cloisonné vase for her mother at a bargain price. It seemed all the children were getting the hang of it.

'You know, I can't stop thinking about Summer,' Jacinta said as she and Alice-Miranda wandered along the market lane together. 'Some of those things she did – I wouldn't have imagined they were humanly possible.'

Alice-Miranda had been thinking about the girl too. Although she hated to imagine there was anything wrong, she kept coming back to that look they'd shared and what it could have meant. Maybe some of what Millie had said was right – not her whole crazy idea about Summer being treated like a slave, but the part about the girl being exhausted. Who knew how much training she had to do? Putting on that incredible show each night would be tiring enough, let alone on top of all the training.

'I wish I could learn some of those tricks,' Jacinta said. She threw her cushion into the air and executed a perfect cartwheel that just missed the top of a passing man's head.

'Probably best not to try them here.' Alice-Miranda grinned. She glanced ahead and caught a glimpse of a familiar-looking girl who was having a heated exchange with a young man. 'Summer!' she gasped, and dashed through the crowd towards her.

'What?' Jacinta squinted into the sun and took off after her friend.

The young man grabbed Summer's arm, just as Alice-Miranda reached her. Summer wrestled against him.

'What are you doing?' Alice-Miranda demanded, calling the man out. 'Leave her alone!'

Summer Tan turned and looked at her in surprise. She said something in Cantonese and the man released her.

'Hello,' he said, his scowl melting into a smile. 'Summer is my . . . sister. We were just discussing what to buy our mother for her birthday.' He then said something to Summer in Cantonese and the girl nodded.

Alice-Miranda looked at the pair, who were now smiling uneasily.

'I'm sorry, but we really must be going,' the man said. He took Summer by the arm and the pair of them hurried off, vanishing like a puff of smoke.

'Who was that?' Lawrence Ridley asked as he caught up to the girls with the rest of the group in tow.

'Summer Tan and her brother,' Alice-Miranda said, her mouth set in a grim line.

'Oh, what were they doing here?' Lawrence craned his neck to see if he could spot the pair, but the crowd of shoppers had swallowed them.

'Buying a present for their mother, apparently,' Alice-Miranda said.

'He was mean,' Jacinta added.

Lawrence grinned. 'Big brothers sometimes are. Well, I'm just glad there was nothing to worry about. I'll call Benny and tell him we saw her.'

'Good idea,' Alice-Miranda agreed. She noticed Sloane and Sep up ahead with Venetia and Caprice, but September, Figgy and Rufus were nowhere to be seen. 'It looks like we've almost reached the end of the market.'

'Who wants an ice-cream?' Lawrence asked, eyeing a vendor's stand. 'This shopping is hard work.' He wiped the perspiration from his forehead with a handkerchief. There was a chorus of yeses, and Alice-Miranda raced off to see if Sloane, Sep and Caprice wanted one too.

The children gathered to survey the unusual selection, with red bean, taro, black sesame and green tea among the more traditional flavours of vanilla and chocolate. While Lawrence organised the orders, the children stood there chatting about their purchases.

'What did you buy?' Jacinta asked Sloane and Sep.

Sloane opened a little bag and held up the same trinkets Alice-Miranda had bought. 'I got some of these,' she said excitedly.

'Me too! I'm going to give them to Mrs Smith and Mr Charles and Mrs Howard.' Alice-Miranda laughed and opened her bag to show Sloane her identical wares. She glanced up and realised that September wasn't with them. 'Where's your mother?' she asked.

'Who knows?' Sloane shrugged. 'She said something about buying fabric and then disappeared.'

'Where are Rufus and Figgy?' Lucas asked, looking around.

'We think they went with Mum,' Sep said. He was desperately trying to salvage his ice-cream, which was melting fast.

'Or they're lost,' Sloane added.

Venetia Baldini stood at the edge of the market, looking at her watch. She turned and walked over to her group. 'September said she'd be back by now. Can you see her?'

The children shook their heads.

'I want to go and buy that bag, Mummy,' Caprice whined.

'Darling, you don't need it,' Venetia said.

'I don't care!' the girl snapped. 'I want it and I'll carry it. You don't have to. Anyway, it's *my* money. Daddy gave it to *me*, so I'm going.'

Venetia looked to the heavens and took a deep breath, summoning patience. 'No, you're not.'

Ambrosia Headlington-Bear walked over to the woman. 'Would you like us to keep an eye on the other kids while you go with Caprice?'

Venetia glanced over Ambrosia's shoulder at her daughter. 'Don't you move, young lady – I won't have you getting lost.' She turned back to Ambrosia. 'I don't know what to do,' she confessed. 'September promised she would only be gone a few minutes.'

'Why don't you go and get Caprice's bag and we'll wait here with the children?' Ambrosia touched Venetia gently on the shoulder. The poor woman looked as if she were about to cry. Ambrosia knew all too well the churned-up feelings between a warring mother and daughter, having been there many times before with Jacinta – although, fortunately for her, things were different these days.

'Thank you.' Venetia smiled tightly. 'Caprice, I'm coming.'

The girl crossed her arms impatiently and pulled a face. 'Hurry up!'

Lucas and Sep compared purchases while the girls strolled inside a stall that carried a range of ridiculously cute stationery. Ambrosia and Lawrence scanned the market and the street beyond.

'There she is,' Ambrosia said as she watched September, her arms laden with bags, tottering towards them in her high heels.

'Sep, come and help Mummy with all these parcels,' September called. 'Who knew that fabric would be this heavy?' She plonked the bags onto the ground, retrieved a tissue from her bra and mopped at her forehead. 'This humidity! I hope we can go back to the hotel for a swim this afternoon. I'm not walking around any silly old gardens in this heat.'

Sep and Lucas ran over to help her. 'Where are Figgy and Rufus?' Sep asked.

September looked at him blankly. 'Who?'

'The other boys in our group,' Sep said with a sinking feeling. 'I thought they went with you to carry your things.'

September snorted. 'I wish! I had to lug all this on my own. I'm boiling and I need a drink. Go and buy me a cola, will you, Sloane?'

Ambrosia and Lawrence looked at one another. 'So if Figgy and Rufus aren't with you, where are they?' Lawrence asked.

'How would I know?' September huffed. 'Venetia said she'd watch the children.'

'Mummy,' Sloane said slowly, 'have you lost boys?'

September threw back her shoulders. 'I didn't *lose* anyone.'

Lucas spied Miss Grimm and her husband heading their way. 'Uh-oh, here's trouble,' he muttered under his breath.

Sloane's mind was racing. If her mother had lost the boys, the headmistress would have a fit. 'You do know that Miss Grimm is going to put you on the first plane home,' she said to her mother. 'And then I'm going to have to leave school again – all because of you.'

'But I didn't do anything,' September bleated, beginning to gauge the gravity of the situation.

Sloane could feel her temperature rising. 'That's precisely my point, Mummy,' she hissed. 'You were supposed to be *supervising* and making sure that everyone stayed together.'

'It's all right,' Alice-Miranda soothed. 'I'm sure they can't have gone far.'

'Why don't I have a look further up the road? They might have followed you,' Lawrence said.

All of a sudden, the market had become very crowded as another busload of tourists surged towards them.

'And I'll stay here to deflect any questions until you get back,' Ambrosia said.

Sloane was fuming. 'You'd better hope that Lawrence finds them, Mummy.'

'They're probably just over there somewhere.' September waved at the melee of traffic and shoppers on the other side of the busy road.

Sep shook his head. He was beginning to think that maybe Sloane hadn't been too harsh on their mother after all.

Chapter 17

Benny Choo flipped open the auction catalogue and ran his finger down the page. There were some beautiful things, and more than a few odd ones, that left him shaking his head. He knew something of antiques – that they were expensive and often their value made no sense at all. His wife, a collector, had filled their house in Beverly Hills with purchases she'd made from all over the world and had threatened to make over their minimalist Hong Kong penthouse too. So far he'd managed to keep her and her extravagant tastes at bay.

Benny unlocked the top drawer of his desk and retrieved a nut-brown leather notebook. Today he would take charge of the situation. He'd caught wind that Monte Carlo Pictures had been sniffing around and enquiring if Beluga was on the market. No doubt they'd be after a bargain, but then again, selling the studio would free up some of the funds Benny needed. There was a message from Beijing that required his attention too. And he was worried about Summer. She was the main attraction of the Circus of Golden Destiny and he relied on her now more than ever.

There was a knock at the door.

'Excuse me, Mr Choo,' Fuchsia Lee said, poking her head around. 'I have sent the gift to Summer.'

'Very good, Miss Lee. I want to make sure that she knows how much I appreciate her,' the man said. He had been relieved to hear the girl had been found. When he'd learned that she was missing, he'd been worried sick.

The woman smiled. 'Of course, Mr Choo. She is so lucky to have a boss as generous as you. I heard that the former owner treated the troupe quite badly, but they are in very good hands now.'

Benny Choo might have been short and round with a particularly antisocial perspiration problem, but there was an air of power about him that Fuchsia respected, and although he could be curt at times, she had come to know him as a man with a good sense of humour and a generous heart.

'Thank you, Miss Lee. Could you hold all my calls for the next hour? I must not be disturbed, no matter what,' he said.

'Of course,' Fuchsia replied. She spotted the auction catalogue. 'Do you have your eye on something special, sir?'

'Perhaps,' he said, a faint waver in his voice.

'Well, if you need any help, Mr Choo, I am more than happy to do some research,' Fuchsia said, then retreated from the room.

Benny Choo picked up the telephone and placed the call he had been dreading.

Summer Tan gently pressed the top of her arm, wondering how long it would take for the bruise to appear. There was something strangely satisfying about the pain – it made things real, because for the past few days she had begun to think that perhaps she had been transported to some parallel universe.

It had started with the letter. She had no idea where it had come from, but the words had ripped at her heart.

> *Your mother's health has been steadily improving; however, in order for her to continue on the path to wellness, there are certain things you must do. Things that will guarantee her a better future.*

Summer had read the page over and over, a chill running down the length of her spine.

> *Should you fail to do what is asked of you, or speak of this to anyone, you will never see your mother again. Know that there are eyes everywhere.*

There was no signature, no postmark, no clue as to where it had come from or what this person had planned. But Summer's stomach had been turned inside out since it arrived. She'd had to get out for a while – to breathe and walk in the sunshine, and to think. She used to go to the market in Kowloon as a child to see her grandparents, who'd had a stall there, but it was long gone and so were they. Now the only family she had left was her mother. Since joining the circus, Summer had few opportunities to visit her, but she did her best to speak to her on the telephone every week. It had been so hard, though, with her mother being unwell – in the nursing home and in hospital – and the circus travelling all over the world for months at a time.

Sadly, her freedom hadn't lasted long. One of the young men from the troupe had found her. How he'd known where to look was anyone's guess, and then those girls who she had met after the show last night appeared out of nowhere too. There was something about the little one with the chocolate curls. Her grandmother would have called the child an old soul – there was wisdom in her eyes. Perhaps she could help me, Summer thought. She wished she could speak better English, then she could get a message to Alice-Miranda. But her English was terrible and the girl didn't seem to understand

Cantonese. Summer dismissed the idea. It was a silly thought and one that would only get more people in trouble.

She sat down on her bed, alone in the room she'd once shared with Tiffany, an acrobat two years older than her, until she was moved to a bunk room with three other girls last week. Summer hadn't wanted her to go – at least when Tiffany was there she had someone to talk to. Now Tiffany and the other girls wouldn't speak to her because Mr Choo had made such a big fuss of Summer being the star of the show.

There was a loud knock on the door. Summer hastily brushed away her tears as Tiffany walked into the room.

'Hello,' Summer said softly.

Tiffany stalked over, carrying a giant basket filled with fruit and other delicacies. 'This just came for you.' The girl dumped the gift on the bed, a look of disgust on her face. 'We all know who is Mr Choo's favourite, don't we?' she sneered.

'Would you like some? I'd like to share it with everyone,' Summer said.

'Don't bother,' Tiffany said with a disdainful flick of her hand. 'We don't need your charity.'

Summer watched her leave, then turned back to the basket. There was a card on top. She opened the envelope.

To keep up your strength. Eat well.
— Mr Choo

What if she told Mr Choo about the letter? He was a powerful man. Surely whoever was behind it wouldn't be able to get to him. He had bodyguards.

Summer grabbed an apple and bit into it, forgetting her twisted stomach for a moment. And then she saw it – an envelope on top of her chest of drawers. It hadn't been there earlier. She took a deep breath and slid her fingernail under the flap, her heart thumping as she pulled out the page.

Chapter 18

Lucille Wong had a spring in her step as she navigated the alleyways to the shop. The owner, an ancient chap called Jiao Long, looked up as the woman walked through the door.

'Good afternoon, Miss Lucille. What can I do for you this fine day?' he asked.

'Three packets of vermicelli and a bag of rice,' she said with a smile.

He nodded, wondering at the source of her

happiness. The woman was a notorious grouch. 'You are in a very good mood.'

'Am I not always in a good mood?' she said, the usual scowl returning to her face.

The old man decided it was safer just to smile. 'Where is Wai Po?' he asked.

'Her bunions are playing up, so I offered to come for her,' Lucille said. Truthfully, she was dying to tell someone her news – she couldn't have cared less about Wai Po's sore feet.

'You are a good daughter,' the man replied.

'She is not my mother,' Lucille snapped. 'My mother would not be seen *dead* in this place.'

'Of course, my apologies.' The man gulped and set to, finding what Lucille had requested.

The woman's eyes wandered around the chaotic shelves of the dusty shop. How Jiao Long knew where to find anything was almost as big a mystery as what some of the ancient jars contained. 'Anyway, soon you will not see us either,' Lucille said, unable to help herself.

Jiao Long frowned. 'What do you mean?'

'We are leaving,' she said smugly.

The man raised his head in surprise. He would never in a million years have thought that the Wongs would leave the *hutongs*. This was their home. 'Is that so? Where are you off to?' he asked.

'That is for me to know and for you to find out in due course,' she said.

'You will be missed,' he replied, handing her the parcel of goods.

'Don't you want to know more?' she asked.

Jiao Long shrugged. 'You will reveal all when the time is right. It is not my business to know the private matters of others. Good afternoon, Miss Lucille.'

Lucille was disappointed. Her attempt at being mysterious had backfired completely. She was bursting to tell someone her news, even if it was just the wrinkly old shopkeeper. She sniffed and walked out into the alley. Surely her father-in-law would make the announcement soon. He couldn't keep the good news to himself too much longer. She wondered why Bernard had said nothing. Even when she prodded him, he refused to take the bait. At least Rou was a reliable, if not expensive, source of information.

The Circus of Golden Destiny was the most prestigious acrobatic troupe in the world, with shows in Las Vegas and New York and all over Europe. At last, Lucille thought, she would get her chance to travel the world and live the life she deserved.

Chapter 19

Lawrence had raced up and down the street searching for Figgy and Rufus, past fast-food outlets and electronics shops, before he had happened upon one of the more interesting areas of the city. He'd stopped to look at the rows of goldfish and other sea creatures trapped in bloated plastic bags and suspended from bamboo racks. Lawrence couldn't help but laugh out loud when a gap-toothed shopkeeper tried to sell him an octopus, suggesting it would be a lovely present for his wife. Finally, after hurrying back across the street, he located the boys outside a dumpling bar. The smell had almost driven Lawrence inside, and it would have if they didn't have mere minutes to get back to the bus.

They sped into the market where the children, Ambrosia, Venetia and September were waiting for them. Ambrosia let out a huge sigh of relief, while September grilled the pair about where they had been. The boys protested that they had gone to help her, but the woman didn't believe a word of it.

'We haven't got time to argue,' Ambrosia reminded them, as Lawrence led the charge. The other parents and children followed hot on his heels, dashing past the stalls to arrive at the bus with exactly ten seconds to spare.

Miss Grimm was tapping her foot and looking mildly agitated. 'Cutting it fine, I see,' she said as the relieved shoppers hastened up the steps and found their seats.

'Never in doubt,' Lawrence said, and gave her a wink.

Ophelia felt a blush rising to her cheeks. That man could get away with anything, she thought to herself. 'Goodness, you've been shopping up a storm, Mrs Sykes,' the headmistress noted.

The woman blinked at her innocently. 'It's not that much.' She held the bags aloft, glad that Sep was carrying the rest of her purchases. 'It would have been better if we'd had more time. There were plenty of other things I wanted to try on.'

Ophelia forced a smile onto her lips. 'Never mind, Mrs Sykes. We mustn't lose sight of why we're here. It's a cultural trip for the children, not a shopping expedition for the parents.'

September rolled her eyes and sashayed down the aisle. As far as she was concerned, holidays were for relaxing. So far all they'd done was rush from one place to the next.

Miss Grimm called the roll while Mr Plumpton did a head count, just to be doubly sure that everyone was on board.

'I've got to take this jumper off soon or I'm going to pass out,' Figgy panted in desperation. He pulled something out from under his clothing and sat it between him and Rufus, careful to hide it from view.

'What are you doing?' Rufus hissed.

Alice-Miranda looked across the aisle at them, wondering what the pair was up to this time. They had a knack for getting into trouble and there was definitely something fishy going on. Figgy wrestled his jumper over his head, which, seeing as though it was glued to his T-shirt with sweat, was difficult. She had thought it rather strange that the lad had been wearing so many layers in thirty-five-degree heat but had put it down to eccentricity.

'Gross! You're dripping,' Rufus said as Figgy bundled his prize under the damp jumper.

'What did you expect?' Figgy grumbled. 'It's about a hundred degrees out there.'

Mr Plumpton yawned and rested his head against the seat. In next to no time, his eyelids flickered shut and he began to snore gently. Livinia smiled adoringly at her husband. She loved the way his cheeks puffed in and out as he slept. The English teacher then turned her head towards the back of the bus, where all but a few of the children were dozing, their mouths agape and eyes closed.

It was probably just as well they were having a rest, she thought. She was going to suggest to Ophelia that they cut back their time at the gardens and zoo to leave earlier for the airport. Catching planes was a tricky business at the best of times, let alone when it came to doing it with a group of this size.

Chapter 20

The bus pulled up outside the terminal just before half past two. Miss Grimm and Miss Reedy had been quite right about the flying visit to the botanic gardens and zoo. By the time they'd eaten lunch, the children had about half an hour to spot a few exotic birds, a two-toed sloth and some monkeys before they had to be back on the bus.

Rufus nudged Figgy. 'What are we going to do?'

The boy bit his lip and looked around. He'd been hoping to snare a carry bag from somewhere.

The children hopped off the bus and trundled their bags inside. Miss Grimm and her husband wove through the crowds, with the rest of the party behind them and Miss Reedy and Mr Plumpton bringing up the rear. Livinia felt like a sheepdog, darting out every few seconds to bring one of the flock back into the fold. If only she could have given September Sykes a nip on the heel, perhaps the woman might have made a more concerted effort to keep up. When they reached the check-in desk, Miss Grimm directed the group to stand off to one side while she spoke to one of the customer-service supervisors. Alice-Miranda was chatting with Jacinta, still trying to convince the girl she needed to make a proper effort to talk to Lucas – sooner rather than later. But the boy was messing about with Sep and Lawrence, garnering the hairy eyeball from Miss Reedy more than once.

Surprisingly, it wasn't long before they were relieved of their luggage and headed for immigration. On the way, they stopped for a toilet break. Mr Plumpton took the boys and Miss Reedy escorted the girls. After a while, when everybody except Figgy was outside and waiting, Mr Plumpton ventured inside again to investigate.

'Are you all right, George?' Mr Plumpton asked, concerned by the boy's grunting noises. He hoped the lad wasn't coming down with something.

'I'll be out in a minute, sir,' Figgy said. There was a squeak followed by a loud expulsion of air.

Mr Plumpton grimaced. 'Good heavens, George! You really shouldn't scoff so many baked beans at breakfast.' He'd noticed the boys eating more than their fair share of the buffet that morning.

'Sorry, sir,' Figgy said, opening the toilet door.

Mr Plumpton watched as the lad was about to bypass the basin. 'Aren't you forgetting something?'

'No, I'm fine,' the lad said.

'Wash your hands, Figworth,' Josiah ordered, shaking his head.

Ophelia Grimm frowned as the pair finally emerged from the bathroom. 'Is everything all right?' she asked.

'Yes, sorry about that,' Mr Plumpton replied. 'Just some gas, I think.' He motioned towards Figgy, who had conveniently disappeared.

'Honestly, Mr Plumpton,' the headmistress spluttered, 'I think that qualifies as far too much information.'

Sloane and Jacinta nudged one another and giggled.

✫

Fortunately, immigration proved a breeze, with some unexpected smiles from the officials. Often they were a stern breed, but it seemed the children had a cheering effect. The group proceeded to the security checks, the queue for which seemed to wind its way through the barriers for miles.

'What did you do with it?' Rufus whispered to Figgy.

The lad looked down at his bulging stomach.

'Good one,' the other boy said with a grin.

No matter how many times she'd done it before, this part of the process always set Ophelia's teeth on edge. She never had a thing to hide, but every country seemed to have a different set of rules these days, and having been pulled up and searched over a tiny bottle of perfume last time she and Aldous had been overseas, she was keen to avoid trouble.

The children chatted in the queue, shuffling forward until, finally, they reached the next set of officials, who instructed them on what needed to go into the plastic tubs for scanning. Suddenly, there was a loud squeak and George Figworth froze. After a beat or two, he shifted uncomfortably from one leg to the other.

Alice-Miranda and Millie were standing behind the lad when Millie gently prodded her friend. 'I think Figgy's sprung a leak,' she whispered, pointing to a dribble of liquid that was fast pooling on the floor at the boy's feet.

Jacinta and Sloane noticed it too. 'Is that what I think it is?' Jacinta gasped.

'Oh no,' Alice-Miranda murmured. 'Poor Figgy.'

Millie grimaced. 'I once wet my pants at school and I wanted to die. Should we say something?'

'Of course we should,' Sloane said. 'He'll leave a trail and that's disgusting.'

Lucas tapped Jacinta on the shoulder. 'What's going on?'

'We think Figgy's wet his pants,' she replied. With a smile, she realised that was the first time she'd spoken to the boy without getting stupidly worked up.

Lucas was aghast. 'No way!'

Alice-Miranda hesitated. 'If we draw attention to things, Figgy might get upset and then everyone will notice. Maybe we should wait until we go through and then see if Mr Plumpton or Uncle Lawrence can say something to him.'

'Do you think so?' Millie looked doubtful. 'He's got to walk through the scanner on his own. Maybe we should see if we can get Mr Plumpton's attention now,' she said, and Sep agreed.

But before the girls had time to do anything, Rufus stepped up, leaving Figgy next in line for the scanner. The trickle seemed to have got worse and Figgy was fidgeting madly with the front of his pants. The security guard on the other side of the machine looked at Figgy and motioned for him to come through.

Jacinta covered her eyes. 'I can't look.'

'What are you all so excited about?' Caprice demanded. She was standing with her mother and Susannah, behind Lucas and Sep.

'Nothing,' Sloane said. The last thing the boy needed was Caprice making a scene.

Figgy did his best to walk nonchalantly through the scanner, but the machine insisted on beeping loudly. The security man frowned and pointed for the lad to walk back out and through again.

Mr Plumpton looked up as Figgy re-entered the machine only to set off the alarm for a second time.

He shuffled past the children. 'Excuse me, is there a problem?' he asked the security officer, who indicated for him to stay behind the yellow line.

'Are you this boy's father?' the man asked.

'No, but I'm with the school group,' he said.

'We have to give him a pat-down,' the man said. 'Do you want to come through? You can supervise.'

'Poor Figgy,' Millie said. 'He must have a really full bladder. This is not going to end well.'

'Surely he can't have much left in the tank,' Lucas said, eyeing the growing puddle.

The guard began patting the lad's arms and then continued down his torso and legs.

Figgy flinched. 'Steady on.'

The security officer stood up and patted the lad's back before asking him to spin around. He tapped Figgy on the shoulders and chest before reaching his stomach. The fellow smiled as Figgy's belly wobbled. 'Too many sweets for you.'

'That's a bit rude,' Mr Plumpton mumbled. He hoped he wouldn't be subjected to the same treatment.

But the pressure had caused Figgy's problem to worsen. Now, instead of a tiny trickle, there was a steady stream.

Josiah Plumpton looked down and was horrified by what he saw. 'Good heavens, Figworth, you just went to the bathroom!'

'This is awful,' Sloane wheezed.

Caprice craned her neck to see. 'What's awful?'

But the security officer wasn't buying it. He looked at the pool and then at the lad's face. He patted Figgy's stomach again and – *whoosh!* – there was an almighty gush.

'Oh, gross!' Caprice looked as though she was about to be sick.

Murmurs rumbled through the queue as everyone strained against the ropes to catch a glimpse of the action. Miss Grimm and the rest of the group were watching, spellbound.

Then, with a delicate *splat*, a small goldfish slid out of the bottom of Figgy's jeans and onto the floor.

'Good gracious! Quickly, someone do something!' Mr Plumpton pleaded, staring at the floor and doing absolutely nothing.

Jacinta scanned the area until she found exactly what was needed. From a standing start, she leapt over Alice-Miranda's head, then snatched a recently confiscated bottle of water from the hands of one of the security officers. She grabbed a Ziploc bag from the pile available and had the top off the bottle and the water in the bag before anyone could stop her. Jacinta closed the bag with a flourish of her hand, then cartwheeled through the checkpoint and scooped the flummoxing fish inside it within seconds.

'Whoa, that girl's awesome,' a boy in the crowd yelled out.

'She sure is,' Lucas agreed.

The goldfish floated motionless in the bag. Everyone stared at it, willing the creature to live.

'Come on, little guy,' one of the security officers whispered, clenching his fist.

Suddenly, the fish twitched. A gasp went up around the room, then a cheer, as it flipped and flopped and began swimming laps. Jacinta and Mr Plumpton exchanged high-fives.

Once the fate of the fish was sealed, it seemed that everyone was keen to get on with their day.

'George Figworth, what on earth were you thinking?' Ophelia said.

The boy licked his lips, trying to summon some moisture into his mouth. 'It was a present for my host family. I heard that goldfish were good luck.'

A security guard grabbed Figgy by the arm.

Ophelia Grimm's jaw dropped. 'What are you doing? We've got a plane to catch.'

'He is being taken in for questioning,' the security officer replied tersely. 'The boy has committed a criminal offence. We must search him for any other contraband. Maybe he has a tortoise hidden in his trousers?'

The headmistress eyeballed the lad. 'Do you?'

Figgy shook his head and fidgeted uncomfortably with his wet underpants.

Another of the guards was on the telephone and it wasn't long before a very official-looking gentleman in a highly decorated uniform appeared and marched towards them. He asked Ophelia to step aside and the pair spent several minutes in hushed conversation. She explained as best she could that, while the boy had done something completely brainless, his intentions had been noble.

'Hurry up, will you?' a chap called from the middle of the line. 'I'm going to miss my plane.'

A chorus of grumbles started up.

The official sighed and glared at Figgy. 'You are free to go, but please ensure that in future you abide by our laws.'

'May I take Gordon?' the lad asked, looking over at the goldfish.

'My children will enjoy looking after him,' the man said.

Figgy gulped and nodded.

Ophelia Grimm thanked the man and took Figgy to join the others. The lad squelched through the checkpoint with everyone but Rufus giving him a wide berth.

'I'm in big trouble, aren't I?' Figgy whispered.

'Yup,' Rufus said.

Figgy frowned. The whole thing was so unfair and now he was going to have sit in wet pants for two and half hours. 'But it wasn't just my idea . . .' he whined.

Rufus swivelled his head and glared at him. 'Don't drag me into this,' he hissed. 'I wasn't the one who chose a stupid goldfish.'

Figgy folded his arms obstinately. 'If I'm going home, you are too,' he huffed.

Rufus stalked away.

Ophelia Grimm looked over from where she had been speaking quietly to Mr Plumpton and Miss Reedy. At this point in time she had no idea what she was going to do, except to hope that the boy's judgement improved considerably by the time they reached the Bright Star Academy in Beijing.

Chapter 21

The flight had been uneventful and mercifully short. Despite being seated together, Figgy and Rufus hadn't exchanged a word since Hong Kong Airport. With no in-flight entertainment, both lads had been bored senseless. Several times they had gone to speak to one another and then stopped themselves, remembering they were in the middle of a fight.

Figgy was wary of Miss Grimm as she seemed to have forgotten all about Gordon, but having seen her in action in Paris, he knew that she'd unleash her fury on him at some point. His parents would be mortified if he was sent home, especially as he knew his mother had been bragging to his grandparents on his father's side (who she couldn't stand) that he'd been specially selected to represent the school in its pilot exchange program with a prestigious Chinese academy. Though it wasn't technically true, it had made his mother very proud.

The group arrived at Pudong Airport, which resembled the shape and bones of a whale's belly. They were met by a petite young woman called Iris, who was to be their guide for the next two days. Iris was a picture of professionalism and efficiency, teaming a smart grey suit with a matching pair of practical trainers. Even her precisely cut bob looked like it meant business. Despite her diminutive size, she soon revealed herself as a force to be reckoned with. Iris welcomed the children and adults to Shanghai in excellent American-accented English and swiftly brandished a stick with a large cut-out red dragon stuck on top. 'Keep an eye on this and you will not get lost,' she instructed. 'Now, follow me.'

As they snaked their way through the airport, Iris's sweet tones transformed.

'Move it, grandpa, I have children coming through,' she barked at a startled fellow, who immediately shuffled aside. 'Look out,' she yelled at a man driving a cart. He slammed on the brakes to allow the children to pass, almost catapulting his disabled passenger through the windscreen.

'Why does she yell at them in English?' Jacinta asked.

'Who knows,' Sloane said, 'but it works.'

It was true. The young woman cut a swathe through the crowd, earning not one word of retaliation. They reached the platform for the Maglev train in what could only be record time, and lined up behind a glass barrier.

'Look at that!' Lucas exclaimed as a sleek train glided into the station.

'Whoa, it looks like something out of a science-fiction movie,' Sep said. 'Or a giant caterpillar.'

Iris laughed and executed a couple of deep lunges, before stretching her arms over her head. 'Then it is the fastest caterpillar in the world.'

'Yeah, this thing's even cooler than the Japanese bullet trains and I didn't think there was anything to rival them,' Lucas said.

The train doors and the glass panels opened simultaneously and Iris ushered everyone on board.

'Find a seat and don't get up while the train's moving,' Miss Reedy ordered. She found herself looking to Iris for confirmation, and the young woman nodded.

'How fast does this thing go?' Lucas asked.

'I believe the top speed is four hundred and thirty-one kilometres per hour,' Mr Plumpton said, 'but when it was tested it exceeded five hundred kilometres per hour.'

'My dad's car goes faster than that,' Rufus scoffed.

'Yeah, and I'm Superman.' Figgy looked at his friend and the pair grinned like idiots. It seemed the frost was thawing.

'How does it work?' Sep asked.

Caprice rolled her eyes. 'Seriously, did you have to ask?' she muttered. 'Here comes another mind-numbing Science lesson with Plumpy.'

Venetia shot her daughter a glare. 'Excuse me, young lady, there is no need to be rude. I, for one, am very interested to know.'

Mr Plumpton stood beside his seat at the end of the carriage, despite his wife's preference that he sit down, and gave a very interesting explanation of the magnetic levitation system employed by the train. His speech was only interrupted by gasps from the children as the speedometer displays quickly shot up to over four hundred kilometres per hour. It was hard to imagine they were going that fast, apart from the speed with which the landscape was changing.

Thankfully, for Caprice at least, Mr Plumpton's speech didn't last long as the entire journey took just over eight minutes.

'I can't believe we're here already,' Mr Grump marvelled. 'Last time I was in Shanghai, I recall sitting in traffic for hours.'

'Yes, much better than the freeways – you can be stuck on them for days,' Iris said.

Millie wrinkled her nose. 'Surely you don't mean that.'

'Oh, yes I do,' Iris replied. 'There was a traffic jam for over two thousand kilometres during Chinese New Year. Some people spent seventy-two hours in their cars. I never go anywhere during holiday periods in China – it's nuts,' she said with a grin.

Millie was struck by the frightening prospect of being trapped on a freeway for days on end. She wondered where the motorists would go to the toilet and what they would eat. Or, even worse, what if someone had a heart attack or a baby? People could die in situations like that.

The group disembarked and, with a wave of her flag, Iris led them to their bus. She regaled them with facts about the area they were travelling through, called the Pudong, as they took the scenic route to their hotel. Millie had been reading about it in her guidebook, and she and Alice-Miranda were busy pointing out the high-rise buildings they recognised from the pictures.

When the woman asked if anyone knew the population of Shanghai, Alice-Miranda jumped in, answering twenty-four million, which, Iris proceeded to tell them, made it the most populous city in the whole of China. She pointed out several other interesting buildings, including one that looked like a giant bottle opener, before their first stop came into view. Iris introduced it as the Oriental Pearl Tower, and in no time the group found themselves inside the giant foyer, where hundreds of red lanterns hung overhead. They lined up for the elevators, which would take them to the viewing platforms housed in the pink spheres that were dotted along the tower's spine. Millie made a beeline for the viewing deck that wrapped around the building.

'Look at that view!' Alice-Miranda exclaimed, stepping out onto the timber deck. Lights twinkled in the distance and the whole city was on display.

Sloane took one look at the section beyond the wooden floor, comprised of a glass-panelled walkway and safety barrier, and clamped her eyes shut. 'Oh, I can't look.'

'What are you talking about, Sloane?' her mother said. 'It's gorgeous out here.' September tottered onto the transparent surface and was completely fine until she glanced down and realised that all there was between her and a very long drop were a couple of inches of toughened glass. September froze. 'Oh no,' she whimpered. 'No, no, no, no. I c-can't b-be here.'

Sloane opened one eye to take a peek. 'Well, come back then.'

'I can't move,' September began to yelp. 'I can't feel my legs. I can't breathe.'

Alice-Miranda heard the woman's cries and hurried over to her. 'You're fine, Mrs Sykes,' Alice-Miranda said. 'Just come towards me and put one foot in front of the other and you'll be back on solid ground.'

'I c-c-can't,' the woman gasped.

'Come along, Mrs Sykes,' Josiah Plumpton said, walking out onto the glass platform. 'Take my hand and you'll be fine.'

September saw her life flash before her eyes and let out a bloodcurdling scream.

'Stop that, Mummy,' Sloane pleaded, feeling the weight of everyone's attention on them. 'You're being *embarrassing*.'

Sep ran over from the other side of the tower, with Lucas and Lawrence hot on his heels. He looked at his mother, whose legs were splayed as if she were about to lay an egg. 'What's the matter?' he asked.

'I'm stuck!' September wailed, now clutching Josiah's arm. 'I can't move.'

'Of course you can,' Sep said. 'Just put one foot in front of the other.'

Mr Plumpton was beginning to look a little peaky too. September's talons were digging into his flesh so hard he was surprised there was only sweat running down his arm.

'Mrs Sykes, please let go of my husband,' Miss Reedy said, a note of panic seeping into her voice.

'No, you'll just leave me on my own,' September wailed. She began to cry – and it was ugly. All the while, her heels had begun sliding apart on the sweat-stained floor, resulting in an awkward and ever-expanding splits position.

Miss Grimm and Mr Grump watched on in bemusement, as did hordes of other tourists who were happily snapping photographs of the frozen pair. One little girl even poked out her head from between September's legs, making a peace sign, while a boy ran over and prodded the woman on the bottom.

Lawrence decided it was time to take action. Although he wasn't all that keen on being out there himself, the situation was getting sillier by the second. He made his way towards the pair as if he were scaling a glacier. 'All right, you two. September, on the count of three, I want you to release Mr Plumpton and grab on to my arm,' Lawrence instructed. 'One, two, three!'

September let go of Josiah and launched herself at Lawrence. The traumatised Science teacher ran towards his wife, who consoled him with a hug.

'Good grief,' Lawrence squeaked, struggling under the woman's weight as she wrapped herself around him like a python around a palm tree. He prised her free and swung her over his shoulder, running to the nearest elevator.

'Well done, Uncle Lawrence,' Alice-Miranda called out, clapping along with the rest of the crowd that had been watching the drama unfold.

'Mama,' said a little boy, tugging at the hem of the woman's dress. 'That was Vector!'

'Don't be silly,' his mother replied with a laugh. 'That was just a pudgy man rescuing his silly wife.'

Iris rounded up the rest of the group and they joined Lawrence and September back on the ground floor.

'Did everyone enjoy the sky deck?' she asked. The woman had missed all the fuss as she'd dashed off to make some telephone calls about their arrangements for the morning.

'It was fantastic,' Jacinta said.

'The view was fabulous,' Alice-Miranda enthused.

'It was horrible,' September whimpered. 'And I broke a nail.'

'Which I think is in my arm,' Mr Plumpton grumbled.

'We have a little while until the bus returns, so may I suggest a tour of the museum? There are some shops at the end of the arcade too,' Iris said.

At the mention of shops, September perked up considerably.

'Oh no you don't, Mummy,' Sloane said, wagging her finger. 'You're staying with us.'

Sep looked at the woman and nodded.

'Perhaps we can all have a look together,' Alice-Miranda suggested.

September pouted like a three-year-old. Even her son had turned against her. Maybe she should look into getting a flight home, the woman thought to herself. She and China weren't getting on very well at all.

Chapter 22

The old man smiled as he hung up the telephone. It seemed that his plan was coming together even better than expected.

'What is that look for, husband?' Winnie asked, standing in the doorway.

'That was the realtor. He said they have agreed to our price for the old school. We will be able to purchase it as soon as the deal is done with the Circus of Golden Destiny. I have made a down payment,' he said.

Winnie walked into the room and closed the door. 'Are you happy?'

'Yes, absolutely. We cannot run the troupe forever and the boys agree this is for the best,' he said. 'Have you changed your mind?'

'Of course not. There are so many children we can help and I can't think of a better way to spend the rest of our days. Perhaps it is time to tell Cherry and Lucille and the children?' She gave him a curious look.

The old man shook his head. 'There is no need, not yet.'

'Are you worried they will not be happy?' his wife asked.

Lionel sighed wearily. 'Tell me when Lucille is ever happy,' he said. 'All she wants to do is spend, spend, spend. Money flows out of her fingers like water. If she were in charge of the funds, we would all be living on the street by now.'

Winnie nodded. 'You are right about that, and she is lazy too. She has done none of the work in preparation for our guests. Wai Po and I have organised everything. And now, with Mr Choo coming to see the show next week, there is too much to do.'

'We will get through, we always do,' Lionel said, patting his wife's hand. 'By the way, Mr Choo telephoned this morning. He was keen to know about the troupe, so I told him that Coco is our best, although she is still a child, and Cherry defies her age. She works so hard and is magnificent not only with her acrobatics but her sleight of hand too. Mr Choo was very impressed. He said he couldn't wait to meet everyone.'

There was a loud knock at the door, and Deng Rou entered carrying a tray with a teapot, two cups and a plate of orange slices.

The old man smiled. 'Ah, Rou, what would we do without you?'

'I hope you're not planning to do without me anytime soon,' she said.

'Of course not.' Lionel looked up and caught his wife's gaze. Winnie rolled her eyes and gave an almost imperceptible shake of her head.

'Well, I'm sure that one day you will want to retire and have a life of your own,' Winnie said.

Rou placed the tray down with a clatter and proceeded to pour the tea. 'Retirement is for ninnies,' she said, sloshing some of the liquid over the edge of Winnie's cup. 'Besides, why would I leave when there is so much excitement ahead for us?'

Winnie and Lionel looked at each other. 'Excitement?' Lionel asked.

175

Rou smiled and wiped up the spill with a cloth. 'I just meant that you are so clever coming up with new routines for the whole family. You must have some more big ideas for the show.'

'Yes, we are having some fun,' Lionel said cautiously. 'There is no one in the world who is as innovative as we are.'

'What about the Circus of Golden Destiny?' Rou asked.

Lionel's brow furrowed. 'What about them?'

'Oh, I just read that they have the most incredible acts, doing things that no one had thought humanly possible,' Rou said, lowering her eyes. She set a teacup down in front of Lionel, then Winnie, and offered the plate of sliced orange.

Winnie didn't believe a word of it. Rou's eyesight these days was terrible – she was always complaining that she could barely read anymore. 'As they aren't allowed to perform in mainland China, I don't think we will see them anytime soon. Unless you would like to go for a long-overdue holiday and watch them yourself?'

It was true that Winnie would love nothing more than for Rou to go on an extended vacation. Deng Rou had been part of the troupe since the beginning, despite Winnie often wishing otherwise. The woman had once been an extraordinary gymnast and had attended the same school as Lionel. They had grown up as close as any brother and sister. When Lionel hit upon the idea of his show, they had started it together. But during one of their rehearsals, Rou had plummeted from the trapeze and, without a safety net to catch her, had almost died. She never performed again.

But she had been determined that her friend Lionel would succeed and, from her hospital bed, managed to get word to her uncle who ran an acrobatic school in the city. He sent a beautiful and talented young woman named Winifred to take Rou's place. Winnie and Lionel formed an instant bond, first in their routines and soon after as husband and wife. The show became a huge success and Lionel visited Rou in hospital every day for months while she recovered. He felt so guilty about what had happened to her that he vowed Rou would have a job for life within the troupe.

As China underwent a massive cultural and economic transformation, Lionel was able to take the show to new heights, from a fledgling troupe performing mostly for government officials and their guests, to one of Beijing's premier tourist attractions. Despite not being able to perform, Rou had made herself useful in other ways. She was a brilliant masseuse and trainer, and she made props and sewed exquisite costumes.

But Winnie felt the sting of resentment from the woman. Rou believed Lionel had become soft, always letting his wife have her way. Although Winnie had never been able to catch Rou out, she suspected the woman was a master manipulator as well as a gossip – so much so that if there was anything Lucille wanted the rest of the troupe to find out, it was Rou she told first. Lionel insisted that Rou was just lonely, but Winnie simply didn't trust the woman. Rou and Lucille were as thick as thieves too, which was another thing that didn't sit well.

'Thank you for the tea, Rou,' Winnie said. 'You need to go and check the sewing basket. I heard Lucille complaining that there were some sequins missing from her red leotard, and I think the hem on Coco's pink frock needs fixing.'

Rou bowed and darted out of the room, closing the door behind her.

Winnie picked up her teacup and slurped loudly. 'She knows something,' she said after a moment.

'I cannot imagine how,' Lionel replied. 'I have sworn Bernard and Charles to secrecy.'

'She probably had her ear to the keyhole. That woman is a meddler and a troublemaker, I tell you,' Winnie fretted. 'The sooner you get rid of her, the better.'

Lionel sighed. 'Must we keep doing this? I promised that I would look after her. Do you want to make me a liar and bring shame upon our family?'

'Of course not. I just want her to move far, far away. Perhaps we could suggest that we put her up in a retirement home,' Winnie said. 'In Harbin.'

Lionel suppressed a smile. 'You know the law as well as I do. If Rou were to retire, she must return to her birthplace to collect her pension benefits. She would hardly move to Harbin, where it is forty below in winter. We are better off making sure that she stays here, in Beijing.'

Winnie closed her eyes. 'Fine. She and Lucille can take care of one another. Heaven knows they deserve it.'

Rou's face scrunched into a ball. 'I'd like to see her try to get rid of me,' she muttered, and pulled away from the keyhole. The laxatives she'd forgotten to add to Winnie's tea went straight back into her pocket. 'Next time,' she sniffed, and stalked off down the hall.

Chapter 23

Grey skies greeted the group when they met for breakfast in the hotel restaurant at nine o'clock. After their late night, almost everyone was glad for a slower start to the day. September, however, was itching to get to the shops. She'd purchased a cheongsam at the arcade in the Pearl Tower and was keen to find a pair of shoes in just the right shade of red to go with it.

Despite Sloane's horror at the idea of her mother trying to squeeze herself into one of the tiny dresses, the wily sales assistant had swiftly located the only extra-large garment in the shop. Even though it was still snug, September thought it very fetching and somehow convinced Ambrosia and Miss Reedy to try some on too. They both looked stunning, and in the end Venetia and Miss Grimm also bought themselves cheongsams; the five women making a pact to wear their dresses on the last night in honour of the trip.

Alice-Miranda greeted Sloane and Jacinta with a bright smile as they joined her and Millie at their table. 'Good morning.'

'Hi,' Sloane mumbled.

'What's the matter with you?' Millie asked.

The girl waved a hand in her mother's direction. 'She's been banging about since half past six and before that she was snoring like a train. So much for getting a sleep-in.' Though she wasn't about to say so, Sloane was relieved that the snorer had turned out to be her mother and not herself.

'The congee is delicious,' Alice-Miranda said, pointing her spoon at the bowl of rice porridge in front of her. 'Especially if you dunk in the Chinese doughnut.'

'I still don't know how you eat that stuff,' Millie said, pulling a face, and went back to her bacon and eggs.

Jacinta dug into her cereal and Sloane nibbled a piece of watermelon.

Lucas and Sep walked towards the girls with their breakfast trays. 'Can we sit with you?' Sep asked.

'Sure,' Millie said.

Alice-Miranda didn't miss the anxious look on Jacinta's face and flashed her a comforting smile.

'Figgy doesn't seem too happy this morning,' Sep said, nodding at the boy sitting on his own at a table for two.

'I saw Miss Grimm and Mr Plumpton speaking to him before we went up to bed last night,' Millie said. 'About the goldfish.'

'At least he's still here,' Lucas weighed in. 'I thought Miss Grimm was going to put him on the first plane home.'

'You have to admit it was a sweet idea to buy a goldfish for his host family, although not well thought through,' Alice-Miranda said. 'They are considered to be very lucky.'

'Not for Figgy,' Sloane quipped, and the others laughed.

'It looks like he and Rufus are back to their silly old selves,' Millie said as the other boy reappeared from the breakfast buffet and frisbeed a croissant at the lad before sitting down opposite him. 'Unlike you two.' Millie eyeballed Lucas first, then Jacinta.

The girl gulped. She raised her eyebrows at Alice-Miranda, who shook her head.

Caprice was sitting on the next table munching on some toast and eavesdropping on their conversation. She couldn't understand why Lucas was so interested in Jacinta. Caprice thought she'd be a much better friend to the boy. She couldn't help herself and leaned over. 'I heard you two lovebirds weren't talking because Lucas has a girlfriend,' she said airily.

'What?' The lad turned to her. 'Where did you hear that?'

'It was all around school,' Caprice cooed. 'Someone saw you with a girl in the village.'

'Caprice, please stop making mischief,' Alice-Miranda said. 'That's not true at all.'

The girl flicked her copper-coloured tresses and smirked. 'Maybe Jacinta's got a secret boyfriend too.'

'I do not!' Jacinta leapt out of her chair, her hands on her hips. 'That's a *lie*. You're lying, Caprice.'

Ambrosia Headlington-Bear and the other adults were enjoying their breakfast in the far corner of the room when they became aware of the ruckus.

Ambrosia looked across the restaurant and lowered her spoon. 'Oh no,' she whispered, recognising the old telltale signs.

Caprice smiled to herself. 'You know, I've heard so many stories about the school's second best tantrum thrower. Perhaps now I'm going to see her in action.'

Jacinta's face was getting redder by the second and she looked set to pounce. 'Why are you telling such horrible lies about us?' she demanded.

Before she unleashed the full force of her rage, Lucas stood up and grabbed her hand, charging out the door into the hallway beyond. Alice-Miranda and Millie went after them like a shot.

'Well, that was disappointing,' Caprice remarked, and went back to munching on her toast.

Jacinta stood in the hallway as stiff as a board. The intense crimson was seeping from her cheeks and her heart rate was beginning to slow. Lucas let go of her hand and stood facing her, wondering what to say.

'Right,' Millie said as she and Alice-Miranda arrived on the scene. 'This is stupid. What's the matter with you two?'

Jacinta stared at the ground and Lucas shrugged.

'Fine. If you're not going to work this out, then I will,' Millie said. She turned her attention to Jacinta. 'Why aren't you talking to Lucas? Has he done something to upset you?'

Jacinta shook her head.

'So why aren't you talking to him?' Millie was dumbfounded. 'What's changed?'

Jacinta took a deep breath and turned to the boy. She hesitated for a moment.

'I'd really like to know if I've done something,' Lucas said.

Jacinta twisted her fingers together. Her stomach was churning. 'You're probably going to think I'm a fool, but I've been worrying myself sick that you don't like me anymore and that you're just being kind because that's the sort of person you are,' she blurted.

'What?' Lucas's forehead creased. 'You and Sep are my best friends.'

Jacinta's eyes filled with tears. 'Do you really mean that? Even after I've been such an idiot?'

Lucas nodded. 'Absolutely.'

Millie dusted her hands and winked at Alice-Miranda. 'Good, that's sorted then. So are you two going to act normal from now on?'

They both nodded.

'But no holding hands, okay? You're still too young for all that boyfriend and girlfriend stuff,' Millie chided. 'We're going to have to put up with that for years sooner or later.'

Lucas grinned at the girl. 'Has anyone told you that you're really bossy?'

'But you've got to admit she's effective,' Alice-Miranda said.

Jacinta leaned in and gave the flame-haired girl a hug, and embraced Alice-Miranda too. 'Thanks, both of you.'

Lucas looked at the girls. 'What about me?' he asked.

Millie grimaced. 'Okay, just this once but don't make a habit of it.'

Jacinta hugged Lucas, and as Alice-Miranda and Millie turned to go back inside, the boy planted a kiss on Jacinta's rosy cheek.

Chapter 24

The children gathered in the foyer after breakfast, armed with their daypacks and drink bottles. Iris was there to meet them and quickly distributed maps, each having been meticulously highlighted to show where the hotel was and the name and number of the attractions they would be going to. She gave them a couple of minutes to look over their arrangements and, in the meantime, did some stretches. It seemed she was very dedicated to her physical wellbeing.

Alice-Miranda studied the page, keen to find out which of the attractions that she and Millie had circled in Millie's guidebook they were actually going to see. She realised their first destination was only a few hundred metres from their hotel. 'Are we walking to the museum?' she asked.

'Oh, I hope not. My feet are already killing me,' September griped.

'Why don't you go and put on some sensible shoes like Caprice's mum?' Sloane suggested, pointing at Venetia.

Her mother looked over and shuddered. 'You know I can't wear *flat* shoes, Sloane. They're not good for my posture.'

'I bet Venetia doesn't have bunions like you do,' Sloane grumbled under her breath. 'Don't complain to me when you can't walk this afternoon.'

September huffed loudly. 'Excuse me,' she said, putting up her hand. 'I just need to duck upstairs for a minute.'

Iris frowned. 'We are leaving in five minutes,' she said as September scurried away. 'To answer your question, miss, we are taking the bus to the museum.'

Their guide then went on to give them a brief history of each of the places they would be visiting that day. Iris finished her monologue as the lift bell sounded and September charged out. All heads turned to look at her.

'Good heavens, what has she got on her feet?' Mr Plumpton's eyes had been immediately drawn to her enormous shiny silver shoes.

'Sorry, I thought I'd better change my footwear to something more appropriate,' she explained.

Sloane groaned and a few of the children chuckled behind their hands. Mr Grump had to turn away and pretend to cough to avoid being caught out.

'Do you like them?' September asked. 'They're all the rage in Barcelona at the moment.'

Sloane closed her eyes tightly, hoping that when she opened them again her mother's giant metallic platform trainers would have morphed into an elegant pair of ballet flats.

'Your mother's right,' Ambrosia said. 'I just wrote a feature on the teenage trend for *Gloss and Goss*.'

'Well, that might be true, but I think my mother has forgotten that she's *not* a teenager and we're *not* in Spain,' Sloane fumed.

Millie considered the offending footwear. 'You know, I think they look pretty cool, Mrs Sykes.'

'Oh, Millie. For the hundredth time, call me September,' the woman simpered. 'Mrs Sykes makes me sound positively ancient.'

They drove past the opera house and turned left into a pretty boulevard lined with flowerpots, arriving at the Shanghai Museum minutes later. An impressive oval concrete structure incorporating a curved facade with squared-off walls protecting the front, the whole place looked as if it glistened with gold.

'There are different exhibitions on each floor – from jade to paintings and ceramics, to clothes and furniture. It's not a race and you don't have to see everything,' Iris said. 'We will meet back here in the foyer in an hour and a half.'

Miss Grimm nodded her approval. 'Very sensible.'

'Oh, and please don't run,' Iris added. 'Just last week the guards tied a young boy to a chair for that very reason.' Jaws dropped all over the place. She burst out laughing. 'I'm only joking, but you wouldn't really want to try their patience.'

'Thank you, Iris,' Miss Grimm said. 'Now, I want you all to enjoy looking around. Many of the antiquities in this building are thousands of years old.' The woman caught Figgy's sly look. 'Yes, even older than me, George. Astonishing.'

Figgy sheepishly turned the other way and pretended he hadn't been about to say a thing.

'See you all back here at exactly fifteen minutes past eleven,' the woman said, and the adults and children proceeded to their allotted starting points.

Chapter 25

'Where do you want to go first?' Alice-Miranda asked Millie.

'We should probably start either on the top floor or here, at the bottom, and work our way through the exhibits,' the girl replied.

Alice-Miranda nodded. 'I can't wait to see the ceramics. I love all the pretty colours and shapes they used in the different dynasties.'

'We are not stopping to look at every single thing,' Millie said, pretending to look sternly over her glasses. 'I don't think my boredom threshold is that high.'

Millie, Jacinta, Sloane, Sep, Lucas and Alice-Miranda decided they would explore the museum together and begin their journey in the ceramics exhibit on the first floor. The pieces were exquisite and Alice-Miranda found several that she absolutely adored. There was one large cylindrical container she thought especially striking.

Sloane tilted her head to one side. 'What would anyone use that for?'

'It looks like an umbrella stand to me,' Millie said, and leaned in to study the plaque beside it. 'Although I don't know if umbrellas were invented way back in the third century.'

'Probably not,' Lucas said. He and Jacinta wandered along the glass-fronted display cabinet to the next exhibit. There were beautiful bowls and jugs and some very unusual porcelain statues.

'It's fascinating to see how people liked to decorate their homes even thousands of years ago,' Alice-Miranda said, eyeing an especially pretty cup. It was only about three inches in diameter with a delicate painting of a cockerel and hens around it.

'That's over five hundred years old,' Alice-Miranda said. 'It's so sweet. Mrs Oliver would love it.'

'If you're into that sort of thing,' Millie said, wrinkling her nose.

'Yeah, boring,' Caprice muttered, from the safe distance at which she'd been following the group.

The children moved from ceramics to bronze artefacts, where giant urns thousands of years old and enormous bells took centre stage, then on to calligraphy. Many of the pieces consisted of long scrolls inscribed with poetry and were often accompanied by exquisite watercolour paintings.

Alice-Miranda stared at one of the scrolls that was several metres wide. 'This is gorgeous,' she sighed. 'I just wish I knew what it said.'

A bespectacled man in a humble suit turned to her and smiled. 'It is a very special story,' he said softly. 'It is a poem called *The Song of Unending Sorrow* about the last Emperor of the Tang Dynasty and his young love. This scroll once hung in the Forbidden City and there was another to match, but the white devils stole it when they sacked the palace during the Opium Wars.'

'Oh, wow. Thank you,' Alice-Miranda said.

'White devils?' Sep asked.

'I mean you no disrespect, young man,' the fellow said.

'Oh, you're referring to westerners. I imagine it did feel like you were being invaded by white devils,' Sep said. 'I've read that they stole lots of the antiquities and treasures. It's such a pity. All Chinese artefacts should be in Chinese museums.'

The man bowed his head slightly. 'If only everyone in the world thought like you, perhaps treasures could be returned to their rightful owners.'

Sep grinned. 'Maybe that's what I should do when I grow up.'

'What? Steal antiquities and take them back to their owners?' Lucas teased.

'I think he meant being some sort of human-rights lawyer who returns important things to their countries of origin.' Millie looked at Alice-Miranda. 'See, I told you.'

Sep frowned. 'Told her what?'

'The other day Millie was making all sorts of grand predictions about what we might do when we grow up, and she said that you'd most likely become a human-rights lawyer,' Alice-Miranda explained, her eyes twinkling. 'It seems she was right.'

'What did she say about me?' Caprice asked, appearing behind them.

'That you'd be a famous singer,' Alice-Miranda said, smiling.

Caprice stared at Millie. She felt strangely touched by the revelation and just a tiny bit guilty about her behaviour at breakfast. Both were uncomfortable feelings. 'Did you really say that?' she asked.

'Among other things,' Millie mumbled.

The group moved on to the sculpture gallery and passed September Sykes on their way.

'Don't waste your time, kids,' she said, rolling her eyes. 'Everything in there is a zillion years old.'

'But that's the point,' Sloane said, aghast.

'Well, then I just don't understand museums. But,' September said, brightening, 'I've had lots of people following me around and taking photographs of my shoes. They're a big hit.'

Sloane and the rest of the group looked over at a gaggle of Chinese schoolgirls who were standing off to the side pointing at September's feet and giggling behind their hands.

'Would you like to take a picture?' she asked, holding one foot in the air to offer them a better view. The girls nodded and gathered around her.

'I suspect they think she's a celebrity,' Alice-Miranda said.

'Of course they do,' Sloane replied. 'No normal person would ever wear shoes like that.'

Alice-Miranda glanced across the atrium at the entrance to the sculpture exhibit. 'Jacinta, isn't that Summer Tan?' She gestured to a slight girl standing beside a young man.

Jacinta looked across. 'Oh my goodness, I think it is. We've got to go and say hello!' she fizzed.

Alice-Miranda and Jacinta hurried around the circular balcony with the others close behind. 'Summer!' Alice-Miranda called.

The girl spun around, but instead of cheerful recognition, the look on her face seemed to be one of sheer horror. The man grabbed Summer's arm and steered her away. The girls had almost caught up to them when a mob of students spilled out of the doorway, blocking their view. By the time they pushed past, Summer was gone.

'That's odd,' Alice-Miranda said, frowning. 'Fancy seeing her twice in a couple of days. She must have boundless energy to be sightseeing as well as performing at night.'

Jacinta's face fell. 'I'm so sad we didn't get to say hello and I wonder why she didn't look that thrilled to see us.'

'She looked terrified, if you ask me,' Millie noted.

Sloane squinted into the distance. 'Who do you think that guy was?'

'There they are!' Lucas pointed at the escalator to the floor below.

'Summer!' Alice-Miranda called again, waving to her. But this time the girl didn't even look up.

'Maybe she just looks like Summer,' Jacinta said, though she didn't sound entirely convinced.

Alice-Miranda couldn't shake the strange feeling in the pit of her stomach. That girl was either Summer Tan or her twin, and something told Alice-Miranda there was something seriously amiss.

The children finished up their tour and slowly made their way back downstairs to the foyer. Iris was there with her red flag, as the children drew around her like bears to a honey pot.

'Did you enjoy the exhibits?' she asked.

There were lots of nods.

'Wonderful. Now, you have about fifteen minutes to look in the shop. There are lots of replicas of things you have just seen, but keep in mind that the baggage handlers aren't always gentle with your luggage on the planes,' Iris said.

'Yes,' Miss Grimm agreed. 'If you purchase anything breakable, you're going to have to carry it with you in your hand luggage.'

'Do you think they'll have those bronze helmets from upstairs?' Rufus asked. 'They were cool.'

'And weigh about half a tonne,' Mr Plumpton interjected.

'I could wear it on the plane,' Rufus said. 'They don't weigh *us*, do they?'

'I don't think you want to do that, buddy,' Lawrence said. 'I had to wear a replica First World War helmet for a movie not long back and, believe me, I was begging to take it off after five minutes. It felt as though I was balancing a brick on my head.'

Rufus pulled a face.

Mr Plumpton felt for the boy. It was a pity to dampen his enthusiasm. 'Perhaps they'll have a pencil sharpener in the shape of a helmet, or something small like that you can buy instead,' he suggested as the group made their way into the shop.

Meanwhile, Jacinta, Sloane and Ambrosia spotted some outfits from the clothing exhibition on the far wall of the shop and walked over to inspect them. Sep and Lucas were busy admiring miniature bronze pots and urns, while Venetia and Caprice were looking at Chinese puzzles which they thought might make good presents for her brothers. September collapsed on a chair in the corner, tired of walking. She couldn't quite come to terms with the fact that there was nothing she wanted to buy. It was a very strange feeling.

'Look, Millie, it's a copy of the cup with the hens on it.' Alice-Miranda picked it up and checked the price, pleasantly surprised. 'I'm going to get one each for Mrs Oliver and Shilly. I think they're adorable.'

'I'll be back in a minute,' Millie said, and headed off to take a closer look at a scroll she thought her mother might like.

As Alice-Miranda queued at the counter to pay for her goods, she felt a tap on her shoulder. She turned around and was taken aback to see Summer Tan standing before her. 'Oh, hello!' Alice-Miranda beamed. 'We thought it was you on the escalator.'

Summer smiled nervously.

'Was that your brother you were with again?' Alice-Miranda asked.

Summer shrugged, clearly not understanding what the tiny girl was asking.

'I'm buying these for my friends Mrs Oliver and Shilly.' Alice-Miranda held out her hands to show the girl what she was getting.

Summer blanched at the sight of the replicas.

Alice-Miranda bit her lip. 'Don't you like them? I thought they were sweet.'

Summer shook her head, but Alice-Miranda still wasn't sure whether that meant yes she did like them or no she didn't. The woman at the counter beckoned for Alice-Miranda to put her purchases forward.

'Excuse me a moment,' Alice-Miranda said, and turned to pay for the goods, then waited while the woman wrapped them carefully.

'These are popular today,' the woman said. 'I think your friend bought one earlier.'

Alice-Miranda smiled politely, wondering who the cashier was referring to. She rejoined Summer and held up her purchases triumphantly. 'All done. So what brings you to Shanghai?'

The same look of terror flashed across the girl's face. Summer scanned the shop. He'd be back any minute and it would be time to go. She tried to remember what she wanted to say to Alice-Miranda, but the words were like a whirligig inside her mind. All she could think about was how her mother's life depended on her silence. So why did she believe this girl could help her?

'Summer, are you all right?' Alice-Miranda asked.

'Yes,' she said quickly, then leaned forward and embraced her, which caught Alice-Miranda completely off guard. 'I must go.' She hesitated for a moment before adding, 'Look after your buys and do not show the authorities.'

Summer looked over Alice-Miranda's shoulder, which caused the girl to turn too. But she couldn't work out what she was focused on. When Alice-Miranda turned back, Summer was gone.

Chapter 26

After midday, the group was back on the bus and heading for their next destination.

'I'm starving,' Lawrence said, a little louder than he'd meant to. Soon, just about the whole group was complaining of hunger pains, although Iris reassured them that they would have lunch very soon.

'I can't believe you got to talk to Summer and nobody else saw her,' Millie said. 'That girl is like a Houdini as well as the world's best acrobat. Was she okay?'

'I think so,' Alice-Miranda replied. 'We didn't really talk much, so it was hard to tell. I still don't know why she was there.'

'Maybe the Circus of Golden Destiny is in town,' Millie said.

'I'm not sure. Perhaps Iris can tell us,' Alice-Miranda said. Their tour guide was sitting at the front of the bus in the seat ahead of them. 'Excuse me, Iris,' Alice-Miranda said, tapping the woman's arm, 'do you know if the Circus of Golden Destiny is performing in Shanghai at the moment?'

'I wish, but the government does not allow visiting entertainment like that as we have many troupes of our own,' Iris explained.

Alice-Miranda thanked her and sat back in her seat. Perhaps Summer was on a short holiday – it wasn't unfeasible, yet it still didn't sit right. Alice-Miranda wished she could work it out. She decided to ask Uncle Lawrence if he could phone Mr Choo again, just in case there was something the matter.

The rest of their time in Shanghai flew by. Lunch was followed by a trip to the Yuyuan Garden, an ancient compound built in the 1500s by the governor of Sichuan. According to Iris, it was the man's lifelong dream, and in the end his greatest folly as the expense of maintaining the vast area completely ruined the family. Over the centuries, the gardens had been impinged upon by suburban sprawl and were now surrounded by tourist shops selling all manner of Chinese knick-knacks, from porcelain and pottery to fans and footwear. There were lots of Western fast-food outlets too, which Alice-Miranda thought looked terribly out of place. In the short time they were there, September managed to add to her impressive collection of silks and clothing, although she couldn't find a single pair of shoes to fit her, no matter how hard she tried to stuff her feet inside. Sloane didn't help matters when she explained to one of the shopkeepers that fitting her mother was like trying to find shoes for one of Cinderella's ugly stepsisters.

In the evening, the group toured the area called the French Concession. It was full of little alleyways and lanes and lots more restaurants and shops. They then took a cruise on the Huangpu River, which wriggled like a dragon's tail from central China to the sea. They boarded the vessel at one of the docks on the Bund, a beautiful area along the river where tourists gathered to get some of the best views of the city's architecture. An impressive fireworks display capped off an extremely busy day.

'I'm exhausted,' Millie said. She laid her head on Alice-Miranda's shoulder as the bus drove back to the hotel. 'I can't wait to start going to school again.'

Alice-Miranda smiled to herself. 'Did you really just say that?'

Millie looked up. 'I think I did. You know, this tourist thing is tiring. At least we get to sit down for an hour at a time when we're at school. If any of our lessons are in Mandarin I might have a nap to conserve my energy.'

'According to the schedule, we only have one full day of school anyway,' Alice-Miranda said.

There was a screech as Iris activated the PA system. 'Thank you, everyone, for a very good day,' she said. 'We have kept together and I have received many nice comments about the lovely children.'

'Well done, kids,' Lawrence said, leading the adults in a round of applause.

'What about the grown-ups? Did you get any compliments about us?' September asked.

'Oh yes, Mrs Sykes, your shoes were a source of constant amazement,' Iris said.

September beamed. 'I'll make sure I wear them again.'

'Good grief, no,' Sloane mumbled, and rolled her eyes.

Millie stared out of the window at the sparkling city lights. 'Shanghai is exciting but I don't know if I could live here all the time.'

'Why not?' Alice-Miranda asked. 'It's got such a great buzz. It's sort of like New York but even bigger and with different smells and arguably much worse traffic.'

'How do people get away from it all? I suppose you wouldn't ever feel lonely,' Millie said.

Alice-Miranda's thoughts wandered back to Summer. 'I don't know – I think a person can still be lonely in the middle of an enormous city.'

The bus pulled up outside the shiny hotel lobby and the children spilled out onto the driveway. Alice-Miranda hung back and waited for the others to walk out of earshot.

'Uncle Lawrence,' she said, walking up to the man.

He looked up and smiled, dusting the crumbs from his pants. 'Hello, sweetheart.'

'I was wondering if you had managed to get hold of Mr Choo?' she asked.

'Afraid not, darling. I've left a couple of messages for him, but he hasn't returned my calls. Don't worry too much. Summer looks like she can take care of herself.'

'You're probably right,' the child said. 'Thanks for trying.'

'Would you mind giving me a hand with something, Lawrence?' Mr Plumpton asked, and the two of them trotted inside.

Miss Grimm gathered everyone around to have a quick chat about packing and ensuring that nothing was left behind. She and Miss Reedy planned to inspect the children's rooms before lights out to check that they were ready to leave swiftly for their flight in the morning.

'We will be going straight from the airport to the Bright Star Academy to meet your billets and start your next big adventure,' Miss Reedy said. She was looking forward to having some nights off with her husband to explore the city.

'I hope our billet's nice,' Susannah said to Caprice.

'They'd better be,' Caprice snorted, 'or else I'll be going to stay with Mummy in the hotel.'

Susannah gulped. 'You wouldn't leave me there on my own, would you?'

Caprice shrugged. 'I suppose you could come with us, but you'd have to sleep on a rollaway.'

'I can't wait to meet Coco,' Alice-Miranda said.

'Me too,' Jacinta fizzed. 'What do you think she'll be like?'

'They're probably as scared about meeting us as we are about meeting them,' Lucas said with a grin.

The sound of a phone ringing interrupted the group. The bus driver hopped off and held it aloft, then said something to Iris.

'Someone left this on board,' she announced.

'That's Uncle Lawrence's,' Alice-Miranda said. 'I'll give it to him.'

Iris passed it over, and the girl was thrilled to see the caller was none other than Benny Choo. Knowing that her uncle had gone inside with Mr Plumpton, Alice-Miranda took the call.

'Hello Mr Choo,' she said. 'It's Alice-Miranda speaking. Uncle Lawrence is busy right now.'

To her surprise, it was a woman who replied. She introduced herself as Mr Choo's secretary and apologised for missing Lawrence's calls. Alice-Miranda told her it was not a worry at all and that Lawrence had in fact been calling on her behalf, that she had seen Summer Tan in Shanghai that morning and wanted to check that everything was all right.

On the other end of the line, Fuchsia Lee faltered. The child had to be mistaken. 'I'm afraid that is impossible,' Fuchsia said. 'Miss Tan is performing this evening in Hong Kong. She cannot be in Shanghai.'

'Oh, I see,' Alice-Miranda replied, her brow furrowing. 'Could you ask Mr Choo to call Uncle Lawrence as soon as he can?'

Miss Lee agreed to do so and hung up the telephone, confused.

Millie took one look at her friend's face and knew something was wrong. 'Is everything okay?' she asked.

'I'm not sure,' Alice-Miranda said with a shake of her head. 'I'm really not sure at all.'

Chapter 27

Coco was out of bed and dressed before the alarm began to beep.

Wai Po pushed open the door into the child's bedroom. 'Good morning, little one.'

'Hello Wai Po,' Coco said brightly.

The old woman smiled. 'You are in a very fine mood.'

'Jacinta and Alice-Miranda are coming today!' The girl jumped up and down on the spot as if she were on a pogo stick, except that, unlike most children, she actually jumped so high she could touch the ceiling and executed a perfect split as she did so. 'Do you like the gifts I have made for them?' She raced to her desk and lifted up the two Chinese knots she'd made.

Wai Po's eyes twinkled. 'They are perfect, but you must not forget that the boys are coming too.'

Coco nodded. 'I told Sunny to make them a gift as well, but he just wants them to play video games with him. I want to show the girls everything.'

'Of course,' Wai Po said, 'but you must not expect too much of them. They might be very shy and it will be a completely different experience for them – especially living here in the *hutongs* with us.'

'I don't mind. I think it's exciting to meet someone from far away,' the child babbled. 'I can practise my English so that, when I go to America, no one will even be able to tell that I'm from China.'

'Since when do you want to move to America?' The old woman frowned, her face crumpling like crushed velvet.

'Because I want to star in movies and on television shows,' the girl said, a dreamy look in her eyes.

'Chinese people can be on the television. You could get a job here on my favourite show, *Amazing Detective Di Renjie*,' the woman said.

Coco scrunched up her nose. 'That's a boring old people's program. I would rather be on *Beijing Youth* – at least they are young and fun.'

'Well, I don't know when you are doing all these things. You are already in the most famous acrobatic show in all of China and it is your family tradition,' Wai Po said. 'Who would take over the show if you and Sunny left?'

Coco shrugged. 'I suppose. Maybe I'll stay if I can do tricks like Summer Tan.' Coco looked admiringly at the poster of the girl, which took pride of place on her wall.

'You are better than her,' said Wai Po.

Coco shook her head. 'Mama said she does things that aren't humanly possible. I wish I could see her perform.'

Lucille pushed open Coco's bedroom door. 'Who do you wish you could see?' she asked, a cheery smile on her face.

'Hello Mama,' Coco replied, wondering the reason for her mother's early visit. She couldn't remember the last time she had come into her room before school. 'I was just telling Wai Po that I wish I could see Summer Tan.'

'Oh.' Lucille's smile broadened. 'You never know your luck, daughter.'

Wai Po looked at the woman, pondering what mischief she was up to today. 'I will get your breakfast, Coco,' the older woman said, and walked out of the room.

'You can get mine too,' Lucille shouted after her.

It was just as well she couldn't see Wai Po rolling her eyes.

'Are you excited about our visitors?' Coco asked, tugging at her mother's hand.

Lucille's smile melted. 'I am embarrassed,' she admitted. 'What will they tell their parents when they return home? That we made them share a bathroom in an alley?'

'Mama, what does it matter? They have come to China to see what life is like here, and this is our life,' the girl reasoned. 'I don't understand why you are always so upset about the way we live. Ye Ye and Nai Nai are so good to us.'

'Yes, I suppose you're right. But our life is going to be so much better when . . .' Lucille trailed off and a strange look settled on her face.

'When what, Mama?' Coco asked. Her mother wasn't usually backwards in saying what was on her mind.

Lucille stared into the distance as though she was in the middle of a daydream.

'Are you all right, Mama?' Coco asked. She was beginning to worry that there was something wrong with her. This was not her mother's usual behaviour at all.

'When we have indoor plumbing, of course,' the woman said. 'Come, we must get to breakfast and then to rehearsal. You don't want to be late for school today.'

'I wish Alice-Miranda and Jacinta would be there when we start school, but they aren't due until lunchtime and by then I think I'll be ready to burst with excitement.' Coco grabbed her schoolbag and raced out the door.

Lucille was just about bursting too. The idea of being part of the world's best acrobatic troupe, staying in the finest hotels and flying all over the globe, was almost too much to think about. If someone in this family didn't say something soon, she didn't know how much longer she could keep it to herself.

Chapter 28

The bus slowed down and veered left off the freeway ramp.

Millie looked at her watch. 'We must be getting close to the school by now.'

'I wonder if they're nervous about meeting us,' Alice-Miranda replied. 'I'm so excited it feels like there are a thousand butterflies doing somersaults in my stomach.'

Millie grinned. 'Maybe that's what's happening in my tummy too. I thought it was just that seaweed biscuit I ate on the flight.'

Lucas and Sep were sitting across the aisle from Jacinta and Sloane, who were both gazing out of the windows at the unfamiliar surroundings.

'At least the traffic doesn't seem as bad here,' Sep said, just as the bus lurched to a halt.

'Good one,' Lucas said, eyeing the long line of cars up ahead.

Sep groaned. 'Maybe I spoke too soon.'

September Sykes was sitting a few rows back, regretting both the large bottle of water she had downed on the plane and the decision to wear her brand-new skin-tight jeans. She was now absolutely busting to go to the toilet. She stood up and walked gingerly to the front of the bus, where she whispered into Miss Grimm's ear.

'I'm sorry, Mrs Sykes, I didn't quite catch that,' Ophelia said loudly.

'I need to go,' September hissed, barely raising her voice. She jigged from one foot to the other like an Irish dancer.

Ophelia shook her head. 'My ears must be blocked from the flight. You'll have to speak up, Mrs Sykes.'

'If we don't pull over right now, I'm going to wet my pants!' the woman screamed.

The entire bus fell deathly silent, then erupted with laughter.

'Mummy, you are so embarrassing,' Sloane shouted. 'I disown you!'

'The feeling's mutual!' September yelled back.

'Did you really have to broadcast that to the entire group, Mrs Sykes?' Ophelia rolled her eyes. She hoped it wouldn't take too long to settle the children down again. She wanted them to be on their best behaviour when they arrived at Bright Star.

The guide who was accompanying them from the airport to the school was an earnest young man named Grant. 'Is there a problem?' he asked.

'Would it be possible to find a toilet?' Ophelia asked.

'Urgently!' September added through gritted teeth.

Grant looked outside and spotted a restaurant. 'Perhaps we can use the facilities there,' he said, pointing at the grungy-looking building.

There wasn't really anywhere to pull over, so the driver simply flicked on his hazard lights and remained in the middle of the road. Horns blasted and cars edged around the vehicle, while motor scooters and cyclists whizzed by on both sides.

Grant took the woman's arm and, after a couple of near misses with speeding motorbikes, they negotiated their way to the restaurant door. At least ten minutes went by before September and Grant reappeared. The woman looked as if she'd seen a ghost.

'Are you all right, Mrs Sykes?' Ophelia Grimm asked, as she stepped back inside.

'No, I'm not,' September sniffed.

'What happened?' Mr Grump asked, noting that their resident fashionista was missing a shoe.

'I had to . . . squat over a hole in the ground, and there was no toilet paper,' September said shakily. 'And then . . .'

'I'm sorry, Mrs Sykes. I probably should have warned you that there are a lot of places in China that don't have Western-style toilets, and it's always advisable to take a packet of tissues with you,' Ophelia said.

'Shanghai didn't have anything like that,' September said as she gratefully accepted a wet wipe from Miss Reedy.

'Where is your shoe, Mrs Sykes?' Mr Plumpton asked.

At the mention of her missing footwear, the woman promptly burst into tears.

Chapter 29

'We're here!' Alice-Miranda exclaimed, gazing out at the white building. Strung beneath the Bright Star Academy sign was a large banner with the words 'Welcome, new friends'.

Ophelia Grimm had only just stepped off the bus when she was almost bowled over by a brunette woman in a smart red suit. Behind them, standing to attention on the front steps, was a long line of smiling children. The two women embraced like long-lost friends.

'It all looks so modern,' Alice-Miranda said to Millie, who was putting her camera away into her backpack.

The children filed off the bus and huddled together.

'Welcome, welcome, friends,' said the smiling woman with dark hair. 'My name is Shauna O'Reilly and I'm the headmistress of the Bright Star Academy.'

'She looks way too young to be in charge,' Sloane whispered to Jacinta, a little louder than she'd intended.

Miss O'Reilly winked at them. 'Why, thank you very much, girls.'

'I thought Miss Grimm and Miss O'Reilly had gone to university together,' Millie said.

Ophelia arched her eyebrow. 'We did.'

'O-kay,' Millie mumbled in a singsong voice.

'We're going straight to the auditorium for a quick assembly, then I'll introduce you to your billets and you'll spend the afternoon doing some activities with them. We've planned a special dinner here at school tonight – one that all the parents will attend,' Miss O'Reilly said, buttoning her jacket.

September's ears pricked up. 'A dinner? Does that mean we have to stay here until then?' She'd quickly located another pair of shoes in her suitcase, but all she really wanted to do was go to the hotel and have a shower.

'Won't that be lovely, Mrs Sykes?' Ophelia Grimm could feel her blood pressure rising every time the woman opened her mouth.

'But . . .' September was about to say something when Sloane gave her a sharp poke in the ribs.

'Please stop it, Mummy. We are guests here and you need to behave accordingly,' Sloane ordered.

Livinia Reedy and Ophelia Grimm smothered their grins. They couldn't have said it better themselves.

'Well, I hope they have proper toilets here,' the woman huffed.

Miss O'Reilly smiled sweetly. 'Of course, Mrs Sykes. We have all of the modern amenities here at Bright Star.'

Millie giggled behind her hand. 'I wonder if Miss O'Reilly and Miss Grimm learned their smiling assassin skills at university together.'

The children walked through the guard of honour that had been created by the Bright Star students. As they entered the formation, the boys and girls bowed to acknowledge the arrival of their visitors, but there were plenty of smiles and giggles too.

Alice-Miranda smiled and waved while Millie bowed, although after a while she felt like that drinking bird toy Mr Plumpton kept in the Science lab.

The children entered the school reception area, which looked more like something out of a space-age corporation. There was a huge television screen flashing a welcome message that was bordered by photographs of each of their faces.

'Gosh, they don't do things by halves around here,' Jacinta said. 'We'd have whipped up a sign in Art class.'

Miss O'Reilly led them into an auditorium, which would have looked more at home inside an opera house than a school. The students from Bright Star spilled in after them and, within a few chaotic minutes, the visitors and hosts were seated. As several Bright Star pupils took turns welcoming their guests, Ophelia was kicking herself for not thinking to have any of her children ready with a reply. Although, at least she'd thought to arrange the presentation of the school pennant.

Millie spotted the teacher waving at them and tapped Alice-Miranda on the shoulder. 'I think Miss Grimm wants you,' she whispered.

Without a fuss, the child stood up and quickly made her way to the end of the row. Minutes later, she thanked their hosts for their generous welcome in near-perfect Mandarin.

✯

After the formal assembly, the children were taken to another reception area to be introduced to their billets. The room was blooming with floral arrangements and centred around a long table laden with afternoon tea. The students fidgeted excitedly as Miss O'Reilly announced each of the hosts and their guests, the children then hurrying towards each other and making speedy introductions.

'Hello, I'm Alice-Miranda Highton-Smith-Kennington-Jones.' The child smiled at a tiny girl whose hair was wound tightly into two panda ears. She offered her outstretched hand before introducing Jacinta too.

Coco shook the girls' hands and bowed. 'I'm Coco Wong and I am so excited to meet you both. Congratulations on your speech, Alice-Miranda. Your Mandarin is spotless.'

Alice-Miranda smiled. 'That's very nice of you to say, but I'm just a beginner. You can be sure that your English is much better than my Mandarin.'

'Well, you made everyone laugh with that story about your friend not wanting to eat scorpions on sticks.' Coco grinned. 'It feels like we have been waiting forever for you to arrive.'

'It felt like that for us too,' Jacinta said. 'Is the traffic always so bad?'

Coco nodded. 'You get used to it.'

'Do you walk to school?' Alice-Miranda asked, wondering how far away they were from Coco's home.

The child shook her head. 'Not usually, but sometimes I walk home – it's not that far. I have to go to the theatre for rehearsals before school.'

'The theatre?' Jacinta's eyebrows raised.

'My family has an acrobatic troupe and we rehearse every morning,' Coco said.

'That's fantastic,' Alice-Miranda gasped. 'We saw the Circus of Golden Destiny perform in Hong Kong and there were some incredible acrobats there. Is that the sort of thing you do too?'

Coco nodded. 'I have never seen them in real life, but they are on the television sometimes. There is one performer – Summer Tan – who is my idol.'

'She's mine too,' Jacinta sighed, finding her voice.

'We met her and she's absolutely lovely and so clever,' Alice-Miranda added.

Coco's eyes lit up. 'You must tell me all about her. What's she like? Is she as tiny as she appears on the television?'

Jacinta nodded. 'She's pretty small and so flexible. I think her bones are made of elastic bands.' The girl's mind raced. 'Can we see *your* show?'

'Yes, of course. My family would be honoured,' Coco said.

Alice-Miranda gave her friend a gentle nudge. 'Jacinta is an excellent gymnast,' she said.

Jacinta's cheeks flushed red and her eyes dropped to the ground. 'I'm not, really.'

'She's just being modest,' Alice-Miranda said. 'Jacinta's a former national junior champion.'

Coco beamed.

'Past tense. I'm not anymore,' Jacinta protested.

'That's still amazing,' Coco insisted. 'Maybe you can train with us.'

Jacinta could feel the excitement rising in her body. This was like a dream come true. 'Do you have a plate-spinning act?' she asked.

Coco's eyes sparkled. 'I also have a special performance using silk ribbons, which is lots of fun. And we do plenty of trampolining and tumbling.'

'Wow.' Jacinta was itching to start right away.

Coco turned her attention to Alice-Miranda. 'And you?'

'Oh no,' the girl said, shaking her head. 'I'm not the least bit flexible.'

Alice-Miranda glanced across at Millie, who was talking animatedly to a girl with two plaits. She and Sloane were laughing as the girl pulled a funny face. Caprice and Susannah were standing nearby with another girl whose thick black hair tumbled all the way to her bottom in luxuriant waves. Caprice didn't look very happy, but at least Susannah was smiling.

'Your headmistress seems like a lot of fun,' Alice-Miranda said. The woman was laughing hysterically with Lawrence Ridley and Ambrosia Headlington-Bear.

'Oh, she is,' Coco gushed. 'We've been on lots of excursions. Last year we camped on a far section of the Great Wall, where we had to get dropped in by helicopters, and another time we spent three days training to be panda keepers in Chengdu.'

'Wow!' Alice-Miranda's eyes widened. 'That sounds extraordinary.'

Jacinta looked over at Lucas and Sep with their billet. 'I wonder who the boys have been paired with.'

'Oh, that's my cousin Sunny,' Coco said. 'He's really more like a brother because we live in the same house and perform together too. I hope you don't mind that there'll not be three children but six.'

'Fantastic!' Jacinta exclaimed. Alice-Miranda smiled, glad that things between her and Lucas were back to normal.

Miss O'Reilly pulled a tiny piccolo from her jacket and began to play a spirited tune, which quickly got everyone's attention. 'Okay, children. I hope that you've had a good chat with your billets, but I'm afraid it's time to make your way to your after-school activities. We'll meet back in the cafeteria at half past five for our early supper. See you then!'

'What about your show?' Alice-Miranda asked Coco. 'Do you have to perform tonight?'

The girl shook her head. 'We only perform Friday to Sunday because Ye Ye – that's our grandpa – says that it would be too much on top of school. Other performers take our place from Monday to Thursday. We'd better be going. My badminton coach doesn't like it when we're late.'

As the children were leaving the auditorium, Alice-Miranda noticed September sitting on her own.

She peeled off and hurried over to her. 'Are you all right, Mrs Sykes?' she asked.

The woman pouted at her telephone. 'Stupid battery's run out and my charger's on the bus. What am I supposed to do until dinner?'

'Why don't you go with Sloane or Sep to their after-school activity?' the child suggested.

'They're not talking to me,' she said.

'Would you like to come with us?' Alice-Miranda asked. 'We're going to play badminton with Coco.'

September realised that all the other students and adults had left the room. Two women in white pinafores wheeled in a trolley and began to clear away the afternoon tea.

Coco smiled. 'We just have to go to the gymnasium next door.'

'I suppose,' September huffed. 'But I hope it's not too far to walk. My feet are killing me.'

Chapter 30

The Bright Star cafeteria more closely resembled an upmarket restaurant than something one would expect to find in a school. Several buffet stations groaned under the weight of far too much food and, to the children's surprise and delight, the fountain in the centre of the room flowed with lemonade. Shauna O'Reilly was busy wandering around introducing the parents of the host children to their adult guests and making sure that everyone had plenty to eat.

Millie picked up a barbecue-pork bun and plonked it onto her plate. 'This food is great,' she announced, as the children shuffled along the line helping themselves to the feast.

'Those dumplings look delicious too,' Alice-Miranda said. She took a small plate of three and added it to her tray.

The afternoon's activities had proven to be a resounding success. Although September Sykes had somewhat reluctantly joined Alice-Miranda and her friends, in the end she'd had a wonderful time, even hitting the court to demonstrate some surprising skills with the badminton racquet. Alice-Miranda had taken the opportunity to have quite a lovely chat with her too. Coco Wong directed Alice-Miranda and Jacinta to a table where Sloane and Millie were sitting with their billet, Selina. Caprice and Susannah were at the table next to them, accompanied by the girl with the lavish curls.

'Are you friends?' Millie asked Selina and Coco.

The pair smiled at each other and nodded. 'We've mostly been in the same classes,' Selina said, 'since kindergarten.'

'How lovely,' Alice-Miranda said. 'Millie and I have been room mates since I started at our boarding school, and Sloane and Jacinta used to be room mates before Jacinta moved over to Caledonia Manor.'

'Now I share with Caprice and it's not nearly as much fun,' Sloane said quietly, although Caprice's radar ears still picked up on her name. The girl leaned over.

'What did you say about me?' she asked.

'I was just telling Selina and Coco that we share a room back at school,' Sloane said.

Caprice rolled her eyes. 'She's so messy. I'm always having to tidy up after her.'

The girl with the luxurious hair scoffed. 'Don't you have a maid?'

'No, of course not,' Sloane laughed.

'But how do you get ready for school in the morning?' The child looked positively bewildered.

'Not everyone lives like you do, Felicity,' Selina said.

Caprice and Susannah looked at one another, wondering what they were going to find when they got home.

'Where does she live?' Millie whispered, when the girls were no longer paying attention.

'In a mansion,' Selina said. 'She invited the whole class to her birthday party last year and we went bowling in the basement, then had a karaoke disco in their very own nightclub. It had shiny disco balls and the dance floor lit up when your feet touched the different squares.'

'Wow!' Millie said, between bites of pork dumpling.

'But please don't expect that we have anything like that. My family lives in an apartment on the thirty-sixth floor and it's very small,' Selina said, almost apologetically. 'We are going to be squeezed into my room like anchovies.'

Millie smiled. 'We don't care what sort of house you live in. We're just happy to be here.'

'It sounds as if the teachers made a good choice matching Felicity and Caprice,' Sloane said. 'But I feel sorry for Susannah.'

Coco bit her lip. All the things her mother had said came rushing back to her. 'Sunny and I live in the *hutongs*,' she said softly.

Alice-Miranda and Jacinta leaned forward, eager to hear more.

'What's that?' Millie asked.

'It means laneways. But there are houses too — they are called *siheyuan*. The *hutongs* are the oldest residential areas in the city,' Coco explained.

'That sounds fascinating,' Alice-Miranda said. She couldn't wait to get there.

Coco was about to say something when she looked up and spotted her parents enter the room. She excused herself from the table and ran towards them. Coco hugged her father and beckoned her parents to come and meet her new friends. 'Mama, Baba, these are our guests, Alice-Miranda and Jacinta,' she fizzed. 'And this is Millie and Sloane. They are staying with Selina.'

Alice-Miranda slipped out of her chair and walked to shake the adults' hands. 'Hello, I'm Alice-Miranda Highton-Smith-Kennington-Jones. I'm so looking forward to our time together, and I hope to learn as much about your culture as possible and to, of course, improve my Mandarin.'

Lucille Wong studied the girl with the tiny mass of cascading chocolate curls.

'It's lovely to finally meet you both and thank you so much for having us to stay,' Alice-Miranda finished, with a smile.

'It is our pleasure to welcome you to Beijing,' Bernard replied, charmed by the small girl. 'We hope that you will enjoy it here.'

'Jacinta is a gymnast,' Coco said proudly. She looked at her mother and added, 'She is even a national champion. Can she train with us? Please?'

'But of course! It would be our honour,' Bernard said with a huge smile.

Coco grabbed Jacinta's hands and the two girls jumped up and down excitedly.

Shauna O'Reilly hurried over to greet the Wongs and asked them to join her and the other adults to have something to eat.

'Your father's like a muscle man,' Millie said.

Coco giggled. 'Both of my parents also perform and Baba has to be strong for the shows. We're actually putting together a new act which will debut at the end of the week, and my grandparents are in it too.'

'Are you serious?' Jacinta breathed.

Alice-Miranda giggled to herself.

'What are you laughing about?' Coco frowned.

The child grinned. 'I was just trying to picture Granny Valentina doing cartwheels in a sparkly leotard. Or Aunty Gee.'

'Ha!' Millie snorted. 'Imagine Aunty Gee on a trapeze.' Millie turned to Coco. 'Your grandparents mustn't be like any other grandparents we know.'

Coco paused for a moment. 'I think you might be right.'

'What will they be doing?' Jacinta asked.

'You'll just have to wait and see,' Coco said with a glint in her eye.

Jacinta could barely contain herself.

Chapter 31

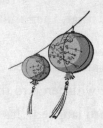

Alice-Miranda gazed out of the window as the van wound its way through the narrow streets towards the Wongs' home. She and Jacinta were with Coco and her parents while another vehicle had come to pick up the boys and Sunny's parents. In the back seat Coco was giving them a running commentary on the local area.

She pointed to a shopfront where lanterns danced in the breeze. 'See that place there? Mrs Chan makes the best wontons in the whole city. Everyone loves her, not only because of her cooking but she tells the best jokes too.'

Alice-Miranda smiled. 'What fun.'

A little further along the roadway the van stopped to let another vehicle go around some parked cars.

'See that man there?' Coco whispered. 'He owns the laundry and he's always picking his nose.'

Jacinta gagged. 'Ew, that's disgusting.'

'Coco, I heard that,' her mother chided from the front.

Coco frowned and hunkered down in her seat. 'Well, he does,' she whispered to the girls.

'It's true,' Bernard laughed. 'It's a miracle the man still has a nose – he was picking it when I was a boy.'

The children laughed.

'I wonder how Millie and Sloane are going,' Alice-Miranda said.

'Selina and her family are really nice. I'm sure they'll have a great time,' Coco said.

'I'd like to be a fly on the wall with Caprice and Susannah at the moment,' Jacinta said.

'Were Felicity's parents there tonight?' Alice-Miranda asked. She thought she'd introduced herself to every one of the parents, but couldn't recall meeting them.

Coco shook her head. 'Oh, they *never* come to school. I've only seen her grandmother or her nannies.'

'That's awful, poor girl.' Alice-Miranda frowned. 'My mother and father wouldn't have missed tonight for the world. They can't wait for you to visit us next year.'

'I hope I'll be able to,' Coco said, darting a quick glance at her parents. 'It will depend on whether I can have some time off from the show. Anyway, I was surprised that Felicity was hosting at all. She's not exactly the easiest person to get along with at school.'

Jacinta grinned. 'Well, she might just have met her match in Caprice.'

Caprice and Susannah stretched out in the back of the gigantic car. It wasn't a limousine as such, but it wasn't an ordinary sedan either. In the back there were four enormous leather armchairs which swivelled so that the passengers could enjoy a panoramic view through the glass panels that made up the roof of the vehicle.

'What sort of car is this?' Caprice asked.

Felicity shrugged. 'I don't know. It's one of Mama's prototypes.'

Caprice and Susannah looked at one another.

'Do you want something to drink?' Felicity pushed a button and a small black box rose up from the centre of the floor. A lid flipped open, revealing an array of coloured bottles.

'What's that?' Caprice asked, leaning forward.

'It's a refrigerator for my after-school beverage,' the girl replied. She pointed to a neon-orange bottle and in seconds a robotic arm reached out and unscrewed the lid, then passed it to Caprice.

The girl sniffed and felt some bubbles tickle her nose. She put the bottle to her lips and took a swig. 'It's like orange soda but bitter,' she said to Susannah, who still looked dubious about the whole thing.

'Do you have any brothers or sisters?' Susannah asked.

Felicity looked at the girl as if she were mad. 'Of course not. My mother and father were only allowed to have one child. And anyway, I'm perfect, so why would they want another?'

For a second Caprice didn't know what to say. The girl was clearly full of her own importance.

'Where were your parents tonight?' she asked, not one for a tactful delivery. 'My mother was hoping to meet them at the dinner.'

Venetia had been disappointed that she'd only got to meet Felicity's grandmother, who had arrived at the very end of the meal. Venetia's attempts at communication were met with a stony silence, but Miss O'Reilly assured the woman that the girls would be in good hands. The Fangs were one of the most prominent business families in China, and their daughter was shrouded in cotton wool, which was covered in bubble wrap with an outer layer of foam for good measure. Still, Venetia would have felt better if she'd at least met one of the parents.

'Daddy is at his hotel and Mummy is at the factory in Shenzhen,' the girl explained with a wave of her hand.

'So your father owns a hotel?' Caprice said.

'Yes, it's like a resort where adults go to play card games and relax,' Felicity said as if the girls should have known it.

'What sort of factory does your mother work at?' Susannah asked.

Felicity flicked at a piece of lint on her uniform. 'She is the founder and CEO of the Wangfang Motor Group.'

'Does her company make cars?' Caprice asked.

'Gold star to the new girl,' Felicity mocked. 'Of course my mother's company makes cars! Where do you think this one came from?'

The vehicle turned into a driveway, where a towering set of gilded gates slid back to reveal a garden to rival the Palace of Versailles. They drove along a tree-lined grove before the house came into view.

'No way,' Caprice breathed, her eyes on stalks as she tried to take it all in. 'This is insane.'

'Insane – doesn't that mean crazy?' Felicity said, her eyes narrowing.

'I meant it in a good way,' Caprice said. She hadn't imagined they'd be staying in the modern Chinese version of Queen Georgiana's palace.

'Are your parents often away?' Susannah asked, unable to take her eyes off the mansion ahead of them.

'I suppose so,' Felicity said. 'But don't worry, there are lots of people to take care of us.'

The car proceeded to an underground car park, and the girls were stunned to see at least fifty gleaming cars, each housed in a glass garage.

The car they were in stopped beneath a giant portico. A uniformed butler stepped forward to open the doors.

'This is the butler,' Felicity informed the girls. 'There are also maids and two nannies. Plus, Chef and his team and three gardeners and the men who wash the cars and the security guards and the drivers.' She paused. 'There are probably others, but don't ask me what anyone's name is.'

'You don't know their names?' Susannah was incredulous. 'Isn't that a bit . . . awkward?' The girl couldn't imagine not knowing the names of everyone at school and not just the teachers and the girls. Mr Charles and Mrs Howard and Mrs Smith weren't just people who worked there. They were like family.

'Why? I don't talk to them,' the girl replied with a shrug. 'And you don't need to either.'

Chapter 32

The van pulled up outside a traditional entrance gate. On the other side was a line of trishaws – bicycles with a carriage for two on the back of them.

Bernard Wong walked up and spoke to several of the drivers. Within a couple of minutes the suitcases were loaded into the first trishaw and the children were sitting three abreast in another, while Mr and Mrs Wong hopped into a third vehicle.

'Do you always go to your house this way?' Alice-Miranda asked.

Coco shook her head. 'We have electric motor-bikes and bicycles and sometimes we walk, but Baba thought this would be more fun. It's the traditional transport people used to travel through the *hutongs* in the olden days. Now they are more of a tourist attraction.'

Jacinta's eyes widened as she took in their surroundings. At first glance, the laneway looked pretty, lined with sparkling lights and Chinese lanterns, but as the trishaw driver pushed on, the girl realised that there was a lot more than fairy lights within that outer wall. Some of the alleys were scattered with junk – there were discarded bicycles, twisted and bent, completely beyond repair, while in other sections there were building materials and bamboo scaffolding wrapped around the perimeter of some of the walls. There were even a few small cars wedged into the narrow laneways. This made the going difficult for the trishaw drivers, who, when they had a clear run, sped through the tight streets.

Alice-Miranda grinned as the vehicle rocked and rolled around every sharp corner. 'What a way to travel,' she marvelled.

They stopped alongside a whitewashed wall interrupted by a glossy red door. Beside it, a flourishing pot of orchids in full bloom brightened the space.

'This is home,' Coco said as she and the girls alighted the carriage. She pushed open the front door, which led straight into the rectangular courtyard with the pomegranate tree in the centre. A covered veranda ran around the perimeter with doors leading to who knew where. Alice-Miranda counted at least ten of them that she could see.

'Oh wow!' Jacinta gasped. 'I imagined a *siheyuan* to resemble the Japanese *ryokan* we stayed in during our time in Tokyo, but this is different altogether.'

'Nai Nai, Wai Po,' Coco called out. 'We're home!'

A tiny old woman with grey hair and twinkly eyes shuffled out of one of the doors close by and nodded at the guests. 'Wai Po,' she said, pointing to herself.

Alice-Miranda dipped her head in return. '*Ni hao*, Wai Po.'

The woman giggled and, to the children's surprise, leaned in and gave each of the girls a hug.

'What is she doing, embarrassing herself like that?' Lucille scoffed under her breath.

A sprightly older man and woman walked out of another room and greeted their guests in the courtyard. Alice-Miranda was mesmerised by the man's triangular beard that reached all the way to his chest.

'I am Lionel Wong and this is my wife, Winnie,' the man said. 'I suspect that you would be most comfortable calling us Mr and Mrs Wong.'

'Thank you for inviting us to your home,' Alice-Miranda said as she and Jacinta bowed.

'Come, you must be tired and hungry after your big day of travelling,' Winnie said with a smile.

'We had dinner at school, Nai Nai,' Coco reminded her.

'Yes, but I have tea and cakes,' the old woman said with a wink.

It wasn't long before the group was seated at a large dining table. Cherry and Charles arrived with the boys and joined them and soon an animated conversation was in full flight. Despite some language difficulties every now and again, the children and adults seemed perfectly capable of making themselves understood to one another.

'Where have you been on your travels so far?' Lionel asked the children.

'Hong Kong and Shanghai,' Alice-Miranda replied. 'I thought Hong Kong was especially beautiful with its steep mountains and the harbour.'

'And Shanghai is modern and slick,' Sep added.

Lionel nodded and stroked his beard. 'Beijing is flat – that's why we have such awful problems with the pollution, and we have many more old buildings, but I think that is part of the charm – the buildings, not the smog.'

'We saw the Circus of Golden Destiny perform while we were in Hong Kong,' Jacinta said. She was dying to talk about the Wongs' acrobatic troupe and find out more.

Lionel's eyes lit up. 'And what did you think?'

'It was incredible. We met Summer Tan, who has the lead role in the production. I don't think I've ever seen anyone as flexible as she is,' Jacinta declared.

'Well, you haven't seen our Coco perform yet, so perhaps you will be in for a surprise,' the old man said, grinning.

Coco's face reddened. 'I can't believe that we would ever be as good as the performers in the Circus of Golden Destiny. And Summer is my idol. She is out of this world.'

'Has everyone had enough tea and cake?' Winnie motioned at the platter, which had been laden with sweet treats. A lot of them were similar to what the children ate at home, but there were moon cakes and egg tarts too.

'I'm full,' Lucas said, patting his stomach. 'I'll be getting a gut to rival my father's if I don't stop eating.'

'It was lovely to meet him this evening,' Charles said. 'What an unexpected honour.'

Lucille looked at her brother-in-law, wondering who Lucas's father was. She didn't remember anything special about the man – only that he needed to lose a few pounds and he would look better without that awful beard.

'It is special for your father to be spending this time with you,' Cherry added.

'Might we know who your father is?' Lionel enquired, his curiosity piqued.

'His name's Lawrence Ridley,' the boy replied.

Lucille spat her tea all over the table. 'It is not!'

It was Lucas's turn to blush. No matter how many times people reacted to such news, he'd never get used to it.

'Uncle Lawrence is preparing for a role and he's had to gain weight and look scruffy,' Alice-Miranda explained. 'I didn't recognise him at first either and he's married to my Aunt Charlotte.'

'I adore his films,' Lucille gushed. 'I hope that we will meet him again before the end of the trip.'

'You will,' Charles said. 'I talked with Miss O'Reilly about bringing the children to the show on Friday night and the parents will come too.'

'Then we must be perfect that night,' Lucille said, fluttering her eyelashes and preening her hair.

'Yes, we must,' Lionel reiterated. 'It seems we will have more than one VIP with us that evening.'

'Now, it is time for bed,' Winnie instructed. 'I do apologise, but we are a family that rises very early in the morning, and tomorrow Coco and Sunny must go to training. We've arranged for your transport to school.'

'Oh,' Jacinta said, her voice tinged with disappointment. 'I was hoping to train with Coco.'

'Could we all go and watch?' Alice-Miranda asked.

'Are you sure you want to be up at five in the morning?' the old woman asked.

There were nods all round.

'We want to see *everything*,' Alice-Miranda assured her. 'After all, what's the point of staying with a family unless you get a proper taste of their life? If your life means getting up very early, then we'll do it too.'

Lionel clasped his hands and grinned. 'Then we should clear the table.'

'Must we?' Lucille groaned.

Wai Po pretended to cover her eyes and waggled her head. 'Oh no.'

'For your safety, please do not move,' Lionel instructed their guests. 'On the count of three, two, one . . .'

Without warning, Coco and Sunny somersaulted across the table, flicking three plates each at their mothers, who caught them with their chopsticks. Meanwhile, Charles had pulled a mini trampoline from under the table. Suddenly, he and his brother were catapulting over the children, scooping up the teacups as they went and stacking them high. Coco and Sunny flipped the plates containing the leftover cakes into the air and Lionel caught them in a tub, then thumped the lid on and tossed the container at his wife at a speed that might well have taken her head off if she hadn't thrillingly caught it under her chin and flicked it at Wai Po. The family finished the show with Coco and Sunny catching the plates from their mothers and spiriting them to the kitchen sink.

'What just happened?' Sep said in bewilderment.

'Teatime pack-up, Wong-style.' Lionel bowed and pressed his palms together. 'You like?'

The four guests clapped and cheered wildly, stamping their feet and marvelling at the precision and skill of their hosts.

'That was incredible,' Alice-Miranda said. 'Do you always do that?'

'Not every night, but it gets things done quickly and we like to practise whenever we can,' the old man replied.

The party broke up, and Coco and Sunny took the children to their rooms. It wasn't long before the girls were settled in their beds and chatting away.

'Your home feels like it's part of a tiny village even though it's in the middle of an enormous city,' Alice-Miranda remarked.

'I suppose it is,' Coco said. She'd worried that the girls may find the bathroom situation tricky, but it was quite the opposite. Alice-Miranda had made friends with three of their neighbours by the time they'd finished brushing their teeth.

'Do you know everyone who lives in the *hutongs*?' Jacinta asked.

Coco thought for a moment. 'Yes, I think so. For Chinese New Year we have a huge party and line the alleys with tables. Everyone cooks and we play games and red packets are given out. There are fireworks too, but last year Au Shen set Jiao Long's roof alight. It was lucky there were so many people to help put the fire out.'

Alice-Miranda was soon drifting off to sleep with visions of parties and fireworks dancing through her head.

Jacinta was almost asleep too. Her mind wandered to Caprice and Susannah and what Coco had said about Felicity living in a mansion. A smile played on her lips. She couldn't help wondering how Caprice would have handled having to share a bathroom in an alley.

Chapter 33

Alice-Miranda was awake early. In the half light of dawn, she threw on her tracksuit and headed to the communal bathroom, where she showered and dressed before Jacinta and Coco had even stirred. She almost bumped into Wai Po as she was re-entering the courtyard. The old woman bowed and smiled, then led the girl by the hand to the dining room, where a wall of cereal boxes lined the centre of the table. 'For you,' the woman said, and bowed again before leaving the room.

Cherry walked in and smiled at Alice-Miranda. 'Good morning,' she said, helping herself to some congee that was bubbling away on a portable hot-plate. 'I am sorry. My English is not as good as the rest of my family. And my mother's is even worse.'

'No, it's *very* good,' Alice-Miranda assured her. 'It's much better than my Mandarin.' The child then ventured to say good morning and asked Cherry if she had a busy day ahead in the woman's native tongue.

The two spoke animatedly for a few minutes before Alice-Miranda faltered. 'I think I've reached my limit,' the girl apologised. 'Have you always been an acrobat?'

Cherry nodded. 'But I am getting too old. My father-in-law is a lovely man, though, and makes sure that we all have a role. Our troupe is different to many others in that way.'

'It sounds wonderful,' Alice-Miranda said.

Cherry glanced at the newspaper that was sitting on the table and let out a tiny gasp.

'Is there something the matter?' Alice-Miranda asked, looking over at it.

'There has been a robbery at the Shanghai Museum,' the woman said. 'It doesn't sound like much, but a wine cup from the Ming Dynasty was stolen. They say it is worth tens of millions of yuan,' the woman said, showing her the article.

Alice-Miranda's eyes widened at the sight of the tiny cup decorated with a cockerel and hens. 'Goodness, we saw that very cup at the museum a couple of days ago. I bought two replicas from the gift shop.'

'It says the ancient artefact was stolen in plain sight, when the museum was open,' Cherry said, her eyes scanning the article. 'It happened two days ago but they have only just discovered that a fake has been sitting in its place.'

Alice-Miranda thought for a moment. 'That's when we were there. How extraordinary. Surely they must have caught the thief on camera.'

Cherry shook her head. 'It does not say, but I would not want to be that person once they are caught.'

'We also saw Summer Tan at the museum,' Alice-Miranda said, forgoing the cereal for congee. She sprinkled some freshly cut scallion on top and sat down.

'She is a remarkable acrobat – but what was she doing in the museum? I thought their show was playing in Hong Kong at the moment,' Cherry said, looking a tad sheepish. 'Coco is not the only one who admires her.'

Alice-Miranda shrugged. 'I was surprised to see her in Shanghai too. She was with a young man. I didn't think she'd seen us, but then she came to speak with me in the shop. Actually, she said something quite strange – I think she must have got her words mixed up.'

Their conversation was interrupted by the crunch of footsteps across the gravel. They were joined by Sunny and the boys, followed by Jacinta and Coco. There was a cacophony of greetings from everyone. Sunny plonked down and poured himself a bowl of cereal and directed the others to do the same.

'Did everyone sleep well?' Cherry asked the group, and they answered with yawns and slow nods.

Coco looked over as her mother entered the room, and noticed that the woman wasn't dressed for training. She wore a pair of skinny jeans and a pretty blouse, not the usual leotard and tracksuit.

'Mama, are you coming to rehearsals this morning?' Coco asked.

'Of course I am,' Lucille snapped.

Coco recoiled and frowned into her bowl of cereal. She wondered what had put her mother in a bad mood already this morning.

Lucille was fuming. After the children had gone to bed last night, Bernard had finally revealed his parents' plans for the future. How dare her stupid father-in-law spend all their money on a school for peasant children? Now they would never move out of the *hutongs*. And when Bernard had told her that, despite being taken over by the Circus of Golden Destiny, they would remain in Beijing and not have to travel, the foolish man had thought she would be pleased. Pleased! What a ninny.

Her mind was racing. The sale had not yet gone through and Benny Choo, the owner of the Circus of Golden Destiny, was coming on Friday night to watch them perform. If she had her way, it would never happen – at least not until her in-laws handed over control of the troupe to her husband and they could sell up and spend the money however she wanted.

★

The children had been ferried in pairs through the *hutongs* on the back of Cherry's motor scooter to the van that would take them to the theatre. Cherry and Lucille were making their own way there and Winnie, Lionel and their sons had left before breakfast.

Even at this early hour, the traffic was starting to build. The van passed a pretty park and Alice-Miranda noticed a large group of older men and women practising tai chi. There were street vendors pushing their carts, and trishaws, their riders peddling furiously to keep up with the flow. The scooter drivers were the most impressive, dodging and weaving through the cars and trucks to find the fastest way to their destinations.

Alice-Miranda gazed up at the giant blue sky with its silhouette of skyscrapers. 'It's such a beautiful day,' she sighed happily, among the honking horns and the drilling at a nearby worksite.

'Make the most of it. It's not like this all the time,' Coco said. 'Last week we had to wear masks and we weren't allowed to play outside.'

'It's hard to imagine that on a day like today,' Sep said.

Sunny grinned. 'Like my cousin said, enjoy it while you can.'

The van pulled up outside a large circular building with a red sign bearing Chinese characters. Beneath it was the word 'Eternity' in English.

'This is it,' Coco declared. She was bursting to show their guests her second home.

'Is that the name of your show?' Lucas asked, pointing to the sign.

'No, it's the name of our troupe. Ye Ye chose it because he wants our troupe to last forever,' Sunny said. 'Our show is called *Believe*.'

'They're great names,' Jacinta said.

The children alighted from the van and followed Coco and Sunny around to the back of the building, where they entered through a steel door.

'How many people are in the show?' Jacinta asked. She could feel the butterflies in her stomach getting busier.

'There are about thirty altogether,' Coco said, 'but some have smaller roles and others much bigger.'

There were a number of doors leading off the wide corridor.

'Are these your dressing-rooms?' Alice-Miranda asked.

'Yes, and that's our grandfather's office.' Coco pointed at another door just as it opened and Deng Rou walked out.

The old woman seemed taken aback to see the children. She spoke quickly to Coco in Mandarin, and before any introductions were able to be made, she hurried away.

'Who was that?' Lucas asked.

'Rou. She's been with the troupe forever,' Sunny replied.

Jacinta frowned. 'Does she perform?' It hardly seemed likely with the limp the woman had.

Coco shook her head. 'No, it's a long story. Nai Nai can't stand her, but Ye Ye says we have an obligation to take care of her.'

Coco knocked on her grandfather's office door but there was no answer.

'I'm here,' Lionel called, waving from the end of the corridor. 'And you need to get started.'

Coco bit her lip. Her grandfather was very particular about no one being in his office if he wasn't there. She wondered what Rou was up to now.

'Coming, Ye Ye,' Sunny called back, and the children thundered down the hall.

Chapter 34

Jacinta's eyes widened as they reached the stage area. The auditorium was cavernous and, much like the Circus of Golden Destiny, there was tiered seating on three sides. Long ropes were suspended from the ceiling and at least twenty young men and women were limbering up, turning cartwheels and walking on their hands.

'I wish I could do that,' Lucas said, staring at a fellow who was resting on his forearms with his legs curled back all the way over his head. His feet almost touched the ground. He held the pose for a while before a young woman lay on his legs. He then straightened up, took one hand off the ground and the two of them hung in the air. Their balance was breathtaking.

Sunny disappeared and returned with several pairs of stilts. 'Would you like to try?' he asked. They weren't old-fashioned timber ones but were curved and springy with an attachment for the feet and a strap for the knees.

'I'm game,' Sep said, stepping forward.

'It's not as hard as it looks. If you have good balance, you'll pick it up in no time,' Sunny said, distributing the apparatus to the four guests.

Several burly young men came and helped the children put on the stilts, then held on to them as they attempted to take a few steps. Alice-Miranda wobbled a little to begin with but was soon walking all over the arena, with Sep and Lucas stumbling after her. Lionel clapped heartily. Bernard and Charles shouted words of encouragement too. Jacinta not only mastered walking in stilts, she swiftly began jumping with no assistance whatsoever.

A huge trampoline was rolled onstage and several young acrobats with taller stilts began springing from the ground onto the trampoline, doing all sorts of flips and splits. Coco and Sunny joined them, and soon there was a trail of at least ten acrobats running and leaping and jumping.

'Do you think I could have a go?' Jacinta asked Lionel, as they both watched from the side of the stage.

There was a glint in the old man's eye. 'Are you sure?' he asked.

Jacinta nodded. She sprang up and down on the spot to get used to the feeling, conscious of the fact that she had to work out how high she could push herself without losing control. Lionel indicated for Bernard and Charles to assist.

Winnie had appeared and was standing with Cherry near the children. Alice-Miranda and the boys sat down while Jacinta prepared herself.

She looked at Bernard. 'My stomach feels a little bit funny.'

'That is a very good thing. I don't ever feel right about a performance unless the butterflies are having a boxing match in my belly,' he said with a smile.

Coco and Sunny stood on either side of the trampoline while their fathers positioned themselves to catch Jacinta should she fall. Jacinta listened carefully as Lionel instructed her on where she should aim to land and how high she should leap beforehand.

'Remember, you can always abort – we would rather abandon than ambulance,' the man said.

Lucille was watching from the shadow of a doorway. 'Oh, father-in-law, you are ever the comedian,' she muttered to herself. 'Or is it the clown?'

'What is the matter with you?' said Deng Rou, appearing next to her.

Lucille looked at Rou with a thinly disguised sneer of contempt. 'Don't pretend with me. I know you far better than that.'

Jacinta stared at the trampoline and the landing spot beyond it. 'Well, here goes nothing,' she said, and began to bounce.

Lucas's heart was pounding. He couldn't take his eyes off the girl. 'Come on, Jacinta,' he whispered.

Jacinta sprang into the air, executing a perfect backflip.

'Woohoo!' Lucas shouted, amid the claps and cheers from the troupe members. 'I knew you could do it.'

Sep leaned over and gave Lucas a friendly nudge.

'That was excellent, Jacinta,' said Sunny's father. 'Are you sure you've never done this before?'

Jacinta was just about bursting. 'Never, but that was incredible. I loved it! I wish I could do it again.'

'Perhaps we can find a guest spot for you in the show on Friday,' Lionel said, glancing at his wife.

'If you think Jacinta can manage it, but remember we have an important guest that evening,' the woman replied.

'Let's see. I can't promise anything, Jacinta, but I think you might be up for one somersault at least,' Lionel offered.

'Perfect,' Lucille muttered.

'Who is our guest, Ye Ye?' Sunny asked. 'You have been teasing us for days.'

'All will be revealed soon, grandson,' the old man said. 'For now, we must practise our finale.'

'Where is that other daughter-in-law of mine?' Winnie looked around, wondering where Lucille had got to this time.

Lucille sighed. 'You will meet me in the first-aid room in ten minutes.'

'Why?' Rou wrinkled her lip.

'Consider it an order.' Lucille drew her shoulders back and stalked across the stage.

★

Alice-Miranda, Jacinta, Lucas and Sep had front-row seats for the next part of the rehearsals. When Winnie peddled onto the stage, riding faster and faster, they held their breaths. The series of tricks was mind-blowing to say the least. Lucille and Cherry spun so many plates that they lost count. In the background, the male members of the family flipped and tumbled, creating human towers and demonstrating their phenomenal strength and balance, with Lionel as the anchor at the bottom.

'Mr Wong is like Superman,' Lucas said in disbelief. 'Can you imagine how strong he must be?'

Sep shook his head. 'My dad can barely lift me on his shoulders in the swimming pool these days, and Mr Wong's got to be at least twenty years older than he is.'

Coco pedalled by on a half-sized red bicycle and began tailing her grandmother. Things were getting busier and faster when, all of a sudden, there was an enormous crash and several of Lucille's plates hurtled to the ground, smashing into thousands of pieces.

The children didn't know where to look as the whole scene began to unravel. Winnie, who had been leaning back on her bicycle, sat up and brought the vehicle to a halt. Coco managed to stop too, and the tower of tumblers leapt gently to the ground.

Bernard raced over to his wife, whose face was flushed a bright red. 'What happened?' he asked.

'I must have slipped,' she said, batting him away.

'Mama, is it your shoulder?' Coco hurried to her side.

'I'll be fine,' Lucille snapped. 'I just need to take a few minutes.'

Lucille hurried off towards the changing rooms.

'Mama!' Coco called after her. She hated the thought of her mother being hurt.

'Leave her,' Bernard said. 'Your mother will be fine.'

'We will take it from the top, but only up to where Lucille and Cherry mount Winnie's bicycle,' Lionel instructed.

'Wow, that was scary,' Lucas said. 'I wonder if there are many injuries.'

Alice-Miranda looked down and realised that her finger was bleeding. 'Oh dear.'

'What happened?' Jacinta asked, looking over at her.

Alice-Miranda clucked her tongue. 'I don't know, but it's just a tiny cut. Maybe one of the plate pieces hit me. I might try to rustle up a bandaid,' she said.

'Would you like me to come with you?' Jacinta asked.

Alice-Miranda shook her head. 'No, stay here and watch. I'm sure I saw a first-aid room in the hall.'

She walked into the tunnel that led to the rooms backstage. Alice-Miranda located the door with the red cross and was about to knock when she heard voices coming from inside. One sounded like Lucille. The two women were speaking in Mandarin. Alice-Miranda knocked gently and the door opened. The old woman they had seen leaving Lionel's office, the one called Rou, answered it.

'Excuse me, would I be able to get a bandaid?' the child asked. 'I seem to have cut my finger.' She waved it in the air.

Rou looked at her blankly, but after a few sharp words from Lucille, she fetched a plaster from a cupboard on the far wall.

'Are you all right, Mrs Wong?' Alice-Miranda asked.

'Yes, I am fine,' the woman replied.

Rou began to speak in Mandarin again. She handed the plaster to Alice-Miranda, her words flowing.

Alice-Miranda frowned. Her knowledge of Mandarin was elementary at best, but what she'd heard had seemed a very strange thing to say. 'Thank you very much. I feel better already,' she said, and walked back to join the others.

Chapter 35

From a very early hour, the Bright Star Academy was buzzing with activity. Students were busy swapping stories amid others rushing to their before-school activities. Somewhere in the building an orchestra was rehearsing; the sounds of their symphony filtering through the halls. Alice-Miranda, Millie, Coco and the boys headed straight to the hall, where they were met by Miss Grimm and Miss O'Reilly, the two headmistresses firing questions like bullets, eager to ensure that everyone had enjoyed their first evening together. As the rest of the visitors and their hosts arrived, Millie and Sloane raced up to Alice-Miranda with Selina in tow.

'We've had the most wonderful morning,' Alice-Miranda blurted. 'We went to training with the Wongs and they taught us how to walk on stilts and Jacinta is going to be in the show on Friday.'

Miss Grimm beamed. 'Oh, Jacinta, that's fantastic news!'

'Ophelia, you won't believe your eyes. The whole family is extraordinary,' Shauna O'Reilly chimed in.

Jacinta's smile couldn't have been any bigger.

'You must be really good,' Selina said.

Coco nodded and gave Jacinta a nudge. 'She is.'

Lucas caught Jacinta's eye and winked. She shivered with happiness. It was good to feel like they were back to normal again, and being able to train with the Wongs was the icing on the cake.

'What did you do last night?' Alice-Miranda asked Millie.

The girl's face lit up. 'Selina's parents took us to a market and I ate a scorpion on a stick!'

'Seriously?' Lucas grimaced.

'Yup, it was crunchy and a bit nutty,' Millie said. 'It honestly wasn't that bad once you got over the thought of it.'

'You're much braver than me, Millie,' Sep said admiringly.

'It was disgusting.' Sloane poked out her tongue. 'I couldn't even watch but I bought this.' The girl produced a cute little toy panda from her pocket. 'Isn't he adorable? And we're going to see the pandas at the zoo after school today.'

'Selina's apartment has the best view. You can see Tiananmen Square and the Forbidden City,' Millie added.

Selina smiled shyly, thrilled that her guests were having such a good time.

Miss Reedy and Mr Plumpton arrived with the other parents.

Lawrence stuffed a half-eaten chocolate bar into his pocket and gave a wave. 'Good morning, kids.'

'Hey, Dad, you're never going to believe what we were doing this morning,' Lucas said. He and Sep rushed up to the man to share tales of walking on stilts.

'Aren't you going to say hello to your mother?' Millie asked Sloane, who was doing her best to pretend that the woman wearing the sky-high boots and what looked like silk Chinese pyjamas tucked into them was not related to her in any way.

September was standing on her own looking a little down in the mouth.

'Not if I can help it,' Sloane mumbled.

Alice-Miranda took the girl by the arm and steered her towards the woman. 'I'm sure your mother would love to know what you did with Selina.'

September looked up and smiled as the girls approached.

'Good morning, Mrs Sykes,' Alice-Miranda said. 'Did you have a nice evening?'

'Yes, it was surprisingly good,' the woman replied. 'I even got to do a little bit of shopping.'

Sloane rolled her eyes. 'Of course you did.'

'Actually, Sloane, I got something for you,' September said, pulling a small white box tied up with a jade-green bow from her pocket. 'I saw it last night and thought you might like it.' She passed the gift to her daughter.

Sloane held it gingerly, as if she was expecting something to jump out and bite her.

September looked at her anxiously. 'Aren't you going to open it?'

'Oh, Caprice and Susannah have arrived. I should go and say hello. I'll see both of you later,' Alice-Miranda said, and hurried away.

Sloane untied the ribbon and flipped open the lid. 'Wow!' she whispered. 'Is this really for me?' She looked up at her mother, who nodded eagerly. 'I love it,' Sloane said, wondering how her mother even knew that she had admired a very similar bracelet in a shop in Shanghai. She lunged forward and briefly hugged September around the middle, working hard to stop the fog that was inconveniently clouding her eyes. 'Thank you.'

Sep glanced over at the pair and almost did a double take. Then he caught a look across the room between Alice-Miranda and his mother and shook his head. That girl never ceased to amaze him.

Alice-Miranda grabbed Millie and the pair wandered over to talk to Susannah and Caprice. 'So how was last night?' Millie asked.

Susannah shrugged. 'It was okay.'

'It was weird,' Caprice said.

'Why?' Alice-Miranda asked.

'When we got home, Felicity took us to our seriously ginormous bedrooms. We both have ensuites with solid gold taps and sitting rooms the size of a tennis court. Her house is like a palace. Felicity showed us how everything worked and told us which number to call if we wanted to order food or needed someone to draw the bath or help with anything and then she disappeared,' Caprice explained.

'So what did you do?' Millie asked. It didn't sound all that bad to her.

'We hung out in my room,' Caprice said. 'Felicity never came back. A maid turned down our beds and brought warm milk and choc-chip cookies, but that was it. We got up this morning and had breakfast in the dining room on our own and another maid told us that the driver would take us to school in one of Mrs Fang's Wangfang concept cars – which has to be the most bizarre thing I've ever seen.'

'Where are Felicity's parents?' Alice-Miranda asked.

'They're both away for work,' Susannah replied.

Millie looked around. 'I think a better question is, where's Felicity?'

'We haven't seen her today,' Susannah said, just as the girl appeared in the doorway.

'Speak of the devil,' Millie said.

Miss O'Reilly clapped her hands and called the group to attention. 'Good morning, girls and boys, parents and staff, what a wonderful feeling of excitement there is in the room. It's been such a treat to hear your stories and I am thrilled that everyone's been getting on so well.' Shauna smiled. 'We'll be leaving in just over an hour to visit the Forbidden City and Tiananmen Square, followed by the Summer Palace. In a moment, though, you'll all be off to Mandarin lessons. Parents, you're most welcome to join the students or have a coffee in the staffroom. Our barista makes a lovely latte. Tomorrow the children will be at school all day, so I understand you've got the day off to explore our fine city.'

'Actually, I have something special planned for us,' Venetia said.

'Hopefully it involves food,' Lawrence chimed in, patting his belly.

Venetia smiled. 'You'll just have to wait and see, Mr Ridley.'

'Will there be shopping?' September trilled.

'Yes, I've got a few things lined up for us in that department,' Ambrosia piped up. 'I'm writing an article on cutting-edge Chinese designers, so I don't think you'll be disappointed.'

'Excellent.' September smiled and gave her daughter a squeeze.

Sloane fidgeted. 'Too much too soon, Mummy,' she mumbled, and September loosened her grip.

'Do we have to go to school on Friday too?' Figgy groaned.

Ophelia Grimm glared at the lad. 'That's George,' she whispered behind her hand to Shauna. 'He of the goldfish-smuggling incident.'

Shauna O'Reilly suppressed a smile. When Ophelia and Aldous had regaled her with the tale the evening before, she'd nearly choked on her dinner. It was the funniest thing she'd heard in years.

'No, Master Figworth. On Friday we're heading up to the Great Wall at Mutianyu. In the evening we're off to see Eternity, the most exciting acrobatic troupe in China,' Shauna explained.

The boy pumped his fist and jostled with Rufus and their billet, Hero, a rotund lad with a quick wit and an extreme love of dumplings.

'Now that that's sorted, could the Bright Star students please take their billets off to class and meet back here promptly at quarter past nine?' Miss O'Reilly instructed. 'Felicity, may I see you for a moment? Caprice and Susannah, would you mind going with Coco and the others? Felicity will be along soon.'

The woman hadn't missed that the girl had arrived quite a while after her guests and wanted to ensure that everything was all right.

The children moved off to class while Ophelia Grimm led the other teachers and parents to the staff-room. She was dying for another cup of tea and would pay a visit to the classroom once she'd got the parents settled. Besides, Miss Reedy and Mr Plumpton could pull their weight a little more.

'I wonder if Miss O'Reilly's going to tell Felicity off for being such a terrible host,' Caprice griped.

Coco frowned. 'I don't think so. She never gets into trouble.'

'Well, she should. She's horrible,' Caprice sighed. So far she didn't think much of her host at all.

'Uh, pot, kettle . . . hello?' Millie whispered, but Sloane heard and was trying not to smile.

'Come on, play nicely, you lot,' Alice-Miranda said. 'Let's just go and enjoy ourselves.'

Chapter 36

Cherry Wong wove in and out of the traffic on her scooter, hoping to get home before the children. She balanced a huge box of pastries on her lap – a special treat for their afternoon tea. As she turned into the entrance to the *hutongs*, another rider shot across and blocked her path. She tooted the horn and tried to get around him, but he moved from side to side, preventing her from going anywhere.

'What are you doing?' Cherry yelled. She tried to catch a glimpse of the rider's face, but he wore a helmet with the visor down.

The rider turned sharply and pulled up beside her. She was about to move off when the man thrust an envelope at her. He then revved the bike and sped away, leaving Cherry completely confused. She turned the envelope over in her hand and found her name typed across it. It was all very odd. How would he have even known who she was? Perhaps he was a fan. She had received a few odd letters over the years from people who had seen the show. One man had even proposed marriage, which her husband, Charles, had thought very funny. But Cherry had felt quite unnerved by the brazen display of affection from a stranger. She tucked the envelope inside her jacket and hurried home.

When she arrived, the compound was eerily quiet. Cherry quickly deposited the cakes on the dining-room table and took out the envelope. She slipped her finger under the flap and opened the letter. Her heart began to beat faster and faster as she read on. Could this be a joke? As she reached the final sentences, her blood ran cold.

'Hello, daughter,' Wai Po said, shuffling into the room. 'Is everything all right? You look as if you have seen a ghost.'

Cherry tucked the letter back into its envelope with shaky hands. 'Of course, Mama. I bought cakes for the children,' she said, and quickly left to go to her bedroom.

She unlocked her camphor chest and hid the envelope in the secret compartment at the bottom. Cherry fought a wave of nausea as she fled through the courtyard and along the alley to the bathroom block, where she reached the toilet just in time.

'Today was so much fun,' Susannah said as she and Caprice rode home with Felicity in yet another state-of-the-art vehicle. This one had doors that opened like wings and seats that felt more like they belonged in a spaceship than a car. Felicity's grandmother had come to school to pick them up but, as was the case the previous evening, she hadn't uttered a single word. 'What did you like best?'

'The Summer Palace,' Caprice said. 'Which was your favourite, Felicity?' She looked over at the girl, who was engrossed in a Sudoku puzzle.

Felicity wrinkled her nose but didn't bother to look up. 'None of it.'

'I suppose you've probably seen it before,' Susannah said. She was beginning to wonder if there was anything the girl did like. Between her and Caprice, they weren't exactly what you'd call doyennes of positivity.

'We have a holiday house bigger than both the Summer Palace and the Forbidden City put together,' Felicity said.

'Where is it?' Caprice asked.

'It doesn't matter,' Felicity snapped. 'You're never going there.'

'I was only asking,' Caprice huffed. 'You don't have to be rude.'

Felicity flung her book of brain teasers across the vehicle, narrowly missing her grandmother's nose.

'It's all right. Caprice didn't mean that,' Susannah said, desperately trying to maintain a semblance of peace amid the developing cold war. Caprice shot Susannah a look that said she absolutely did. 'So what are we doing tonight?' Susannah asked in a weak attempt at diverting their attention.

'Whatever you want,' Felicity said.

'I thought you might want to show us around a bit,' Susannah said hopefully.

Felicity shook her head. 'Pierre will be waiting for me, then Brian is due at five and Soo-Lin is coming at six o'clock, so I will be busy until at least seven o'clock. If you really insist on spending time with me, we can eat dinner together.'

Thankfully, no one noticed Caprice pretending to gag.

'Are they your tutors?' Susannah asked. She'd heard a few of the children at school this morning talking about their after-school tuition.

'Pierre is my French teacher. He lives in Paris but flies in once a week for our lesson. *Il me dit que je suis si intelligente.* Brian is my ice-skating coach and Soo-Lin is my manicurist.' The girl inspected her perfect nails and frowned.

'An ice-skating coach?' Caprice blanched. 'But where do you practise?'

'In our rink, of course,' Felicity said, rolling her eyes.

Susannah and Caprice looked at each other. They both had a funny feeling that they had only seen the tip of the iceberg when it came to the Fangs' estate.

The car pulled up at the gates just as a helicopter came into view, hovering over the front lawn. Felicity shouted at her grandmother, who turned her palms in the air and shrugged.

'What's the matter now?' Caprice asked.

'My mother is home,' Felicity spat. A dark look swept across the girl's face.

Susannah smiled. 'That's great! It would be lovely to meet her.'

'Don't be so sure about that,' Felicity sniped as the car sped along the driveway and descended into the parking garage below.

Susannah shot Caprice a worried look. Surely Felicity's mother couldn't be any less hospitable than her daughter.

Chapter 37

Thursday came as something of a relief to the visiting students. After a whole day of intensive sightseeing, they were all ready for the less harried pace of school lessons. Bright Star Academy was one of those schools where fun went hand in hand with learning and there were surprises around every corner. Spread over three storeys, the building's traditional exterior housed the most futuristic of spaces. With wide hallways and classrooms that resembled high-tech play centres, the visiting students and staff were savouring each new experience.

Livinia Reedy stepped out of the library, a look of pure bliss on her face. Her husband was walking towards her, having just spent the past hour touring the Science laboratories. 'Josiah,' she gasped, 'you're simply not going to believe this.'

At the very same time, he exclaimed, 'Darling, I've just seen the most extraordinary things!'

They met in the middle of the corridor.

'You go first,' Livinia said.

'No, you go. I insist.' Josiah reached out to hold her hands, his face pink with excitement.

Livinia took a deep breath. 'There are shelves and shelves of first editions and original manuscripts. The Brontës and Orwell and Dickens.' Just verbalising what she had seen brought a tear to the woman's eye. 'And they have a writer-in-residence. This year,' she said, lowering her voice, 'it's our *favourite*.'

'It's not,' Josiah breathed, his jowls quivering. 'Did you *see* her?'

Livinia shook her head. 'She's teaching at the moment, but Miss O'Reilly said that she'd arrange for us to have a cup of tea.'

'Well, you're never going to believe this,' Josiah said. 'They have their own fully fledged research facility and an operating theatre with robotic patients that are so lifelike I had to look twice – more than once!'

The pair stared into each other's eyes.

'I wonder if we'll ever teach in a place like this,' Josiah sighed. Livinia was thinking the exact same thing when a door marked 'Computer Science' opened into the hallway and a tall man with a mop of closely cropped brown curls walked out.

'Good morning, sir,' the children sang as he turned and gave them a wave.

'Hello,' he greeted Josiah and Livinia in a Californian accent.

The woman's eyes spun and she promptly fainted into her husband's arms.

The school day sped past, and before long the last bell echoed through the building.

'Your Science teacher is a genius,' Millie said as the girls poured out into the corridor. 'Her experiments were awesome. I hope Mr Plumpton was taking notes.'

'Yes, I believe I did pick up a few useful things in there,' Josiah Plumpton said from behind the girl. 'Perhaps my investigations will be more successful in the future.'

Millie cringed and turned around. 'I didn't mean it like that, sir. I just . . .'

'It's all right, Millie. I know my limitations, but at the heart of teaching is a willingness to learn. I might be an old dog, but I think I could master a few new tricks,' the man said. 'And honestly, I've been quite overawed by the things I've seen here at Bright Star. I'm feeling absolutely inspired, to say the least.'

'Good for you, Mr Plumpton,' Alice-Miranda said. 'My granny says that we should keep learning no matter how old we get, and you're not terribly old at all – well, not compared to my granny.'

'I couldn't agree more.' The man grinned. 'Have a good afternoon, everyone. Miss Reedy and I are off to meet the parents for a lesson on how to make dumplings.'

There was a chorus of yums from the students.

Jacinta could feel the excitement rising inside her already. There would only be two more rehearsals before the show tomorrow night and she really wanted to be included in the stilt stunt.

As the girls collected their bags and walked to the front doors, they spotted Caprice and Susannah with Felicity and a very glamorous-looking woman. She wore oversized sunglasses with a beautifully tailored white dress. The bodice was long-sleeved and fitted with a perfect circle skirt landing just above the knee. Her long hair fell in loose waves over her shoulders, partially hiding a small telephone earpiece in her right ear.

'Who's that?' Sloane asked.

'That's Felicity's mother. I don't remember her ever setting foot on the school grounds before,' Selina said. 'I've seen her on television sometimes – always on boring business shows.'

'She's gorgeous,' Millie said. She could see where Felicity got her model looks from.

Alice-Miranda waved and walked over to them. 'Hello, I'm Alice-Miranda Highton-Smith-Kennington-Jones. It's very nice to meet you.'

The woman stared at her, wondering if all the overseas guests were as forthright as this impertinent child. Coco and Selina greeted the woman shyly too.

'It's nice to meet you all too. I'm Barbie Fang,' the woman said. 'Tell me, are any of your parents famous like Caprice's mother?'

Caprice rolled her eyes. She was becoming increasingly annoyed with the woman. Last night, when they had met Mrs Fang, she hadn't been remotely interested in either Caprice or Susannah until Susannah spilled the beans that Caprice's mother was Venetia Baldini. Apparently, Venetia was something of an idol to Mrs Fang and her friends, who not only wanted to cook like her (or at least for their chefs to) but to look like her as well. Mrs Fang hadn't actually asked Caprice or Susannah a single thing about themselves. While Caprice was proud of her mother, she didn't feel the need to talk about her all the time. She had a sinking feeling the only reason Mrs Fang had accompanied the driver to school was in the hope that she would meet Venetia in person.

Millie shook her head. 'Not mine.'

Jacinta shrugged. 'My mother writes for fashion magazines.'

'Oh?' Mrs Fang turned on the girl. 'What's her name?'

'Ambrosia Headlington-Bear,' the child replied. When Mrs Fang looked at her blankly, she added, 'But she writes under the name Rosie Hunter.'

A flicker of recognition passed over the woman's face. 'She writes for the Highton's magazine. I like to study the publications of successful businesses, and although car manufacturing and retail are quite different, Highton's is one of the best companies in their field. Her stories in their magazines are always interesting and on trend. That being said, I would much prefer to meet Cecelia Highton-Smith and pick her brains about their strategies.'

Alice-Miranda smiled. 'I'll mention that to Mummy,' she said.

'I knew your name was familiar! Is Cecelia Highton-Smith your mother?' Mrs Fang demanded.

'Yes, she is,' the child said. 'And Hugh Kennington-Jones is my father.'

'So that means Charlotte Highton-Smith is your aunt and Lawrence Ridley is your uncle!' Mrs Fang was getting incredibly excited.

Lucas, Sep and Sunny reached the group just as the woman finished her exclamations.

'What did you say about Dad?' Lucas smiled and looked around. 'Is he here? I thought we weren't seeing our parents again until tomorrow morning.'

'No, Mrs Fang was just asking, that's all,' Alice-Miranda said.

'If you'd bothered to come to dinner on Tuesday night, Mama, you would have met lots of them there,' Felicity sniped.

The woman shrugged. 'You know I was busy at work.'

'I mean, of course you couldn't possibly miss seeing another new car roll off the production line to be with your only child,' Felicity said, wrinkling her nose.

The woman turned back to the others. 'We must have you and your parents over for dinner,' she said to the children.

'I'm afraid they have plans this evening and then tomorrow night we're all going to see Eternity,' Alice-Miranda explained. 'We're leaving on Saturday.'

The headmistress of Bright Star was surprised to see Mrs Fang and decided to walk over to greet the woman. 'Hello Mrs Fang, it's such a pleasure to see you,' she said.

For the second time in as many minutes, the woman looked completely blank.

'It's my headmistress, Mama,' Felicity hissed.

Barbie Fang laughed. 'Of course, Miss O'Grady, I didn't recognise you with your new hairdo.'

Shauna O'Reilly felt a smile tickle her lips, but she managed to keep it from settling there. She hadn't changed her hair in years, nor her name for that matter. 'Are you and Mr Fang coming to see the show with us tomorrow night?' she asked. 'I'm sure Felicity would love for you to be there.'

'I don't think we can manage it,' Barbie replied, clearly scrounging for an excuse, 'but I would like to host the visitors for dinner beforehand at our home.'

'I'm afraid that won't be possible, Mrs Fang. There's not enough time and, as you know, the traffic is a nightmare, but we are having a special farewell reception for everyone afterwards. It will be a little late, but the Wongs have insisted. It was in the letter I sent to the host families – in fact, I'm sure that you replied to say that you and your husband were coming.'

Barbie Fang's mouth twitched. Her husband was due home in the morning and she knew he would be furious if she didn't tell him that there was a chance to meet Lawrence Ridley – his favourite actor in the world.

Felicity looked at her mother. She could tell that the woman was still trying to come up with reasons not to attend.

'I'm so pleased you'll be joining us, Mrs Fang,' Shauna said sweetly. 'And it will be lovely to finally meet your husband too.'

'Yes, of course. We wouldn't miss it for the world.' Barbie Fang's lips turned upwards, but you'd have hardly called it a smile.

Chapter 38

As Jacinta and Coco set off for the showers after another intense rehearsal, Alice-Miranda sat down on her bed and pulled out the small bag of gifts she had bought for everyone back home. There was a fan each for her mother and grandmother, a tiny cloisonné vase she thought she might give to Mrs Greening, and a little plate for Daisy. She still had to find something for her father and Mr Greening and she was keen to get a gift for Jasper and Poppy and their parents too. Up until now she'd completely forgotten about Max and Cyril. She hoped there would be some time to hunt for souvenirs during their excursion to the Great Wall tomorrow.

Alice-Miranda was just about to take a look at the cups she'd bought at the Shanghai Museum when she heard a faint knocking. She hurried to the front door and opened it to a rather frazzled-looking delivery driver.

'*Ni hao*,' the child said.

When the man replied in frantic gestures, Alice-Miranda shrugged apologetically. 'Would you like me to go and get someone?'

He tapped his pen on the clipboard, clearly in a hurry.

'Do you want me to sign for it?' she asked, scribbling in the air.

He nodded and tapped his watch.

Alice-Miranda read the label and saw that the small package was addressed to Cherry Wong. She marvelled at how hard it must be to find residents in the *hutongs*, with the houses boasting very few identifying features. As she accepted the parcel, Alice-Miranda noticed that one end of the box was crushed and there was a section of cardboard missing. The man realised her look of concern and indicated that she should give the box a shake. There were no sounds of anything broken, so the girl thanked the man and bid him farewell.

Alice-Miranda passed Wai Po preparing dinner in the kitchen, and poked her head into the sitting room, but it was empty. So was the dining room. She decided to try Cherry's bedroom next and knocked gently on the door.

Cherry opened it just a little. Her face was blotchy and it looked as if she'd been crying.

'I'm so sorry to disturb you, but are you all right?' the child asked with concern.

'Yes, of course,' Cherry said, forcing a smile to her lips.

'A parcel just came for you,' Alice-Miranda explained, holding up the box. 'I'm afraid it's a little damaged, but the delivery man assured me that the contents are still in one piece.'

A deep frown line appeared across the top of Cherry's nose. 'Thank you.'

'You didn't hurt yourself at training, did you?'

'No, I am fine,' Cherry said. She reached out to take the parcel, brushing Alice-Miranda's hand. Suddenly, Cherry's face drained of all colour. She wobbled and looked as if she was about to fall over.

'Here, you should sit down.' Alice-Miranda took the woman by the arm and guided her to the bed. The package fell from Cherry's hand and landed on the floor with a thud and a crack.

'Oh no!' the woman sobbed. 'No, no, no. What have I done?'

'Goodness,' Alice-Miranda said. 'I'm sure that whatever is broken can be replaced.'

Cherry shook her head. 'You don't understand. They are in danger.' She clasped a hand over her mouth, realising that she had already said too much.

'Who is in danger?' Alice-Miranda looked at the woman, whose face was marked with fear. 'Mrs Wong, please tell me. I'll do whatever I can to help.'

Cherry gulped. 'I don't know what to do. There are eyes everywhere, and if I don't do as I'm asked terrible things will happen.'

Alice-Miranda grasped the woman's hands. 'What are you talking about?'

Cherry sat up and opened the box. Inside it were four cups, just as she had expected when the second letter had arrived this morning. But now one of them was broken.

'These are replicas of the cup that was stolen from the Shanghai Museum,' Alice-Miranda said.

'You told me about the article in the newspaper yesterday.' Her brow wrinkled. 'I have two as well, remember? I'll show you.'

Alice-Miranda fled from the room and across the courtyard to Coco's bedroom, where Coco and Jacinta had just arrived back from the shower.

'You're in a hurry,' Jacinta said as she stuffed her dirty clothes into her suitcase.

'I was just going to show Sunny's mother the gifts I've bought everyone,' Alice-Miranda said.

'Do you want to come for a walk to the shop with us?' Coco asked. 'Wai Po needs some things for dinner.'

'No, you go ahead. I'll see you when you get back,' Alice-Miranda said. She quickly gathered up the bag and hurried to Cherry's bedroom, where the woman was still sitting in the same spot. Alice-Miranda pulled out the package and was surprised to find there was only one cup. 'Oh dear, I know I bought two of these,' she said, unwrapping it carefully. 'I wonder what happened.'

Cherry turned one of the cups that had just been delivered over in her hands. On the bottom were three words: Made in China.

'That's funny,' Alice-Miranda said. 'Mine is different. It almost looks as if it could be . . .'

Cherry stared at Alice-Miranda, then slowly took the cup from her hand. The two of them gasped and at that moment they both knew: they'd inadvertently become a part of something big, much bigger than they could handle on their own.

Fuchsia Lee looked at the clock on the wall and decided she might as well do some tidying up. It would be at least a couple of hours until her boss was safely on his flight to Beijing and she could leave for her appointment at the hairdresser. She had been glad to see him go. Now she could turn the air-conditioning back to a reasonable temperature instead of the arctic climate he'd insisted on that morning. Even then the man had had to change his shirt twice before he left. That reminded her – she needed to drop off his washing at the laundromat downstairs. Whatever Benny was doing, it was certainly making him sweat more than usual.

Fuchsia walked into Benny's office and surveyed his desk. She was sorting through the mass of papers when a nut-brown leather notebook fell out of the middle. Fuchsia reached down to pick it up. It wasn't one she'd seen before. Benny was quite adamant that only black notebooks be used, all of which were lined up along the bookshelf on the back wall of his office. Fuchsia flipped open the cover.

At first it just looked to contain a series of numbers and a few names, but then she turned one more page and stopped. Tucked inside was an itinerary for plane tickets to Shanghai for Summer Tan and a second person whose name she didn't recognise, for earlier in the week. Her mind quickly turned to the little girl she'd spoken to on the phone the other day and began imagining all sorts of scenarios. Perhaps Summer needed medical treatments they couldn't risk anyone knowing about, or maybe a member of her family was in prison! Each thought grew more far-fetched than the one before it, so much so that Fuchsia began entertaining the idea of trying her hand at writing one of those soap operas she loved to watch. She had enough time to while working for Benny.

Fuchsia sat down in her boss's chair and turned the page. This time there were diagrams and more names and times. 'What are you up to, Mr Choo?' she mumbled to herself, and returned to the beginning to pore over every page.

By the time she'd finished, her heart was pounding. Benny Choo was not the man she'd thought he was. The phone at her desk outside began its shrill ring, and she set the notebook down and walked out to pick it up.

'Hello, Fuchsia Lee speaking,' she said. The woman's forehead puckered as she listened. 'Please, Alice-Miranda, you must slow down.'

Chapter 39

Caprice Radford pushed open the door she thought would take her back to the games room where she and Susannah had been playing air hockey. They were waiting for Felicity's massage to finish, although now that they'd been shown some of the more audacious rooms in the house, Caprice didn't really mind if the girl showed up or not. Apparently, like her manicurist, the chiropractor and masseuse visited weekly. And on top of the French teacher from Paris and the ice-skating coach, Felicity also had lessons in robotics and English, violin, piano and pipa, which was a pear-shaped Chinese guitar. Susannah had asked Felicity how many extra activities she undertook each week but Caprice had tuned out by the time the girl had reached fifteen.

When Mrs Fang had arrived the evening before, she'd insisted on taking the girls on a tour of the house, but Caprice suspected they'd still only seen a fraction of the estate as it seemed to go on and on forever and they hadn't yet spotted the ice rink. This afternoon Caprice and Susannah had enjoyed a swim in the heated pool, which had a waterslide to rival any theme park and came complete with an on-duty lifeguard. When it got dark, a maid introduced the girls to the games room, bowling alley and movie theatre. Unfortunately, Caprice had neglected to ask her where the toilet was and now she was completely lost.

The room she was in looked a bit like an art gallery. Paintings lined the walls and several bronze busts of important-looking men stood on tall plinths, each with an accompanying description.

'Probably Felicity's ancestors,' the girl scoffed, as she leaned in to inspect one gentleman wearing a funny squashed hat.

She moved to the end of the room, wondering if there was a secret door somewhere. Surely there was a toilet – or twenty – on this level of the mansion. There seemed to be an abundance of bathrooms everywhere else, including in the pool house that was about half the size of their boarding house.

Caprice pushed on a panel and was surprised to find it was actually the most enormous door. It pivoted and she walked through, trying not to think about the fact that she was getting a bit desperate. Soft lighting emanated from beautiful timber showcases that housed what looked to be artefacts. One wall contained parchments and scrolls while another displayed jade carvings in various shapes and sizes. The far wall was reserved for ceramics, but all the cups looked the same. In among the collection were three blank spaces and underneath were the words 'Shanghai Museum', 'Beijing Museum' and 'Po Collection'.

Caprice rolled her eyes. Who would collect lame, old cups? It seemed that the Fangs weren't as smart as they were rich, the girl thought to herself.

'Excuse me, miss,' a voice boomed. 'What are you doing in there?'

Caprice jumped. 'Who's that?' she said, looking around.

'I am in the control room,' the voice answered. 'You should not be there. The door was locked.'

'No it wasn't,' Caprice reported. 'I just pushed the panel.'

'May I help you back to the games room?' the voice asked.

Caprice huffed. 'I need to go to the toilet, which is why I was here in the first place.'

'Please, miss, just listen to my instructions and you will soon be there,' the voice said.

True to their word, Caprice soon located a toilet and was then swiftly directed back to Susannah and the games room.

Caprice had just beaten Susannah for the third time in a row when Felicity arrived in the room.

'Would you like to play?' Caprice asked the girl.

'No, I can't do anything strenuous for the next few hours until my back is properly rested,' the girl replied. She stretched her neck from side to side and arched her spine. 'Anyway, it's time for dinner.'

Caprice and Susannah put their paddles down and followed Felicity out of the room and into a lift. 'Where are we going?' Caprice asked.

'To the roof,' the girl said.

Seconds later, the lift doors opened and the girls walked out onto a terrace with the most incredible view of the city. The rooftop was positively palatial, with separate areas for seating and dining, a full kitchen and bar area and even a dance floor. The sky was so clear it looked as if you could reach up and touch the stars.

'What happened to the clouds?' Caprice asked. She remembered it had started to rain when she and Susannah got out of the pool.

'That's not the sky, it's a roof,' Felicity said as she led the girls towards the smallest of several dining tables. 'It's an exact replica of the real night sky but without any clouds or pollution.'

'Is there anything you don't have in this house?' Caprice asked.

Felicity shrugged. 'I don't think so.'

Several waiters were already rushing about and it wasn't long before the girls were offered a tray of colourful fruit drinks. Caprice took one and ate the pineapple pieces from the stick first before she sipped the delicious beverage.

'Good evening, girls,' Barbie Fang said as she walked out to join them. She was dressed in a stunning floor-length gown of peacock-blue. Diamond earrings the size of Christmas baubles adorned her lobes. 'Felicity, you are not dressed for dinner.'

Caprice and Susannah looked at one another in their jeans and blouses, which were about the best things they had brought with them on the trip. Felicity was wearing a white cotton drop-waisted dress with a blue sash, obviously made of the finest material, well cut and perfectly sewn.

Susannah's cheeks flushed red with embarrassment. 'Sorry, Mrs Fang. We weren't told that we would need to bring evening wear with us for the trip.'

The woman nodded sympathetically. 'I understand completely,' she said, the word 'peasants' rolling around in her head as she spoke. 'But Felicity knows better than that.'

'I'd rather wear jeans too,' the girl snapped.

'And if you would like to continue as a member of this family, those words will never come out of your mouth again.' Barbie Fang smiled sweetly.

Felicity rolled her eyes and glared at her empty plate. Susannah gulped and Caprice tried not to grin. That Felicity was a piece of work and then some.

'What have you girls been up to this afternoon?' Mrs Fang asked.

'We had a swim and then played in the games room,' Susannah said.

Mrs Fang arched an eyebrow. 'No study? How interesting.'

'I visited your museum,' Caprice said quickly. Although she hadn't meant to go there, she thought she'd mention it so Mrs Fang didn't think they'd wasted their time on frivolous pursuits.

Barbie Fang almost choked on her drink. 'What did you say?' she sputtered.

Caprice frowned, wondering what she'd said wrong this time. 'The museum at the bottom of the house. To tell you the truth, I found it when I was looking for the toilet. It's got lots of interesting stuff.' That was a lie, but Caprice thought she should try to be polite.

'No one is allowed in there except Baba,' Felicity said fiercely. 'The doors are always locked. That's Baba's special place and he would be extremely angry to know that you were anywhere near it.'

'I told you, I didn't mean to go there. It's just that your house is so big I found it by accident,' Caprice said.

'You must have broken in,' Felicity accused.

'I did not!' Caprice could feel her blood begin to boil. She may have been a guest of the Fangs, but they had no idea how to make a person feel welcome.

'What did you see?' Barbie didn't like where this was headed at all. She hadn't been in there for years and really had no desire to know of its contents or their origins, yet at this point it was important she understood what the girl had seen.

'Just lots of old junk,' Caprice spat. 'I wasn't really interested because I was busting to go to the loo. It was just as well some security guy noticed I was in there because he helped me to find one, or I would have peed all over your precious imported marble floor!'

Barbie Fang stood up and walked to the end of the terrace where a thickset man in a black suit stood at attention. She began to whisper in Mandarin but it wasn't long before she was shouting and moments later he disappeared. She composed herself and walked back to join the children while four waiters descended upon them with plates of steak and salad.

'Caprice and Susannah, it is very important that you do not speak of my husband's collection to anyone. Ever.' There was an icy tone to the woman's voice that sent a shiver down Susannah's spine. 'Mr Fang is a very private man and he would not like his personal collections discussed. How much will I need to pay for your silence?'

Caprice's jaw dropped. 'What?'

'You must be rewarded for your discretion,' Barbie eyeballed the girls.

'We don't need money,' Susannah said. 'We're both very reliable. Aren't we, Caprice?'

Caprice was still reeling from the offer. She felt like she was in the middle of a gangster movie. Caprice nodded, apparently rendered speechless.

'What honourable girls you both are,' Mrs Fang said as she shot them one last terrifying look.

Chapter 40

Cherry Wong gathered her wits about her and tucked the two letters into her jacket. From what Fuchsia Lee had told Alice-Miranda, they needed to speak to the police as quickly as possible. But how to do that without arousing the suspicion of the rest of the family was tricky.

Alice-Miranda had an idea. 'If we tell Charles, he could take me to the police station and I can explain everything,' the child said.

Cherry thought for a moment. 'Not Charles. I would rather tell Winnie. Her cousin is very high up in the police department and she is the most level-headed of the Wongs. Winnie will take it all in her stride and the fewer members of the family who know about this, the better,' Cherry said. 'We just have to work out a reason for Winnie to take you out on your own.'

Alice-Miranda bit her lip, wracking her brain for a solution. 'We could tell them that my mother asked me to buy her some silk pyjamas from a manufacturer that's close by. That she's thinking about asking them to supply to Highton's, and the others won't be interested because it's just business.'

Cherry hugged her. 'Alice-Miranda, I swear you are a genius. Wait here and I will fetch my mother-in-law.'

Winnie Wong was as shocked to learn about what was going on as Alice-Miranda and Cherry had been. Especially as she had trusted Benny Choo with her and Lionel's life's work. Winnie explained that they were planning to sell the troupe to become part of a Chinese franchise of the Circus of Golden Destiny. She and Lionel had put a down payment on a school, where they intended to provide scholarships for underprivileged children – not only training them as acrobats but ensuring that they had a sound education. The rest of the family were to have a place in the troupe for as long as they wanted and nothing was going to change.

'Well, the deal is off now,' Winnie said. She was furious that she had been taken in by the smooth-talking man.

'What about the school?' Alice-Miranda asked.

'We will find another way,' Winnie assured her. 'It has been a lifelong wish of ours, and you don't just abandon your dreams because someone has taken you riding.'

Alice-Miranda giggled. Winnie reminded her a little of her own Granny Valentina. Benny Choo wouldn't have stood in her way either.

Cherry handed the woman the letters and Alice-Miranda rewrapped her chicken cup.

'I would rather we leave that here, but I think the only way they will believe our story is for us to take it along,' Winnie said.

'It's all right,' Alice-Miranda said. 'It will be safe inside my jacket.'

It was just before six when Winnie announced to Wai Po that she was taking Alice-Miranda out for a short while. If they weren't back in an hour, she instructed, the rest of the family should have dinner without them. The woman was slightly apprehensive that perhaps the police would want to detain the child, seeing that she was in possession of such a valuable object, but surely they had enough evidence now with Fuchsia Lee going to the Hong Kong Police too.

Alice-Miranda placed the letters Cherry had received on the table along with the priceless antiquity. Winnie's cousin, Superintendent Lu, immediately called one of his colleagues from the Ministry of State Security to join them on this matter of national importance. It wasn't long before a woman in a smart grey suit arrived and was introduced to them as Agent Cheng. She wore no make-up and her hair was wound into a perfect bun at the back of her head.

'So you believe that Benny Choo is behind the Shanghai Museum theft and perhaps another in Hong Kong,' Superintendent Lu said.

Alice-Miranda nodded. 'And Cherry is supposed to steal another of the cups tomorrow at the Beijing Museum.'

'But why does he want them?' Agent Cheng asked. 'He cannot possibly sell them on the open market.'

'There must be a collector,' Superintendent Lu said. 'We know this sort of black-market trade goes on, but it is a game only for those with extreme wealth.'

'There was another name in the book, but Miss Lee wasn't sure if it was of any significance to you,' Alice-Miranda said. 'Have you heard of Elon Fang?'

Agent Cheng gasped. 'If this man is who I think he is, we have been after him for years. He is more slippery than a catfish and more cunning than a fox.'

'Who is he?' the child asked. 'What's he done?'

'He owns The Blue Whale Casino in Macau,' Agent Cheng said. 'But his name has cropped up in association with many criminal activities, from money laundering to illegal property deals and even the black-market sale of weapons.'

'What did it say about him?' Superintendent Lu asked.

'Nothing – it was just a name,' Alice-Miranda said. 'Are you going to arrest Mr Choo?

Agent Cheng looked at Winnie. 'He is on his way to Beijing now?'

'He's coming as our guest,' Winnie said. 'We are supposed to be signing the contracts for the sale of the troupe tomorrow evening after the show.'

'Perhaps he's also making a drop of the goods that are already in his possession,' Agent Cheng said, 'and intending to collect the one Cherry is to steal tomorrow.' She pulled her phone from her pocket and made a quick call. 'Benny's flight has just landed,' she said.

A young man entered the room and handed Superintendent Lu a piece of paper. He scanned it and shook his head.

'Except that now Mr Choo only has a fake and perhaps the other one, which I have just had confirmed as stolen from a residence in Hong Kong two nights ago,' Superintendent Lu said.

'I wonder if Summer was involved in that as well,' Alice-Miranda said. She thought about that look on her face in the dressing-room. It was obvious now that the poor girl was terrified.

'We will speak with our colleagues in Hong Kong. It wouldn't do to bring her in for questioning until we have our man,' Agent Cheng said. 'I imagine Benny's men will be watching her.'

Alice-Miranda exhaled loudly. 'Please don't do anything that will put her in danger. I can only imagine how scared she is. Especially if her family was threatened too. I was so stupid when I saw her in Shanghai and she obviously switched our goods. She must have been trying to tell me to go to the police, but I didn't understand what she meant.'

The superintendent smiled at her. 'You are far from stupid, Alice-Miranda. If it weren't for you, who knows how long this would have continued for.'

Winnie reached over and gently squeezed the child's forearm. She looked at her cousin. 'What are we to do now?'

Superintendent Lu rested on his elbows and inhaled deeply. Agent Cheng bit down on her thumbnail. For several minutes the room was silent.

'You have to go on with the show,' Alice-Miranda said decisively. 'Maybe Mr Choo will lead you to his buyer and then you can catch them both.'

Agent Cheng smiled at the girl. 'You should think about becoming a detective, Alice-Miranda. You have read my mind. I have sent some agents to follow him from the airport.'

The woman's phone rang. She picked it up and took the call.

'What do you mean he's not there?' she spat. 'Find him! And don't lose sight of him again!' Agent Cheng ended the call, shaking her head. 'Imbeciles!'

'At least we know where he's going to be tomorrow night,' Alice-Miranda said.

'Wait until I see that swindler,' Winnie fumed. She caught her cousin's eye and sighed. 'Don't worry – you know I wouldn't do anything to jeopardise the investigation. But once you have your man, I want ten minutes alone with him. Is that a deal?'

Superintendent Lu nodded. 'You have my word. In the meantime, you must both keep all of this completely to yourselves and call me if you hear anything that could be of use.' He pressed a hand-written number into Alice-Miranda's palm. 'I do apologise, but I don't think it would be helpful if anyone saw you with a card from the Superintendent of the Beijing Police – it might create questions.'

Alice-Miranda grinned. 'I think you're right about that.'

Chapter 41

The children chattered as the bus wound through tiny roadside villages on the way to the Great Wall. Alice-Miranda stared out the window, watching the traditional houses pass by in a blur. She was trying to concentrate, but her mind kept returning to what had happened the night before.

'Hey, I think I just saw the Wall,' Millie said, pointing out the window. 'I can't wait to get up there. It's going to be amazing.'

Alice-Miranda turned to her friend. 'Sorry, Millie, what did you say?'

'What's the matter?' Millie asked. 'You've been acting weird all morning.'

Alice-Miranda hesitated. She wanted to tell Millie what was going on, but she'd promised Cherry and the others that she wouldn't breathe a word. There was far too much at stake. 'I think I must be tired. I didn't sleep well last night,' the girl said. At least that was the truth.

Inside the bus were the ten students from Winchesterfield-Downsfordvale and Fayle, the teachers and parents, along with Miss O'Reilly, the five host students, plus the rest of their class and the Science teacher from Bright Star. They'd left school just after eight o'clock and were going to a slightly less popular area of the Wall at Mutianyu. Miss O'Reilly had been there recently and decided that it was no less spectacular than the section at Badaling, but there would likely be fewer visitors.

The headmistress of Bright Star stood at the front of the bus and delivered a fascinating introduction to the Great Wall and welcomed any questions from the students.

'The Great Wall is almost nine thousand kilometres long as it currently stands, although the official length is over twenty-one thousand kilometres – it's just that a lot of it has fallen down,' she said, referring to her sheet. 'Oh, and here's an interesting one. It's said to be the world's longest cemetery.'

'What do you mean?' Figgy called out.

'Over one million people died while working on the Wall and many of them were buried inside it because there was no time to take them anywhere else,' the woman explained.

'Cool, so it's like a zombie wall.' Figgy did his best impression and garnered a few snickers. 'Do they ever attack?'

'Only if visitors are disrespectful,' Miss O'Reilly said, with a completely deadpan expression.

Figgy thought for a moment before breaking into a grin. 'You're joking, right?'

The headmistress arched an eyebrow and shrugged. 'Now, it's a bit of a two-stage process to get there. First, we'll stop at the visitors' centre and take another bus. Then we'll walk a little way and hop on the cable car, which will take us to the Wall,' Shauna O'Reilly said. 'When we're up there, please be very careful. There are no security fences and the stones can be slippery. I'd hate to have to add to that body count,' she said, winking at Figgy.

Ophelia giggled as Shauna sat down beside her. 'You're dreadful, you know,' she said. 'Figgy's going to have nightmares about his trip to the Wall for months.'

'Oh well, no doubt he'll be on his best behaviour for the trip home.' Shauna grinned. 'I don't imagine he'll try to smuggle a stray cat in his luggage.'

The bus came to a stop outside a large entrance gate across from several buildings including a visitors' centre and museum and, further beyond, rows of shops and market stalls.

'This is unexpected,' Lawrence Ridley said. Dotted throughout the market was a smattering of Western fast-food outlets. 'Is that a doughnut stand over there?'

'Dad,' Lucas chided. 'You can't be hungry already.'

The man had eaten two packets of prawn crackers and half a bag of chocolate frogs on the drive up.

September craned her neck to see past Ambrosia, who was glad to have reached their destination, having had the woman talk at her the whole way. 'I can see shoes,' September whispered excitedly.

'We've got about forty-five minutes until we head off, so you can wander about, but please stick with your buddies and make sure you can see a teacher or parent,' Shauna advised.

The children spilled off the bus and quickly divided into their groups.

Lawrence spotted his niece and wandered over to say hello. 'Did you have a good night, sweetheart?'

Alice-Miranda spun around, launching herself at his middle.

Lawrence hugged her back. 'To what do I owe such grand affection?' he asked.

'I just thought you looked like you could do with a hug,' she said. Though the truth was, so could she.

'I've been missing my cuddles with the twins, that's for sure,' he said, and gave Alice-Miranda an extra squeeze.

'What did you do last night, Uncle Lawrence?' Alice-Miranda asked, determined to keep her mind off her own worries.

'Venetia arranged the most fabulous cooking class, then Ambrosia took us to a shopping district where I bought way too many presents for your cousins and maybe one or two for you as well,' he said with a grin. 'September was in her element. I don't know how she's going to fit everything in her luggage for the plane trip home, but thankfully she seemed to enjoy herself. She did find the most spectacular pair of high-heeled trainers to replace the ones she lost.'

Alice-Miranda grimaced. 'I'm sure Sloane will be very impressed.'

'They're so shiny I think September could use them as a make-up mirror,' Lawrence laughed.

The groups set off for the museum first before wandering through the avenues of shops. Alice-Miranda consulted the list she'd made about who she still needed to buy gifts for when she suddenly remembered that she'd have to get something for Shilly and Dolly to replace what she'd lost. She picked up some silk scarves and promptly paid for them.

'Who are those for?' Millie asked.

'Shilly and Dolly,' the girl replied, without thinking.

'But you already bought them those chicken cups in Shanghai,' Millie said.

'Oh, that's okay,' Alice-Miranda said, recovering quickly. 'I can give these to Mrs Greening and Daisy instead.'

Half an hour later, they were riding the cable cars to the Wall. It was another short but steep climb to get onto the structure.

'Whoa! Look at this thing!' Rufus shouted. The party of adults and children stared at the Great Wall, which traversed the contours of the land as far as the eye could see. It rose steeply in some parts and dipped like a roller-coaster in others.

'It's magnificent,' Jacinta said. 'Don't you just want to walk along the edge there?'

Coco nodded. 'I think Miss O'Reilly would have a heart attack, though, and I don't want to be responsible for killing our headmistress. We love her,' she said with a grin.

Millie pulled out her camera and began snapping pictures as soon as they reached the Wall. Jacinta and Coco were walking up ahead, investigating every nook and cranny while Sloane explored with her brother and Lucas. Alice-Miranda found herself wandering along beside Caprice.

'Have you had fun with Felicity?' the child asked.

'Let's just say it's been an experience I'll never forget,' Caprice replied.

Alice-Miranda was impressed that the girl was being rather uncharacteristically diplomatic. 'Why? What happened?' she asked.

'Her family is *nuts*,' Caprice whispered, knowing the girl was right behind them.

'What did you say?' Felicity demanded. It seemed bionic hearing was another of the girl's many talents.

'The truth,' Caprice replied hotly. She had just about had enough of the little princess. After dinner the night before, Felicity and her mother had disappeared again, leaving her and Susannah on their own until bedtime.

Felicity's eyes narrowed and little flecks of spittle began to pool in the corners of her lips. 'Well, you are the rudest guest we have ever had!'

'Well, you're the rudest host I've ever met. And seriously, who flies their French tutor from Paris every week and has a manicurist and chiropractor and masseuse? That's ridiculous!' Caprice shouted.

'You forgot my ballet teacher and hair stylist and acupuncturist and life coach and all the others! Idiot!' Felicity was furious.

'You know what you really need is an etiquette instructor – that's someone to teach manners, just in case you weren't familiar with the word,' Caprice said, and stamped her foot for effect.

'It's French, you imbecile – of course I know what it means!' Felicity retaliated.

Mr Plumpton and Miss Reedy were busy taking pictures of themselves by the first watchtower when they heard the awful screeching. They looked to the others who were ahead of them, but everything seemed peaceful. When they checked the opposite direction, they spotted Caprice and Felicity staring each other down like two bulls in a ring.

'You haven't played with us or made us feel welcome at all,' Caprice continued. 'If your guard hadn't realised where I was yesterday afternoon I probably would have died down there!' Caprice's desire to reach out and shove the spoilt brat off the Wall was rising at a steady pace.

'Calm down, both of you,' Alice-Miranda ordered. She could only see this ending badly.

'You think you are so clever because your mother cooks on television. My mother runs the biggest motor corporation in China!' Felicity shouted, and pushed Caprice against the edge of the Wall.

'How dare you? My mother is a genius and she's loved all over the world. Your mother just loves *herself*! And as for that ridiculous museum – your father could be feeding half the starving nations of the world with what that stuff must be worth. Who has a whole collection of cups covered in silly chickens, anyway?'

Alice-Miranda's eyes widened. 'What cups?'

'Like that one in the Shanghai Museum you loved so much,' Caprice said.

'You promised not to tell anyone!' Felicity charged at Caprice, but Alice-Miranda threw herself between the pair just in time.

'Stop it!' she shouted. 'Or someone is going to be badly hurt.'

Mr Plumpton puffed and blew as he reached the girls. He looked at Felicity and then at Caprice. 'Right, come with me. It's back to the bus for the two of you.'

A small group of tourists had begun to take some pictures of the dishevelled pair.

'Please move along,' Miss Reedy said, steering them away. 'There's nothing to see here. Nothing at all.'

Alice-Miranda's heart was racing and her mind was churning. She needed to find a telephone – and fast.

Chapter 42

Felicity and Caprice sat next to their respective headmistresses on the trip back to school. Both of them were in a terrible sulk and it hadn't helped that Venetia Baldini, upon hearing about the ruckus, had given Caprice a solid scolding, warning her that she should apologise to Felicity or she would never go anywhere with the school again. Miss Grimm had been most impressed by the woman's fervour and it was a relief to see that she was under no illusions about her daughter. Although, perhaps if they'd had time to hear the whole story, including what had transpired the night before, they might not have been so harsh on the girl.

As the bus neared the turn-off to Bright Star, Miss Grimm and Miss O'Reilly stood up. 'Why don't you girls sit together for a moment?' said the headmistress of Bright Star.

Caprice really didn't feel like apologising to the brat, but the fact that she had broken a promise niggled at her. Seriously, she must have been getting soft in her old age.

Caprice looked at Felicity, who was staring out the window. She took a deep breath and readied herself to eat humble pie. 'Sorry about what I said up there,' she mumbled.

'What was that?' Felicity's head swivelled faster than a cobra about to attack.

'I said that I'm sorry,' Caprice repeated. 'I don't want to fight with you.'

Felicity glared. It seemed like she wasn't the apologising type either.

Susannah peered at them through the tiny gap between the seats. 'I'm sure Caprice didn't mean it,' she offered.

'Did you?' Felicity spat.

'What?' Caprice didn't know what she was asking.

'Mean it? What you said up there?' the girl demanded.

Caprice thrust her hands under her thighs and crossed her fingers. She knew it was a lie but she didn't feel like being in any more trouble today. Besides, they had the acrobatic show tonight and it wouldn't be any fun if she was still in a fight. 'No, I lost my temper and I'm sorry,' she said. 'I shouldn't have said all those things.'

Susannah smiled with relief. 'See?'

Felicity exhaled loudly. 'All right, I forgive you. But if you say another word about my family, I won't let you off again.' She held out her hand and Caprice reluctantly shook it. 'Now, move,' Felicity ordered. 'I want Susannah to sit with me, and this afternoon we're going to decide what we play and you may or may not be invited to join us.'

Caprice stood up. 'Fine,' she said. In all honesty, she didn't give two hoots what happened. Tomorrow they were going home and she'd never have to see Felicity Fang or her scary mother ever again.

Deng Rou walked out of the equipment room with a smug grin on her wrinkled lips. Soon Lucille would be handing over a month's pay for her trouble. A shadow crossed her path and she almost jumped out of her skin. 'Oh, hello. I didn't see you there. Is everything all right?' Rou asked.

'One day you think you know where you are heading and the next, things are not so clear,' the old man said, half to himself. It suddenly dawned on him how foolish he sounded. 'But of course you know that better than most people.'

She snorted. 'That is true. But what is it that's troubling you?'

Lionel sighed. 'Our plans are lain to waste.'

'What plans?' Rou asked, feigning ignorance.

'There is no need to pretend,' he said with a wry smile. 'I am well aware of your love of listening in keyholes.'

Rou smiled. 'What will happen to me?' she asked.

'Nothing, because we are not going through with it,' he said.

Rou swallowed hard. 'What do you mean? Have you changed your mind?'

Lionel stroked his beard. 'Let's just say that all was not what it seemed.'

'But . . .' Rou began to huff and blow.

'I thought you would be happy to hear the news,' Lionel said.

Behind her, several of the acrobats had begun laying out the equipment for the evening's performance. Rou jiggled up and down on the spot and bit her lip.

'I must go and supervise,' the old man said. 'And there is food to prepare. We are hosting a reception after the show for Sunny and Coco's school group.'

'And your VIP guest?' Rou frowned.

'He will be here,' Lionel said, 'but perhaps not for long.'

Now the woman was completely confused. If the VIP guest was still coming, then why wasn't the sale going ahead? She had to get back to the equipment room before it was too late.

'Rou, what are you doing out here?' Winnie screeched from the doorway. 'I need you upstairs helping with the food. Now!'

Rou gulped and hurried to her duties. She could feel the trickle of perspiration on her forehead and the unfamiliar grumbling of guilt in her belly.

Alice-Miranda sat in the back of the dressing-room as Coco put the finishing touches to Jacinta's make-up.

The girl leapt from her chair and spun around in her fabulous red catsuit that sparkled every which way she turned. 'How do I look?' she asked.

Alice-Miranda was jolted back to reality. She'd been lost in thought about how the night's events would unfold, knowing that the audience was to be peppered with police and government agents, ready at any moment to make their move. She had managed to borrow Uncle Lawrence's phone earlier and had called Superintendent Lu as soon as Caprice had blurted out what she'd seen of Felicity's father's antiquities collection. It was no wonder the name had been niggling at her, but Fang was a very common surname in China. Alice-Miranda had confirmed with Miss O'Reilly that the Fangs were indeed attending the performance. And now the trap was set.

Alice-Miranda smiled. 'You look beautiful. I can't believe you're going to be out there tonight.'

'I can't either, and I didn't tell Mummy,' the girl said, 'so please make sure that she doesn't have a heart attack when she realises it's me.'

Alice-Miranda chuckled. 'I'll do my best.'

'I love your dress,' Jacinta said, admiring the cheongsam the Wongs had given Alice-Miranda. Just before they'd left for the theatre they had all exchanged presents, and Alice-Miranda's favourite among them was the intricate Chinese knot that Coco had made for her. Jacinta had received her outfit for the performance and the boys had been given sets of magic tricks. Coco had loved the gold bracelet the children had given her and Sunny didn't want to leave his video game. The adults had vowed to open their gifts when they returned home.

There was a sharp rap on the door. 'Fifteen minutes to showtime!' a voice boomed.

'We need to go and warm up,' Coco said.

Jacinta rushed over and gave Alice-Miranda a hug. 'Wish me luck.'

'Wish us all luck,' Coco said with a grin. 'We're debuting our crazy family act tonight, remember.'

'You'll be brilliant,' Alice-Miranda said, and the two girls hurried out the door and down the hall. She waited until the horde of gymnasts had gone past before stepping out into the corridor herself. She spotted Lucille standing over Rou and it didn't look as if they were exchanging pleasantries of the day.

Lucille hissed a few last words and then ran past the doorway to join the rest of the troupe. The dressing-room door opposite opened and Cherry poked her head outside.

The child looked at her. 'All set?'

'Yes, we are ready. Winnie has told Lionel,' Cherry said.

Alice-Miranda hugged the woman. 'Good luck.'

'You too.' Cherry smiled, then raced off to join her fellow troupe members.

Chapter 43

Alice-Miranda scanned the growing crowd from the side of the stage. The students had been allocated excellent seats in the centre, a few rows from the front. She could see Miss Grimm and Mr Grump already in place. Figgy and Rufus were there with their host, Hero, and his parents. She gave Millie a wave as the girl trotted down the steps to take her seat beside Sloane and Selina, with September Sykes and Selina's parents too. Uncle Lawrence and Ambrosia had just walked down together and taken their seats beside Mr Plumpton and Miss Reedy. It seemed most of the group was there but as yet there was no sign of Caprice and Susannah. Alice-Miranda allowed herself a small smile as she realised that the teachers and mothers were wearing their cheongsams just as they had promised to do on the last night, although September had teamed hers with her new silver platform trainers, which was something of a unique look.

Alice-Miranda's heart pounded as she saw Lionel Wong guiding Mr Choo to his seat. There was much shaking of hands and patting of backs and Mr Wong was doing a wonderful job of keeping up the pretence. Unlike the first time Alice-Miranda had met him, Mr Choo didn't look to have any bodyguards in tow. Lucas and Sep were sitting at the other end of the front row and Alice-Miranda's vacant seat was right beside Mr Choo.

Lucille was watching from the other side of the stage. 'So, Mr Choo, are you really sure that you want to buy the clumsiest acrobatic troupe in the world?' she hissed under her breath, and hurried away to her position. The lights dimmed and the slow beat of drums began to sound. It was two minutes to showtime according to Alice-Miranda's watch. She walked to her seat, beside the film producer. 'Hello Mr Choo,' she said to the man, who was fidgeting with his tie and clinging tightly to his briefcase.

'Oh, what are you doing here?' he said, taken aback. 'Is your uncle here too?'

'Yes.' She nodded and pointed towards Lawrence. 'Would you like me to have someone check your bag?' Alice-Miranda asked.

Benny gripped it more firmly. 'No, thank you. That will not be necessary.'

A spotlight shone onto the middle of the ceiling, where Coco was wrapped tightly in a glowing purple ribbon. An eerie tune began to play as she swayed back and forth before the ribbon around her suddenly started to unravel at a great pace. She stopped with her face just centimetres from the floor. The crowd erupted and the show began.

Unlike the Circus of Golden Destiny, the Eternity troupe's performance didn't really weave a narrative. Instead, it consisted of a series of incredible feats, each one even more impressive than the last. There were jugglers and tightrope walkers, crazy convoys of cyclists, the tumbling Wheel of Death and human towers ten men high and, of course, the noisy and smelly motorcycle globe with its buzzing riders zipping dangerously close as they sped around and around and up and down.

Alice-Miranda was trying to pay attention to the show, but her mind was racing. Sunny and Coco performed a highwire act together, garnering whoops and applause from around the arena. When Alice-Miranda looked back across the row, she breathed a sigh of relief to see a thin man sitting beside Benny Choo. Mrs Fang and Felicity were next, then Caprice and Susannah. Alice-Miranda was trying not to make it obvious, but she was desperate to see if the two men had acknowledged one another at all.

Cherry was standing in the wings, offstage. Alice-Miranda caught her eye and nodded, and Cherry bowed her head.

In the darkness, the stage was quickly reconfigured yet again, this time with a giant trampoline in the centre. As the lights came up, stilt-walkers bounced around the stage, their antics growing more and more extravagant as they leapt higher and higher, kicking their legs and executing perfect splits.

Ambrosia gasped. 'Is that Jacinta?'

Lawrence peered at the stage and laughed. 'You know what? I think it is.' He shovelled another handful of popcorn into his mouth.

Millie turned around and nodded. 'It's her, all right.'

'Oh my goodness, that daughter will be the death of me.' Ambrosia's heart was in her throat as Jacinta bounded across the stage, although, really, she couldn't have been more proud.

Moments later, the stilt-walkers were bouncing over the trampoline, then on the next round they tumbled and twirled. As Jacinta approached the apparatus, a huge cheer went up from her friends. She sprang up high and turned two backwards somersaults before nailing a perfect landing. The crowd went even wilder.

'Go Jacinta!' Lucas shouted, louder than everyone else.

Alice-Miranda peered into the darkness at the rear of the stage and thought she saw Rou's face. She wondered what the woman was up to and hoped it didn't have anything to do with that odd comment she'd made when Alice-Miranda was getting her bandaid the day before.

As the stilt-walkers exited the stage, Winnie sped into the arena on her red bicycle – her perfect French roll neatly in place as she raced faster and faster. Then she lay back on the bike. Lionel Wong and his sons catapulted over her, from one side of the stage to the other. Meanwhile, Cherry and Lucille joined her on their bicycles, but this time they were riding while spinning plates with both hands.

Alice-Miranda looked over at Rou in the wings. The old woman clutched at her head as a strange look came over Lucille's face, almost as if she were waiting for something to happen. And then it did. Several of the towering sticks Cherry was spinning plates on top of, collapsed. Out of the shadows a figure in black tumbled at speed across the floor. She dived for the plates, catching them all just millimetres from the ground.

'What are you doing, you stupid woman?' Lucille hissed.

'The sale is off. I tried to tell you that before but you would not listen,' Rou shouted back. It was just fortunate that most of the audience couldn't hear them above the music and applause.

But Benny Choo had. 'What's this?' he muttered to himself.

'What were you trying to do?' Winnie demanded, glaring at Lucille. 'We will discuss this later.'

Rou darted from the stage, not forgetting to take a bow as she left. Rapturous applause filled the arena once again, with people shouting for more.

Lucille glowered at Lionel, who was standing centre stage, giving them all the secret signal to abandon their tricks and come together. 'This is not what we rehearsed,' she murmured.

A long table was pushed onto the stage, set with plates and bowls and teacups too.

'What's this, Ye Ye?' Coco asked loudly. Her question garnered hoots of laughter from the audience.

'Ah, granddaughter, does this remind you of anything?' the man asked, his voice echoing around the arena.

Coco looked at the table. 'Home,' she said.

The audience laughed again. It was a fun change of pace for a show that had, until now, proceeded at breakneck speed. Alice-Miranda wondered if Coco and the others had been let in on the secret, but from Lucille's reaction it didn't seem likely.

'Ladies and gentlemen,' Lionel said, 'as you know, Eternity boasts some of the world's best acrobats. We are always trying to improve our skills and take things to new heights, and after thirty years, we are going to perform our most thrilling act ever – something that we do at home most nights.'

He held up one of the cups for the crowd to see.

'Ordinary crockery. Oh dear!' He tugged at his beard and grinned. 'I think this might actually be my wife's china.'

The audience laughed again.

'It had better not be, husband,' Winnie said, playing along. 'What will we use for our breakfast tomorrow?'

A man in the audience guffawed loudly, which set off the rest of the crowd.

'It would be no fun at all just juggling our everyday tea set, so we had a special delivery from the museum today. My good friend Mr Weng Jun has given me something very special to add to our collection,' Lionel said.

He looked at Benny Choo in the front row and at the man he assumed to be Elon Fang beside him, but both remained stony-faced.

'Among these pretty cups is a priceless antiquity that is over five hundred years old, dating back to the Ming Dynasty. Here, I will show you which one it is.' One of the cameras that was set up to catch all the action on the stage zoomed in on the relic. The image of the tiny wine cup decorated with chickens was projected onto two giant screens. 'We will prove beyond doubt that we are the best jugglers on the planet. If we break this cup, we will be bankrupt – out of business. So, family, please keep an eye on the prize,' Lionel boomed.

The audience gasped.

Figgy held his breath. 'What are they thinking?'

Millie frowned. 'That's crazy.'

Alice-Miranda felt Benny Choo tense up beside her. She peered around him and noticed that Mr Fang was tugging at his tie as if he were choking.

The Wongs started tossing the cups and plates and cutlery at each other with lightning speed. Coco juggled six cups, then flicked them effortlessly to Sunny, while his mother and aunty spun plates and the men threw knives and forks at each other. Sunny threw the cups higher and higher until it looked as if the boy miscued completely and sent one crashing to the ground.

'Oh no,' Lionel shouted, clutching his cheeks. 'I hope that was a fake, Sunny, or we are done for.'

The audience held their breath as the boy picked up the broken pieces and showed them to his grandfather. The camera zoomed in on it.

'Oooooh,' Lionel let out a longwinded gasp. 'We Wongs are lucky tonight, but next time be more careful.' The old man pretended to give the boy a kick in the bottom, which brought howls of laughter from the crowd.

'I think we should make this more difficult,' Winnie said, and an identical set of crockery was wheeled in from the side of the stage.

Winnie threw them like missiles across the table and the family launched into action once again. The crowd was mesmerised. When another cup crashed to the ground, Elon Fang jumped up from his seat.

'Stop! Stop!' he cried, running towards the stage. 'You must stop this madness at once! Give that to me.'

Felicity's jaw dropped. She had never seen her father act like this before, nor move so fast. Her father did everything at a glacial pace – as opposed to her mother, who was always moving at full speed. 'What on earth is Baba doing?' she said, turning to her mother.

Barbie Fang was so mortified it looked as if she'd been snap-frozen.

But the Wongs did not stop.

Alice-Miranda glanced at the man beside her. Benny was shifting in his seat at such a rate she was sure he was about to make a run for it. Having learned a thing or two in the past few days, the tiny girl shouted to Cherry, then grabbed his briefcase and hurled it towards the woman. Cherry leapt from her seat and caught it with one hand.

'What are you doing?' the man screamed.

'Open the case!' Lionel boomed. 'I think we should sign our contracts now.'

'What?' Lucille glared at the side of stage. 'Just wait until I get my hands on Rou. She has ruined all my plans.'

'But . . .' Benny Choo's eyes were bulging out of his head.

Elon Fang looked at Benny. 'What have you done?'

Cherry tried to pop the locks but there was a combination dial.

'What's the number, Mr Choo?' Alice-Miranda demanded.

The man was shaking like a leaf in the wind. 'I am not telling you that. It's my private business in there.'

Meanwhile, Elon Fang was still trying to intercept the cups and managed to get in the way with one deflecting off his hand and crashing to the floor. 'No!' he cried, pulling at his hair in horror. He ran to pick up the pieces, quickly identifying it as a fake and throwing the remnants back down.

Alice-Miranda looked over to the wings and gasped. Standing beside a woman in a striking fuchsia-coloured suit was Summer Tan. She gave the girl a wave and Summer waved back. All this time, Cherry rolled the dials on the case in vain. But Deng Rou had a better idea. The old woman scurried onto the stage, whipped a hairpin from her bun and within seconds the locks sprang open. Cherry lifted the two cups from the case, turned them over in her hand and held them above her head.

'No!' Elon Fang screamed. 'They're mine!'

'Look out, Cherry!' Alice-Miranda shouted as he rushed towards the woman.

Summer hurtled from the wings, flipping and twirling across the stage. Elon Fang connected with Cherry, tackling the woman to the ground. The cups flew out of her hands and up into the air.

The audience drew a huge breath, but Summer caught the first cup in her right hand and the second under her chin. Then she executed a knockout kick, which saw Elon Fang stagger left and right before he fell into the arms of a woman in a charcoal pants-suit. Agent Cheng whipped out her handcuffs and forced him to the floor.

'Give me my cups,' the man wailed. 'With these last three, my collection is finally complete.' Elon Fang might have been physically onstage, but from the strange look in his eyes, he wasn't really there at all.

Agent Cheng shook her head. 'No, Mr Fang, your collection will never be complete.'

Alice-Miranda turned around just in time to see Benny Choo trying to make his getaway up the aisle. She leapt to her feet. 'Stop that man!' she shouted, pointing at Benny.

September Sykes blanched as the sweaty fellow lumbered up the stairs towards her. She stuck her foot into the aisle, and for a second the man was blinded by the light reflecting off her shiny platform shoes. He reeled, shielding his eyes, before losing his balance and stumbling backwards. The entire audience watched as Benny Choo rolled down the aisle like a glistening beach ball. Lawrence Ridley clambered over several seats, puffing and blowing, before he threw himself on Benny's back, pinning the man to the floor. He might have gained a few pounds, but he could still remember some of the moves from his superhero role as Vector.

'What are you doing, Ridley?' Benny shouted.

'I don't know what you've been up to, old chap,' Lawrence grunted, 'but if my niece says that you need to be stopped, then stopped you will be. Anyway, consider this payback for what your bodyguards did to me in Hong Kong.'

'Arrest him,' Agent Cheng ordered her colleagues who appeared from all over the theatre, helping Lawrence to his feet before handcuffing Benny.

The entire crowd was silent, watching the show unfold in front of them. Miss Grimm and the rest of the adults in their group were utterly gobsmacked. Although they were still unaware of the gravity of the situation, it was clear something big had just gone down.

Lionel Wong looked at the woman onstage. 'Agent Cheng, would you like to explain what just happened here tonight?'

'Well, Mr Wong, I think all anyone needs to know is that, after many years of trying, we have finally netted ourselves a whale.' She pointed at Elon Fang, then looked up into the audience at Benny Choo, who was standing shamefaced. 'Or perhaps two.'

Figgy and Rufus looked at each other. 'This is better than a movie,' Rufus gasped.

The audience began to clap, slowly at first, but soon they were on their feet cheering and shouting.

Lionel bowed. 'I think we should give our guests one final show stopper.' The old man nodded at his family. 'Miss Tan, we would be honoured if you would join us.'

The applause reached a crescendo as a waterfall of fireworks cascaded down the back of the stage.

'Places, everyone,' Lionel called out, clapping his hands.

The Wongs quickly assembled and went on to perform the greatest sequence of tricks by three generations of a family, plus one very special guest, that the world had ever seen.

And just in case you're wondering . . .

Elon Fang was taken into custody and charged with receiving the stolen cups. When the authorities executed a search warrant on his mansion they found tens of millions of yuan of black-market antiquities lining the walls of his secret museum. His wife pleaded ignorance to the whole affair, and as there was nothing to link her to any of his shady dealings, escaped their censure. Felicity was annoyed that her father had humiliated her in public, but his absence didn't change her life at all. He'd barely been there in the first place. Anyway, she was now busier than ever. After seeing the exploits of Coco and Jacinta, Felicity had decided to add acrobatics to her weekly schedule of activities.

Elon Fang is currently enjoying an extended stay in a prison north of Beijing. His collection of antiquities, many of which had been stolen from museums around the world, have since been returned to their rightful owners.

It is a slight understatement to say that Benny Choo had made some seriously bad errors of judgement. He'd been in way over his head at The Blue Whale Casino, owing Elon Fang a fortune beyond anything available to him. This debt had prompted his attempts to sell Beluga Studios. Upon learning that Benny had purchased the Circus of Golden Destiny, Elon Fang had come up with an outrageous plan. Unfortunately, Benny hadn't thought it too crazy either, having made The Lobster movies years ago and knowing a bit about burglaries. He thought that if he was successful in bringing Elon Fang the last remaining Ming Dynasty chicken cups to complete a collection he'd been obsessing over for years, it would clear his debt. Benny was not a malicious man, just a stupid one. His love for card games far outstripped any ability he had. He managed to cut himself a reduced sentence in exchange for testifying against Elon Fang.

Fuchsia Lee suddenly found herself elevated to a

management position. Although she was ultimately part of his undoing, Benny realised her exceptional skills and put her in charge of the running of his business ventures until he served out his sentence.

Summer Tan faced no charges for her part in the Shanghai robbery. On the contrary, the museum extended an invitation for her to come on board as a consultant security specialist. They reasoned that there was no one better for the job than the person who had managed to pull off, without any detection, the biggest daylight robbery China had ever seen.

Lucille Wong found herself in serious trouble with her mother-in-law for sabotaging the show. Winnie gave her extra duties for twelve months, which included volunteering her for the weekly cleaning of the communal bathroom. For once in her life, Lucille seemed genuinely remorseful. She'd realised that her actions had risked the wellbeing of others and carried out her punishment gladly.

Cherry felt sorry for her sister-in-law and called a family meeting. Ultimately, it was decided that if indoor plumbing was the answer to Lucille's bad moods, then indoor plumbing they would have.

Deng Rou's sneaky ways had almost ruined their reputation but, having saved the day, all was forgiven. Well, almost. Winnie is still hoping she retires soon.

The Wongs continued with their show and for a while it looked as if their plans for the school would have to be put permanently on hold. But as the Chinese government had been after Elon Fang for years, there had been a large reward for his conviction. It was to be divided between Cherry Wong, Fuchsia Lee and young Alice-Miranda Highton-Smith-Kennington-Jones. Fuchsia couldn't believe her luck and immediately invested her share of the bounty in real estate. Cherry handed her cheque straight to her in-laws and, with Alice-Miranda promptly donating her funds too, the fate of their school was assured.

September Sykes decided that the trip hadn't been so bad after all. Sep and Sloane were proud of their mother for helping to catch Benny. Sloane even agreed to go home for the next term break, whether she had a better offer or not.

The first Winchesterfield-Downsfordvale–Fayle–Bright-Star exchange was declared a huge success. The children can't wait for the return visit of their friends. That is, all except Caprice, who has vowed that there's no way she's hosting a girl as awful and spoilt and mean as Felicity Fang. Figgy's already warned the kids they'd better leave the goldfish at home.

Cast of characters

Winchesterfield-Downsfordvale Academy for Proper Young Ladies staff

Miss Ophelia Grimm	Headmistress
Aldous Grump	Miss Grimm's husband
Mrs Louella Derby	Personal secretary to the headmistress
Miss Livinia Reedy	English teacher
Mr Josiah Plumpton	Science teacher
Howie (Mrs Howard)	Housemistress of Grimthorpe House
Miss Benitha Wall	PE teacher
Mrs Doreen Smith	Cook
Charlie Weatherly (Mr Charles)	Gardener
Petunia Clarkson	Housemistress of Caledonia Manor
Fudge	Much-loved cavoodle puppy

Winchesterfield-Downsfordvale students

Alice-Miranda Highton-Smith-Kennington-Jones	Only child, nine years old
Millicent Jane McLoughlin-McTavish-McNoughton-McGill	Alice-Miranda's best friend and room mate

Jacinta Headlington-Bear	Friend
Sloane Sykes	Friend
Caprice Radford	Friend of sorts
Susannah Dare	Student

Fayle School for Boys staff and students

Professor Wallace Winterbottom	Headmaster
Mrs Deidre Winterbottom	Professor Winterbottom's wife
Parsley	Professor Winterbottom's West Highland terrier
Mr Harold Lipp	English and Drama teacher
Lucas Nixon	Alice-Miranda's cousin
Septimus Sykes	Lucas's best friend and brother of Sloane
George 'Figgy' Figworth	Student, mischief-maker
Rufus Pemberley	Figgy's frequent partner-in-crime

Brave chaperones of the first Winchesterfield-Downsfordvale–Fayle–Bright-Star exchange

Lawrence Ridley	Famous actor and Lucas's father
Ambrosia Headlington-Bear	Jacinta's mother
September Sykes	Mother of Sloane and Septimus
Venetia Baldini	Caprice's mother

Bright Star Academy staff and students

Miss Shauna O'Reilly	Headmistress
Coco Wong	Talented acrobat and student
Sunny Wong	Talented acrobat and Coco's cousin
Felicity Fang, Selina, Hero	Students

Others

Lionel Wong	Owner of Eternity circus troupe and Coco's grandfather
Winnie Wong	Lionel's wife
Bernard Wong	Lionel's elder son and Coco's father
Lucille Wong	Bernard's wife
Charles Wong	Lionel's younger son and Sunny's father
Cherry Wong	Charles' wife
Wai Po	Cherry's mother
Deng Rou	Member of the Eternity troupe
Elon Fang	Felicity's father
Barbie Fang	Felicity's mother
Benny Choo	Owner of Beluga Studios and the Circus of Golden Destiny
Fuchsia Lee	Benny Choo's secretary
Summer Tan	Star acrobat
Iris	Tour guide
Superintendent Lu	Winnie's cousin
Agent Cheng	Ministry of the State Security
Au Shen	Neighbour of the Wongs
Sun Ming	Neighbour of the Wongs
Jiao Long	Shopkeeper
Grant	Tour guide

About the
Author

Jacqueline Harvey taught for many years in girls' boarding schools. She is the author of the bestselling Alice-Miranda series and the Clementine Rose series, and was awarded Honour Book in the 2006 Australian CBC Awards for her picture book *The Sound of the Sea*. She now writes full-time and is working on more Alice-Miranda and Clementine Rose adventures.

www.jacquelineharvey.com.au

Jacqueline Supports

Jacqueline Harvey is a passionate educator who enjoys sharing her love of reading and writing with children and adults alike. She is an ambassador for Dymocks Children's Charities and Room to Read. Find out more at www.dcc.gofundraise.com.au and www.roomtoread.org/australia.